BLACKSTONE AND THE ENDGAME

The Inspector Sam Blackstone Series from Sally Spencer

BLACKSTONE AND THE ENDGAME

An Inspector Sam Blackstone Mystery

Sally Spencer

severn House

This first world edition published 2013
in Great Britain and the USA by
SEVERN HOUSE PUBLISHERS LTD of
19 Cedar Road, Sutton, Surrey, England, SM2 5DA.

British Library Cataloguing in Publication Data

Spencer, Sally
  Blackstone and the endgame. – (A Sam Blackstone mystery ;
  10)
  1. Blackstone, Sam (Fictitious character)–Fiction.
  2. Police–England–London–Fiction. 3. Great Britain–
  History–George V, 1910-1936–Fiction. 4. Detective and
  mystery stories.
  I. Title II. Series
  823.9'2-dc23

ISBN-13: 978-0-7278-8289-9 (cased)

All Severn House titles are printed on acid-free paper.

Severn House Publishers support The Forest Stewardship Council [FSC],
the leading international forest certification organisation. All our titles that
are printed on Greenpeace-approved FSC-certified paper carry the FSC logo.

Typeset by Palimpsest Book Production Ltd.,
Falkirk, Stirlingshire, Scotland.
Printed and bound in Great Britain by
TJ International Ltd, Padstow, Cornwall

16th December 1916

For days, the wind blowing off the Thames covered half of London in a cold, damp overcoat. Women who had forgotten how much their bones could ache were suddenly reminded just how bad winter could be. Men who had boasted about being in the rudest of health were starting to cough up bloodied phlegm. And the children, whose natural life was always on the street, found themselves huddled over the fireplace in their cramped kitchens when their parents could afford the coal – and sometimes, out of habit, even when they couldn't.

But at least there was no fog, people said, in an attempt to sound philosophical – at least they'd been spared that.

And then the fog came. It was what was called a real pea-souper – though, in fact, it was more yellow than green. It held, within it, particles of carbon and sulphur which were eager to find new homes in the lungs of the weak and feeble. It wrapped itself, like poison ivy, around every building and lamppost. It slowed London down, but it did not halt it, because life still had to be lived, even in the middle of a poisonous cloud.

Southwark's New Cut street market had been as much a victim of the fog as everywhere else, and customers floated like ghosts between the stalls and barrows, guided only by the fuzzy light provided by the paraffin lamps which each stall holder had brought with him.

But now some of those lights were going out, Harry Danes noted. Now, some of the other costermongers were packing up and going home.

It was the ones who sold second-hand clothes and tools who were leaving, Danes told himself.

And they might as well. If they stayed, they would probably sell nothing more that night, and their merchandise – as unattractive as it was – would still find ready buyers amongst the poor, who had no other choice, in the morning. But if you sold fruit and veg – like he did – you had to stay until the bitter bloody end, however slight your chance of making a sale, because your goods were rotting even as they sat there.

Not that there was much left to sell, he thought, looking down at the miserable offerings laid out on his barrow. Not that, in all honesty, there'd been much to sell when he'd *started* the night's trading.

Life had been hard before the war, but nothing like as hard as it was now. The German U-boats were partly to blame – Danes had lost count of how many merchant ships they'd sunk in the last few months. But it was also due to the fact that instead of working on the land, all the young men were busy dying on the Western Front – and because the government was spending so much money on killing foreigners that it had none left to look after its own people.

It was as he speculated on the total futility of war that he first noticed the tramp, although – for all he knew – the poor sod could have been standing there for some time.

The tramp was tall – over six feet. He was as thin as a rake and had a bushy grey beard and watery eyes.

There were some tramps who loved the vagabond existence – positively thrived on it – Danes thought, but this wasn't one of them.

'Can I help you, mate?' Danes asked.

The tramp hesitated. 'I'd like some food—'

'I can give you a turnip, if you like,' Danes interrupted him. 'It's not much, I know, but it's all I can spare.'

'It's very kind of you, and I do want it,' the tramp said, then added firmly, 'but I don't want it *now*.'

'No?'

'No. You look to me like a man who's got a family to support . . .'

'You're right there, pal, I have. But one little turnip isn't going to make much diff—'

'. . . so if you can sell it, then that's what you should do. I only want it if you'll definitely be throwing it away.'

He was a strange tramp, Danes thought – very strange indeed.

'Don't I know you?' he asked.

The tramp shook his head.

'I'm sure I do,' the costermonger insisted. 'Didn't you used to be . . .'

'I have to go,' the tramp said. Then he turned awkwardly and disappeared into the fog.

Danes scratched his head. '. . . a copper?' he said, completing his sentence, though now there was no one to hear it. 'A detective inspector from Scotland Yard?'

His week on the run had taken its toll, Sam Blackstone realized, as he pushed his aching body to its limits in an effort to put as great a distance between himself and the costermonger as possible.

He had spent his nights shivering in dark, dank corners, and his days watching out for the policemen who he knew must be searching for him. He had fed on cabbage leaves and stalks he had picked up outside restaurants. Once, he had found a squashed – but still burning – cigarette end on the ground, and it had taken all his discipline – all his remaining self-respect – not to bend down and pick it up. And finally, on what was now his seventh day as a fugitive, he had given in to the demands of his growling stomach and risked the visit to the New Cut.

But it wasn't really much of a risk, now was it? asked a mocking demon hidden deep in the back of his mind. *You're only taking a risk if you've got something to lose, and what does a dying man* have *to lose?*

'I'm not dying,' Blackstone said, in a voice that was weak and cracked, but still loud enough to cause several people to turn their heads.

He stopped walking and clung to the nearest lamppost for support.

'I'm not dying,' he said again – though in a softer tone this time.

Yet he knew that he was.

He had fought Afghan tribesmen and New York gangsters – he had been shot at, stabbed, and beaten – and he had survived. But now he was dying.

He would probably not die that night – or even that week. He might live for a month or two, but, in the end, the hunger and the cold – adding to the desperation and the disappointment that already weighed him down – would see him off.

And dying was not even the worst possible ending.

Far more terrible was the prospect of being caught.

He had a vision of himself standing in the dock while the prosecutor tore his story apart with a contempt reserved only for the most despicable criminals. He could see the disgust in the eyes of the jury as the story unfolded, and hear the cold, vengeful tone in the judge's voice as he passed sentence.

What happened after that – whatever sentence was imposed – didn't really matter. It was the trial he dreaded. It was those few days when everything he had ever worked for – everything he had ever believed in – first rounded on him and then condemned him.

'How did I ever get into this situation?' he wondered.

But it was only a rhetorical question. He *knew* how he had got into it. He even knew exactly when and where it had started – could pin it down to that moment when he first looked across the desk at Superintendent Brigham.

PART ONE
Openings

ONE

9th December 1916

It was just over two weeks to Christmas, and Blackstone stood at his office window looking down on the ragged men on the Victoria Embankment who were attempting to sell Christmas trees to the people passing by.

It wouldn't be a very joyous Christmas that year, he thought. How could it be, when almost every family in the country had sent its young men to fight on the Western Front – and so many of those families had already learned that their young men wouldn't be coming back.

'I think there should be a law making it illegal for criminals not to work over Christmas,' said a voice behind him.

Blackstone turned around to look at his sergeant, Archie Patterson, who was sitting back with his size-ten boots resting on his desk, and tearing a piece of paper into tiny strips.

'What was that you just said, Archie?' he asked.

'It's always the same,' Patterson complained. 'It gets to this time of year and the criminal fraternity decide they don't want to be nicked and spend Christmas behind bars. So what do they do? For two or three weeks, they act just like ordinary decent citizens. And where does that leave us – the guardians of law and order? I'll tell you where it leaves us, Sam. It leaves us stuck here in this bloody office – and it's not right!'

Blackstone grinned. 'I'd never thought of it quite that way before,' he said. 'But you're spot on – the criminal fraternity should be a little more considerate of our needs. So why don't we go out and find a couple of bank robbers, point them towards the nearest bank, and—'

'You're just being silly, now, sir,' Patterson said, still sounding aggrieved at life in general.

There was a knock on the door, and a uniformed sergeant entered the office.

'I'm sorry to disturb you, sir, but Superintendent Brigham wants to see you right away,' he said.

'Who?' Blackstone replied, mystified.

'Superintendent Brigham – the new head of the Special Branch,' said Patterson, who kept track of all kinds of people in his head. 'He was a major in the army, served in India with the Worcester Regiment for a number of years, lives in Peckham and has two grown-up children, one of whom has just started training to be a lawyer.'

'Anything else?' Blackstone asked.

'No, that's about as much as I know,' Patterson admitted.

'And you're sure it's me that Superintendent Brigham wants to see?' Blackstone asked the sergeant.

'Yes, sir. He was quite definite about it.'

'Well, you *are* going up in the world, sir,' Patterson said.

Yes, wasn't he? Blackstone thought. The Branch – originally formed to combat Irish terrorism – had always regarded itself as a cut above every other department in Scotland Yard, so why would it even bother talking to a lowly detective inspector like him?

'He did say *immediately*, sir,' the sergeant persisted nervously.

'Well, it's been nice working with you, sir – and I hope you remember us little people with affection when you've been raised to new and dizzying heights,' Patterson said.

'Oh, do put a sock in it, Archie,' Blackstone said, as he headed towards the door.

Superintendent Brigham had a bullet-shaped head, to the top of which a thatch of iron-grey hair clung on precariously. There was no evidence of great intelligence in his cold grey eyes, nor any hint of humour in his tightly drawn mouth. And though he was making some effort to contain it, he was clearly very angry.

But if he was angry, if he really didn't want this inferior being from one of the lower floors in his office – and he clearly *didn't* – then why was the meeting taking place at all?

The superintendent gazed at the inspector for nearly a minute, almost as if he was a butcher assessing how much the other man would fetch per pound.

'So you're Blackstone,' he said finally.

'Yes, sir.'

'They tell me you once saved the life of our late Queen,' Brigham said in a voice that suggested it seemed unlikely that any man wearing a second-hand brown suit would ever have been capable of such heroism.

'It was a long time ago,' Blackstone replied.

'But you *did* save her?' Brigham persisted, as if expecting Blackstone to be decent enough to make some modest disclaimer, on the lines of him only being one small cog in a very large machine.

'Yes, I did save her,' Blackstone replied, because while he wasn't going to brag about it, he wasn't going to lie about it, either, and the fact was that but for his actions – and his actions alone – Queen Victoria would have died on the very day she was celebrating her Diamond Jubilee.

'Hmm,' Brigham said disapprovingly. 'Still, none of us can live for ever on our past glories, can we?'

'No, sir,' Blackstone agreed.

'Tell me, Inspector, what do you think is the main threat to this country at the moment?' Brigham asked. 'What do you think is really worrying our masters in government?'

When a man like Brigham asked a big question of an underling, Blackstone thought, it was usually because he believed he himself had the answer – and the underling didn't.

'I should imagine that the strength of the German army along the Western Front is causing them some concern,' he said, playing along with the superintendent's game.

'You are wrong,' Brigham told him. 'The German army might seem formidable, but our brave British Tommies will overcome the cowardly Huns in the end.'

'There are brave men in the German infantry, too, you know,' said Blackstone, who had been to the Western Front and seen the bloody stalemate there with his own eyes.

'I consider that to be a very unpatriotic statement,' Superintendent Brigham said angrily.

'Do you, sir?' Blackstone asked calmly. '*I* consider it to be no more than a statement of fact.'

'The real threat is from the German navy – and, specifically, its U-boats,' Brigham said, brushing aside Blackstone's comment as if it had never been uttered. He paused to light up a cigarette, though he did not offer one to his guest. 'We are a small island,

Inspector. We cannot grow enough to feed ourselves, and so much of our food must be imported. And as the damned Huns keep sinking our supply ships, we are edging perilously close to starvation.'

He sat back in his seat, as if he was waiting for his visitor to applaud his brilliant insight.

'Ah, that probably explains why there's not much food around – at least, not in the poorer areas,' Blackstone said.

Brigham scowled. 'Are you trying to be funny?' he demanded.

'No, sir,' Blackstone replied. 'I'm just agreeing with you that there's not much food around.'

'In order to sink these U-boats, we first need accurate intelligence on their exact location,' Brigham continued, backing out of the blind alley which, it seemed to him, Blackstone was trying to lead him up, 'and, fortunately, that intelligence is now almost within our grasp. We have a source – or, more accurately, *I* have a source – in the German high command. He has already given us a sample of the kind of material that he will be able to provide on a regular basis, and the Admiralty assures me that it is first-class.'

Blackstone was growing tired of the man – and tired of his self-serving conversation.

'With the greatest respect, sir, I don't see what any of this has to do with me,' he said.

'Perhaps if you'd shut up and listen, you'd find out,' the superintendent snapped. 'Our source wants twenty-five thousand pounds in return for further intelligence, and you are to deliver that money to him.'

'Why me?' Blackstone asked, puzzled. 'Couldn't one of your lads in Special Branch do it?'

'Yes,' Brigham said, the anger now clearly evident in his tone, 'one of my highly trained officers most certainly could, and I would much rather entrust it to an officer under my command than to an inspector who has had what can be called – at best – a chequered career. But that option is regrettably not open to me. The man insists that you should be the go-between. He simply refuses to accept anyone else.' Brigham coughed awkwardly. 'He seems to believe that you are an honourable man and that he can trust you.'

Blackstone's mind sifted through the names of all the Germans he had had dealings with over the years and attempted to isolate any who might conceivably have ended up in the German navy.

'What's the man's name?' he asked.

'He is known to us as Max.'

'Max what?'

'No more than that – simply Max.'

Blackstone gasped.

'So you're prepared to hand over twenty-five thousand pounds to a man you don't know, on the basis of the one piece of information he's already given you?' he asked incredulously.

'That is the decision that has been taken,' Brigham said stonily. 'Here are Max's instructions. This afternoon, you will go to Harrods department store, where you will purchase a leather attaché case and—'

'Max said that explicitly, did he?' Blackstone asked. 'He wants *me* to purchase the case?'

'Yes, that is what he said.'

'But why does it matter *who* buys the case?'

'That's of no importance,' Brigham said airily.

Meaning, 'I've absolutely no idea why it matters,' Blackstone translated in his head.

'Has Max laid down what size or make of attaché case I should buy?' he asked aloud.

'No. He seems happy enough to leave the choice to you.'

'So he insists that I buy it and that it's bought from Harrods, but he doesn't care what kind of attaché case it is,' Blackstone said, to make sure he'd got it quite right.

'You are allowing yourself to get bogged down in details,' Brigham said irritably. 'I, on the other hand, am able to focus on the bigger picture – which is perhaps why I am a superintendent and you are a mere inspector.'

It was the little details that *made up* the big picture, Blackstone thought – but he said nothing.

'You will take the case to the corner of Denmark Street and Cable Street, arriving at midnight on the dot,' Brigham continued. 'There, you will be handed the twenty-five thousand pounds, which you will put into the case. After that, you will proceed to the Western Dock, where you will meet Max.'

'It's a big place, the Western Dock,' Blackstone said, almost whimsically. 'Is there any particular part of it in which the meeting is supposed to take place?'

'Max would not say. You are to go to the dock, and he will find you. You will hand him the money, he will give you the documents, and then you may return to the job you are best suited for – which is chasing petty criminals.'

Well, if it had to done, then at least he could make sure it was done properly, Blackstone thought.

'I would like my own man, Sergeant Patterson, on the team that's covering my back,' he said. 'In fact, I shall insist on it.'

'You're in no position to *insist* on anything,' Brigham told him. 'Besides, there will *be* no team.'

'What!'

'One of the conditions that Max has laid down is that you go in alone. He has made it crystal clear that if there are any police officers within five streets of the docks, he will not make the exchange.'

'So there won't even be any coppers guarding the dock gates?'

'When I said *any* police officers, I meant, of course, any officers who would not normally be in the area at that time,' Brigham said, stung. 'Max accepts the need to maintain the officers on the gates, but he has specified that the only thing they should be told is that when you appear, they are to allow you to enter the dock.'

'For their own protection, they should be warned there could be trouble,' Blackstone said.

'There will be no trouble,' Brigham said confidently. 'We want the plans that Max has in his possession, and he wants the twenty-five thousand pounds you will be carrying. There is no reason why it shouldn't all be as smooth as silk.'

'There's a hundred ways the thing could go wrong,' Blackstone told him. 'The whole idea is insane.'

'Do I take it from what you've just said that you are refusing to obey a direct order?' Brigham barked.

'Oh no, I'll do it,' Blackstone replied. 'I'll even do it the way you want it done – but that doesn't make it any less crazy.'

There were many things about the Goldsmiths' Arms to recommend it as a watering hole, but the one that Blackstone and Patterson particularly liked was its location. It stood at the corner of Lant Street and Lant Place, which was far enough from the Yard to ensure that when the two of them wished to have a serious conversation, they need have no fear of being overheard by any other coppers. And so they had become a familiar sight in the pub, and when they entered it – and they were easy to spot, since Blackstone was half a head taller than most of the other customers, and Patterson fifty per cent wider – the locals, accepting their need for privacy, would edge to other end of the bar.

They were having a serious conversation that lunchtime, though it was Blackstone who had done most of the talking so far.

'What's got me really puzzled,' he said, when he had finished briefing Patterson on the meeting with Brigham, 'is why this Max should have insisted on me as the courier.'

'Didn't the superintendent mention something about Max thinking you were an honourable man who he could trust?' Patterson asked.

'Yes, he did,' Blackstone agreed. 'That's exactly what he said. But Max must know that since *Brigham's* in charge of the operation, *Brigham's* the man he needs to trust, and looked at from that perspective, it's irrelevant who's actually chosen to carry the money.'

'You've got a point,' Patterson admitted.

'If there's a trap, it's Brigham who'll set it. If the deal goes through as planned, it will be because Brigham has decided that's what should happen,' Blackstone continued. 'You could train a dog to carry the money and pick up the plans – so why does it have to be me?'

'Another good point,' Patterson agreed.

'And then there's the fact that he insists I'm the one who buys the attaché case,' Blackstone said. 'Why should it matter who actually buys the bloody thing? And why, in God's name, do I have to buy it from Harrods?'

'I don't know,' Patterson said. 'But what I *do* know is that what he's asking you to do is well above and beyond the call of duty.'

'I'm not sure there *is* anything above and beyond—'

'And in my opinion, sir, you should have turned him down flat the very moment he asked you to do it.'

'*Ordered* me to do it,' Blackstone corrected him. 'But say he *had* merely asked – if I'd turned him down, he'd only have sent some other poor bugger in, wouldn't he?'

'Exactly!' Patterson agreed, as if he thought he'd just won the argument. 'He'd have sent some other poor bugger in! In other words, he wouldn't have sent *you*.'

'And if things went badly in the docks, would this other poor bugger be able to deal with them as well as I could?'

'Of course not!' Patterson said sarcastically. 'You're the great Sam Blackstone – there's not a copper in the world could deal with things going wrong half as well as you could.'

Blackstone grinned. 'After all the years we've worked together, it's wonderful to hear you finally acknowledge just how bloody good I am,' he said.

'For God's sake, Sam, be serious,' Patterson said exasperatedly. 'You can't keep on taking everybody else's responsibilities on your own shoulders. No man can. I know somebody has to be on the firing line – that's just the way things are – but it doesn't always have to be you.'

'I've told Brigham that I'll do it, so there's no more to be said,' Blackstone said firmly.

Patterson shook his head, which was as round as a football and as pink as a peach. 'Then, if you insist on doing it, at least let me come along and shadow you,' he said.

'I appreciate your offer of support, but I'll be fine on my own,' Blackstone said.

'It's because of my size, isn't it?' Patterson said. 'You don't want to use me because I'm like a barrel of lard.'

Blackstone took a step backwards and looked his sergeant up and down. Archie had already been a rather large young man when they'd begun working together, nearly twenty years earlier, but over that time – during which he had married a pleasantly plump wife and produced three pleasantly plump children – he had positively ballooned.

'You might as well admit that's the reason, because I can see it in your eyes,' the sergeant told him.

Patterson was trying to make him feel guilty, Blackstone realized – using the emotional blackmail of their friendship to persuade his boss to let him tag along.

'It's nothing to do with your size,' Blackstone said.

'Barrel of lard,' Patterson repeated.

'You're a lot nimbler on your feet than some of the men who are half your weight.'

'Then why won't you use me?'

Because, Blackstone thought, *however much I need you – and, God knows, I've got such a bad feeling about this that I really* do *need you – your plump little family needs you more.*

But aloud, he said, 'I won't use you because it isn't necessary to use you. Brigham thinks it will all go like clockwork – smooth as silk was the term he actually used – and I agree with him.'

'You're storing up a lot of trouble for both of us, you know, Sam,' Patterson said.

'How can I be storing up trouble for *you*, when you won't even be involved?' Blackstone wondered.

'I don't know,' Patterson said ominously. 'It's not logical at all, but I can feel it in my gut that what you're about to do will land both of us in the shit.'

TWO

L ondon was a city that had conquered the night, just as it had conquered so much else that nature had thrown at it, Blackstone thought with a true Londoner's pride. When dusk fell there, it did not plunge the city into darkness in the way that it all-but blacked out so many provincial towns. Instead, the lights came on – gas lamps in the poorer areas, the more modern electric street-lighting in the prosperous ones – and London glowed. He'd read somewhere that night-time London could be seen from space, and though he doubted that was true, he nourished the hope that when mankind finally found a way to travel beyond the planet Earth, he'd be proved wrong.

But London did not glow that night – it hadn't glowed since early in the war, when fears of German Zeppelin attacks had been raised – and as Blackstone made his way along Denmark Street, he was guided only by the light of a pale moon.

The four men who were waiting for him on the corner of Denmark Street and Cable Street all had flashlights, and were huddled together like schoolboys hatching a conspiracy against an unpopular master. As Blackstone approached them, both their excitement and nervousness were tangible.

One of the men raised his flashlight and shone it full into Blackstone's face.

'You took your time getting here,' he said, in a voice that Blackstone recognized as belonging to Superintendent Brigham.

So the head of the Special Branch had defied both convention and protocol, and become personally involved at the operational level, Blackstone thought, as spots of light danced before his eyes.

But then, he supposed, it was hardly surprising that Brigham *was* there, because this wasn't just *any* operation; it was the one that would make Brigham's name – and he would want to ensure that no one else snatched any of the glory away from him.

'I said, you took your time,' Brigham repeated, the tension evident in his voice.

'Back in your office, you said that I should be here at midnight on the dot, sir,' Blackstone replied.

'I know I did, but it must already be much later than that,' Brigham replied bad-temperedly.

And no sooner had he spoken the words than some distant clock began chiming twelve.

'Have you got the bag?' Brigham said.

'Yes.'

'Then give it to my inspector.'

The inspector held out his hand, Blackstone handed him the attaché case he'd bought from Harrods, and while a second Special Branch officer held a flashlight over the case, a third began filling it with banknotes.

This could all have been done much more easily in Scotland Yard, Blackstone thought, and yet Brigham had deliberately chosen a dark corner of the East End, instead.

The man was an idiot, because only an idiot tries to draw drama from a situation which – for the safety of everyone involved – should be kept as cut and dried as possible.

And perhaps that was why Max had chosen Brigham as the conduit for the exchange, rather than selecting the head of the secret service, someone in the Admiralty or an official in the Ministry of War.

Perhaps he had known that only the head of the Special Branch – with his obvious liking for the dramatic – could have sold this preposterous scenario to the Treasury.

But that still didn't explain why he had chosen an ordinary copper to be the courier, or why he had insisted the ordinary copper buy the case.

The transfer had been completed, and the inspector closed the case and handed it back to Blackstone.

'You are now holding twenty-five thousand pounds in your hands,' Brigham said gravely. 'Guard it with your life.'

It wasn't going to work, Blackstone thought – he could feel it in his bones that it wasn't going to work.

But it would be wasting his breath to tell the superintendent that.

'Are you armed, Inspector Blackstone?' Brigham asked.

'I have my revolver with me, yes.'

'Max has made it quite clear that he doesn't want you carrying a weapon, so I must ask you to hand it over to my inspector.'

'Oh, for God's sake,' Blackstone said, as a sudden wave of anger hit him. 'Did you have *any* say at all in the way this operation is to be run – or are you just prepared to jump through every hoop that Max holds up for you?'

'That's quite enough, Inspector Blackstone,' Brigham said. 'Max and I have reached an agreement that is acceptable to us both, and I will see that it is carried out to the letter.'

'You haven't reached an *agreement* at all,' Blackstone countered. 'Max – whoever he is – has told you what to do, and you're bloody doing it. And if he'd told you he wanted me to paint my arse yellow, you'd probably have said that that was acceptable, too.'

'I could have you charged with insubordination, and if you do not surrender your weapon immediately, I will do just that,' Brigham said, his anger matching Blackstone's own.

Giving in to the inevitable, Blackstone reached into his coat, took his gun from its holster and handed it to the inspector.

'This is a very simple operation, and there is no reason why you should not be back here within the half-hour,' the superintendent said.

'Unless I hit trouble,' Blackstone pointed out.

'There will be no trouble,' Brigham told him – and though he had probably intended to make it sound as if he had complete confidence in the whole operation, the words came out more like a prayer.

As Blackstone walked down Pennington Road, the leather attaché case in his hand, the whole area was as quiet as the grave.

But he knew it would not stay like that for much longer. Two hours before dawn, a line of ragged and desperate men would begin to queue up in front of the Western Dock's big wooden gates. They were called the 'casuals', and they would be well aware that though they were the first in line, they would be the last to be offered whatever work was going that day, because only after the 'ticket' men had been placed would they get their chance. And so they would stand there, stamping their feet against the cold, wishing they could afford a cheap cup of acorn coffee from one of the temporary stalls, and praying that they would leave the docks that day with some money in their pockets, so that they would be able to pay for a roof over their heads that night.

By the time the ticket men arrived, just as the sun was rising, the queue of casuals would stretch right along the road – almost to St Katharine's Way – and mumbled, hopeful rumours would run up and down the queue that ships were expected and there would be work for all who wanted it.

It was all wrong, Blackstone thought, as he got closer to the dock gates. There was dignity in labour, and no man should be forced to beg for work. And perhaps things would change. Perhaps once this war – which had already cost millions of lives – was finally over, the government would recognize the sacrifice the people had made, and treat them with respect.

And perhaps, too, elephants would learn to fly, and best bitter would come gushing out of the spouts in public fountains.

It was when he was a hundred yards from the gates that he began to be concerned.

At that distance, he told himself, there should have been some indication that there were constables on duty there.

It didn't have to be much of an indication. A dark shape moving along the dock wall, a whisper of conversation caught on the breeze, the glow of a surreptitiously smoked cigarette, a flash of light as one of the constables checked his watch – all these things would be enough to reassure him.

But there was nothing!

It was not until he was almost at the gates that his growing suspicions could actually be confirmed as certainties.

What had happened to the constables?

Had they been removed as the result of a last-minute instruction from the mysterious Max – an instruction that Superintendent Brigham had not considered it necessary to tell him about?

Or had Max 'taken care' of the officers because they did not fit in with that part of his plan that he was keeping secret from the superintendent?

Blackstone felt his rage erupting again. One of the most important responsibilities of any high-ranking officer was to protect his men, and if the two constables had been killed because they had not been aware of the danger they might be facing, then Brigham should be punished.

'And the bastard *will* be punished,' Blackstone promised. 'I'll see to it myself. I'll . . .'

Thoughts of revenge could come later, he cautioned himself. What he had to do at that moment was decide how to deal with this new situation.

There were two alternatives. One was to enter the docks as he'd been instructed and let Max find him. The other was to turn around and walk back to Cable Street.

But the more he thought about it, the more he realized that if Max was intending to simply *snatch* the money – and he now believed that was exactly what Max *was* intending to do – it didn't really matter which of the alternatives he chose, because the German would already have armed men posted along Pennington Road, cutting off his retreat.

'In which case, we might just as well stick to the plan,' Blackstone told himself.

The big dock gates were closed, but when he turned the handle, he found that they were not locked. He pushed one of the gates open slightly and stepped inside.

In the pale moonlight, he could see the outlines of the skeletal cranes and the bulky warehouses, and he could hear the water swishing against the sides of the docks. He reached automatically into his jacket and felt his fingers brush against his empty holster.

'You bastard, Brigham,' he said aloud. 'You weak, ineffectual – *dangerous* – bastard!'

A strong wind blew up from nowhere. It howled around corners and rattled the slates on the dockland roofs. It picked up detritus lying on the ground and sent it manically hurtling through the air. And then, as suddenly as the wind had arrived, it was gone.

Blackstone moved slowly and cautiously towards Wapping Basin. Wherever Max was now, he would not have arrived there from the street, he thought. For safety's sake, the German would have come by river, and that was how he would make his exit, too.

Blackstone heard a furtive scuttling to his left and again reached for his revolver, even though he knew it was probably a water rat. But the revolver was not there, he was forcibly reminded. It was being held by an inspector in the Special Branch – because that was what Max wanted.

'You hav' der money?' asked a voice to his right.

Blackstone turned and saw the dark outline of a large man.

'I have the money, and I'll give it to you the moment you've handed me the documents,' he said.

The other man laughed. 'Yes, ve could certainly do it that vay,' he agreed, 'but I have an alternative plan.'

'An alternative plan,' Blackstone repeated. 'And what alternative plan might that be?'

'Tell me, Inspector,' Max said, avoiding a direct answer to the question, 'how does the thought of one thousand pounds appeal to you?'

The clocks all over London were striking one.

'He should be back by now,' Superintendent Brigham said, walking nervously up and down.

'Yes, sir, he should,' the inspector agreed.

'Do you think we should go down to the docks and find out what's happened?' Brigham asked.

'I don't know, sir,' replied the inspector, who was far too wily a bird to fall into the kind of trap that would lead to him being held responsible for whatever happened next. 'You're the senior man here – it's your operation – so you're the one who should take the decision.'

'If we go down to the docks now, Max may take it as a sign of bad faith,' Brigham said.

He paused to give the inspector time to agree with him – but the inspector said nothing.

'But if it's Max who's shown the bad faith,' Brigham fretted, 'if he's double-crossed us, then the longer we leave it . . .'

Another pause.

Another lack of response from the inspector.

'We'll give it half an hour,' Brigham said, on the verge of panic. 'Whatever problems he's encountered in the docks, Blackstone must surely be back by then.'

Brigham, his inspector, and his two sergeants, reached the dock gates at a quarter to two, and though the night air was cold – and they had been standing around in it for some considerable time – the superintendent was sweating.

'There are no constables on duty,' he said frantically.

'No, sir,' his inspector agreed.

'Do you think they might be helping Blackstone? Or do you think Max might have told them to go away?'

'I've no idea, sir.'

'Well, for the love of God, let's get inside there and find out what's happened,' Brigham screamed.

They found the two constables – who should have been on duty at the dock gates – behind one of the cranes. They had been securely bound and gagged, but they were still conscious, and the moment they saw their rescuers approaching, they began to kick their legs and grunt as loudly as they could.

'Get these lads untied,' the inspector said to the two sergeants.

'There's no time for that!' Brigham screamed. 'We have to find Blackstone and the money.'

'It's below freezing now, sir, and if we don't untie them, they'll probably die of exposure,' the inspector said in a voice as cold as the air – a voice that suggested he was perfectly prepared to disobey his superior, should that prove necessary.

'Very well, then, untie them – but make it quick,' Brigham said. 'And then go and find that bastard Blackstone.'

The constables needed assistance to stand up, but once they were on their feet, they did not seem to be in any danger of falling over.

'Go!' Brigham told his team. Then he turned his attention to the constables. 'What the hell happened here?' he demanded.

'There were these two blokes with guns, sir,' said one of the constables, rubbing his wrists in an attempt to improve his circulation. 'They came out of nowhere. They told us that they'd kill us if we didn't surrender immediately. We didn't have any choice.'

'You didn't have any choice!' Brigham barked, as a voice in his head screamed that someone would have to take the blame for this fiasco, and that – unfairly – it would probably be him. *'You didn't have any choice!'*

'No, sir,' the constable mumbled.

'You're supposed to be members of the finest police force in the world,' Brigham ranted. 'You should have used your moral authority to make the men put down their guns. And if that didn't work, then you should have unsheathed your truncheons and charged them.'

'But . . . but if we'd done that, they'd have shot us down like dogs, sir,' the constable protested.

'Well, at least then you'd have died with honour,' Brigham said. 'As it is, you're nothing but a disgrace to your uniform.'

It was ten minutes before the inspector and the two sergeants returned.

'Have you found him?' Brigham asked.

'The docks are a big place, sir,' the inspector said. 'We'll have to wait until it gets light before we can carry out a proper search.'

'In other words, you *haven't* found him,' Brigham said bitterly.

'No, sir.'

'Have you found *anything*?'

'We found this, sir,' said one of the sergeants, holding up a warrant card.

'Is that . . . is that . . .?' Brigham gasped.

'It's Inspector Blackstone's, sir.'

'So how is it you couldn't find a big man like Blackstone, but you managed to come across a small thing like his warrant card?' Brigham demanded.

The sergeant looked to the inspector for help, and the inspector nodded that he'd be glad to oblige.

'We don't think Inspector Blackstone is still here, sir, but the warrant card was lying right there in our path,' the inspector said. 'And no doubt the thing that's concerning you the most at the moment is whether or not there was any blood on the warrant card.'

'What?' Brigham asked, as if he had no idea what the inspector was talking about.

'Blood,' the inspector repeated. 'You'll be eager to find out if an officer under your command has been injured.'

'Yes, yes, of course,' Brigham said. 'Was there any blood?'

'No, sir, there wasn't.'

'Then if he wasn't hurt, what the bloody hell was Blackstone doing dropping it?'

I'll put in for a transfer the first thing in the morning, the inspector promised himself.

'Why did he drop it, sir?' he repeated innocently. 'I expect that was because he didn't think that he'd be needing it any more.'

'You think . . . you think he's done a runner with the money?' Brigham asked tremulously.

'It's certainly looking that way, sir,' the inspector replied.

THREE

10th December 1916

Had it not been for the steam hammer that was pounding away relentlessly in his head, Blackstone might almost have felt as if he was doing no more than slowly awakening from a deep sleep.

But just *where* was this slow awakening taking place? he wondered.

He was lying on something hard. That was indisputable – but it didn't get him very far.

The idea floated through his mind that he was in New York City, working on the case of a murdered stockbroker – the Wolf of Wall Street, they'd called him – with Detective Sergeant Alex Meade . . .

No, that was years ago.

He was in the English trenches, on the Western Front, inves-
tigating the death of Lieutenant Fortesque . . .

That was closer – *much* closer than New York – but still some
considerable time in the past.

The events of the previous evening slowly began to filter back
into his aching brain.

The Western Dock . . .

A man who called himself Max and was proposing a deal
quite unlike the one he had previously made with Brigham . . .

Blackstone had still not opened his eyes, but now he was
becoming more aware of what was going on around him. There
was the noise of cart wheels, bouncing off the cobbles. There was
a buzz of conversation as people walked past him. And there
was the strong smell – the stink – of whisky.

Now he did open his eyes. His vision was blurry at first, but
as it began to clear, he saw that he was lying on a bench on the
Victoria Embankment, not far from New Scotland Yard.

But how the hell had he got there?

He raised himself on one elbow – taking care not to roll off
the bench – and observed two uniformed constables walking
quickly (but warily) towards him.

Why should they be wary? he wondered fuzzily.

He had never worked with either of them directly, it was true,
but he knew them well enough to exchange a greeting in passing,
and – more importantly – they knew him.

As the constables drew closer, they separated, so that the taller
one was now approaching him from one end of the bench, and
the shorter from the other.

And still Blackstone couldn't work out what was wrong!

The taller constable came to a halt, three feet from the bench.

'We don't want any trouble, now do we, sir?' he asked, in a
soothing yet authoritative tone.

'Trouble?' Blackstone repeated, mystified – and was surprised
at how weak and cracked his voice sounded.

'What I'd like you to do now is get into a sitting position and
hold your hands out in front of you,' the constable said.

'Why should I do that?' Blackstone asked.

'So that we can handcuff you, of course,' the constable replied.

*   *   *

Blackstone was standing in front of Superintendent Brigham's desk, still wearing the handcuffs. Behind the desk sat Superintendent Brigham himself and ex-Assistant Commissioner Todd.

Blackstone had crossed swords with Todd a number of times in the past. To be fair to him, he had never deliberately gone out of his way to make the Assistant Commissioner look like a fool, but since Todd undoubtedly *was* a fool, it might sometimes have seemed that way.

Now, the rumours buzzing around the Yard had it, Todd was dying of cancer, and looking at him, Blackstone had no doubts that the rumours were true.

Todd's skin was yellow, and he had lost some control over the muscles in his cheeks. But though he probably knew he had only weeks to live, there was a look of triumph on his face.

'We know *now* why Max wanted you to deliver the money, don't we?' Brigham demanded.

'*I* don't know anything,' Blackstone said. 'Somebody in the dockyard knocked me unconscious, and everything's a blank after that.'

'Somebody knocked you unconscious,' Brigham repeated, his voice heavy with contempt. 'And then what did he do? Did he carry you to a bench on the Victoria Embankment?'

'I couldn't say,' Blackstone admitted. 'But I'm pretty certain that he drenched me in whisky.'

'Would that be before or after you made your deal with Max – before or after he had given you the one thousand pounds that we found in your pocket?' Brigham asked.

'Do I look like an idiot?' Blackstone demanded. 'If I'd really had a deal with Max, don't you think the first thing I would have done would be to get the hell out of London?'

'A greedy man, who suddenly finds himself in possession of one thousand pounds, will often behave stupidly,' Brigham said. 'Shall I tell you what actually occurred?'

Blackstone shrugged. 'Will it make any difference to you if I say no?' he asked.

'No, it wouldn't!'

'Then, by all means, please feel free to go ahead.'

'I'm now inclined to think your friend Max is not the master spy I once assumed him to be,' Brigham said. 'The truth is probably that he's no more than a *minor* official in the German

navy, who, purely by chance – or the carelessness of others –
found himself in possession of a secret document. His first thought
was to sell it to us, but because it was so limited in its scope,
he realized he would never get more than a thousand pounds for
it. And since there was no prospect of him acquiring any more
documents, a thousand pounds was all he'd ever get. Then he
came up with a brilliant idea – he'd give us that document for
nothing and offer to sell us much more of the same for a considerable sum.'

'Yes, that probably is what happened,' Blackstone agreed.

'So you admit it!' Brigham said, pouncing like an overeager
cat.

'Of course not! I had nothing to do with any of it, and I warned
you yesterday that the whole idea was crazy.'

'Max needed an accomplice for his plan, and he chose you,'
Brigham continued, as if Blackstone hadn't spoken. 'Together,
you ambushed the two constables on the dock gate—'

'They'd already gone when I arrived,' Blackstone interrupted.

'All right, then,' Brigham said, impatiently waving the objection aside. 'Max and *some other* accomplice tied up the two
constables—'

'So they're still alive,' Blackstone interrupted. 'Thank God for
that!' And then the policeman in him took over his mind, and
he continued, 'But why didn't he *kill* them?'

'You'd have liked him to have killed them, wouldn't you?'
Todd asked, with another badly timed pounce.

'No, I wouldn't,' Blackstone said seriously. 'I'd have been
appalled if he'd killed them. But in his position, that would have
been the safest thing to do – and since, if he's caught, he'll
probably hang anyway, he had nothing to lose by it.'

'We are not here to debate what Max did or did not do,'
Brigham said. 'This interrogation is solely concerned with your
part in the affair.'

'Apart from obeying your orders to the letter, I *had* no part in
the affair,' Blackstone protested.

'To continue,' Brigham said firmly. 'You met Max at the
docks. You handed him the money, and he gave you back your
share, as you'd previously arranged. You knew that you'd have
no trouble making your escape, because there were no policemen

in the area except for my team – and we wouldn't come to investigate what had happened for at least an hour.'

'The reason there were no coppers anywhere near the docks was because of the agreement *you* had with Max,' Blackstone pointed out.

'And that agreement was a consequence of the arrangement that you made with him earlier,' Brigham said.

'So if, according to you, I'd set the whole thing up for making my escape, why *didn't* I escape?' Blackstone asked.

'You were fully intending to flee London – perhaps you had a car waiting somewhere – but before you left, you thought you might as well have a little drink to celebrate. But one drink didn't seem quite enough, did it? So you had another and then another. And by the time you were halfway down the bottle, you'd almost forgotten who you were or what you'd done.'

Brigham had been trying to make him angry from the very start of the interrogation, Blackstone thought, because the superintendent knew – as did all policemen – that an angry man had no control and would reveal things that a calm man would wisely keep to himself.

But the ploy hadn't worked so far, and there was no reason why it should start working now.

'Yes, those people who think you're a good copper are quite wrong,' Brigham taunted him. 'All you really are is a drunk.'

There was a click in Blackstone's brain – as if a trap had been sprung or a trigger squeezed.

'Talk to the people who know me,' he heard himself say. 'They'll tell you I care far too much about being on top of the situation to ever drink half a bottle of whisky.'

'No doubt they would tell me that,' Brigham agreed, savouring his triumph, 'but, you see, they only know the *old* Sam Blackstone, not this new one, with a thousand pounds in his pocket.'

Don't mention Vladimir, said a warning voice in Blackstone's head. *For God's sake, don't mention Vladimir. It'll only make you look desperate.*

'Just after the failed assassination attempt on Queen Victoria, I was approached on the Embankment by a Russian secret agent called Vladimir,' Blackstone said, ignoring the warning because – whether or not it made him seem desperate – the truth *was* the truth. 'He offered to give me five thousand pounds.'

'And why would he have done that?'

'As recognition of my part in foiling a plot in which Russia might have been unfairly implicated.'

But that wasn't the whole story, of course.

It is a cold, dark night on the Embankment, and Blackstone is looking down into the river – which is the heart of the city he loves – when he hears the Russian's voice behind him.

'Don't turn around,' Vladimir says.

And Blackstone doesn't.

'Since you have undoubtedly saved my country from a ruinous war, I have been authorized to offer you five thousand pounds,' Vladimir says, 'provided, of course, that you agree to sign an undertaking to never again mention the name of Count Turgenev.'

Turgenev, the fanatical aristocrat behind the plot, has already been killed, but the Russians fear he could cause as much trouble dead as he had alive. And Blackstone – who has seen enough wars to know he never wants to see another – agrees with them.

'Turgenev offered me ten *thousand pounds to let him go ahead with his plans,' Blackstone says.*

'Perhaps we could match that,' Vladimir answers.

'And if I asked for fifteen?'

'That might be considered a little greedy.'

Blackstone laughs. 'You're already sighting your pistol at me, aren't you? There's no need to. I promise not to tell anyone about Turgenev – but I don't want your money.'

'I did not take you for a fool,' the Russian says.

'I've been a fool all my life,' Blackstone tells him. 'But even a fool can learn his lesson, given time. I'm sick of the games you people play. Sick of being a pawn in them – and of all the people around me being pawns. I'm tired of the whole pack of you.'

'Isn't there a saying in English that you must either run with the fox or the hounds?' Vladimir asks.

'Yes, there is.'

'The wiser man will always choose the hounds.'

'The truly wise man will stay at home and tend his vegetables.'

'I am not sure my superiors will accept that,' Vladimir says.

'They would be much happier if they knew you were on our side. And the best way to prove that you are is to take the money.'

'I'm going to walk away now,' Blackstone tells him. 'There's no one around, so if you're going to kill me, now's the time to do it.'

And he does walk away, confidently expecting to suddenly feel the bullet which never comes.

'So, according to you, this Russian offered you money, and you turned it down,' Brigham said. 'And what exactly is that meant to prove?'

'I should have thought it was obvious. Vladimir offered me five thousand pounds – and then raised it to ten. I could have taken the money, and no one would ever have known about it. But I didn't. So do you really think I would risk everything I've ever worked for – everything I've ever stood for – for a mere thousand quid?'

Brigham smirked. 'Do you have any proof that any of that actually happened?' he asked. 'Can you produce this Vladimir as a witness in your defence?'

'No, I can't do that,' Blackstone admitted, wishing – now that he'd calmed down a little – that he'd listened to the voice in his head.

'Why not?'

'Because I don't know where he is.'

'Then why don't you tell us what his surname is, so that we can find him ourselves?'

'I don't know his surname. Even his Christian name is probably false,' Blackstone said.

And given the sort of life he's led, he's probably dead by now, he added silently.

'I'm tired of this fantasy,' Brigham said. 'Let's get back to what actually happened, shall we?' He lit up a cigarette. 'By two o'clock in the morning, you were blind drunk and staggering along the Embankment. Then you saw a bench and decided to rest for a while. And it was on that bench that you were found by two of the constables I sent out to search for you.'

'Make him the offer,' suggested Todd, who was clearly finding just sitting there an exhausting process.

'You're in very deep trouble, Blackstone,' Brigham said. 'You have consorted with the enemy in a time of war . . .'

'Max isn't the enemy,' Blackstone said. 'He's just a con man – and you're the man he's conned.'

'. . . consorted with the enemy in a time of war, which is treason,' Brigham said. 'By rights, you should hang for that, but –' he paused for dramatic effect – 'if you were to tell us where Max is, and if, based on that information, we are able to both arrest him and get the money back, then Commissioner Todd and I will do all we can to see that you are spared the rope.'

'I can't tell you where he is because I don't know,' Blackstone said. 'I've been fitted up – anybody with half a brain can see that.'

'I've always known you were corrupt, Sam Blackstone,' the dying ex-Assistant Commissioner Todd said in a rasping voice. 'And now – finally – we have clear and indisputable proof.'

FOUR

S ince it was in the Goldsmiths' Arms that Blackstone had revealed the details of the mission which would land him in so much trouble to his sergeant, a man of a more fanciful nature than Archie Patterson's might have considered it highly appropriate to hold his crisis meeting with Ellie Carr there, too. But such a thought had never occurred to Archie – he left the fanciful to those who could afford the luxury of indulging themselves in it – and he had selected the pub simply because it was convenient for both of them.

Now, they sat at a corner table in the best room, the bulky sergeant towering over the wiry doctor.

'I warned him,' Patterson said. 'I told him it would go wrong. But you know Sam.'

Ellie Carr nodded. She did, indeed, know Sam. They had been bedding each other – on and off – for well over a decade, and though the word 'love' had never passed between them, they shared an affection which was – as near as damn it – just that.

'If I can get access to the docks, I just might be able to come up with something that will help Sam,' Ellie Carr said.

'You'd be wasting your time even trying,' Patterson replied.

'I'm a good forensic scientist, you know,' Carr said, bridling.

'You're the best there is,' Patterson said.

And so she was. Ellie Carr had been doing brilliant work in the field of forensic science before there'd even been – officially – a field for her to be brilliant in, and when Patterson thought back over the years, he could recall at least a dozen cases that he and Blackstone would never have solved without her help.

'So if I *am* the best, why would I be wasting my time down at the docks?' Carr demanded.

'The money's long gone,' Patterson said. 'That's obvious to everybody – even Brigham knows it really. But he's so desperate that he has to keep believing there's a slim chance it's still somewhere in the Western Dock, so he's had fifty men there all morning – turning over anything that can be turned over.'

'And destroying any forensic evidence in the process,' Ellie Carr said gloomily.

'Exactly,' Patterson agreed.

'Then if that won't work, we need to get Sam one of the top lawyers in London.'

'Can you afford that? Because I know I can't.'

'Of course I can't afford it,' Ellie said. 'Since I've been knocking around with Sam Blackstone, I've been donating half my salary to his precious Dr Barnardo's Orphanage.'

Despite the situation, Patterson smiled.

'Half your salary,' he repeated. 'I didn't know that.'

'No, you wouldn't know,' Ellie agreed. 'I've been keeping it very quiet, in case people thought I was as crazy as Sam.' She paused for a moment. 'So we can't *pay* for a top lawyer,' she continued, 'but I might be able to persuade one to work for us for free – in the interest of justice. I'm very good at persuading people to do things they don't want to.'

'I do know that – from all things you've talked me into doing,' Patterson said. 'But even if you manage to get an outstanding lawyer, it won't do any good.'

'Why not?'

'Because Brigham needs to see Sam go down, in order to save himself. And because Assistant Commissioner Todd is determined to get his revenge on Sam before he dies. Together, they'll do anything they have to do – and that includes manufacturing evidence – which means that by the time the case gets to court, it will be as solid as a rock.'

'So if there's no evidence to save him, and it's pointless getting a lawyer, what can we do?' Ellie Carr asked despondently.

'I'll think of something,' Patterson promised.

'Like what?'

'I don't know,' Patterson admitted. 'But something *will* come to me – because it bloody well *has* to!'

It was late afternoon when they led Blackstone from the cell in the basement to the central courtyard. There were two of them in his escort – a sergeant and a constable. They communicated with each other only by gestures and refused to look their prisoner in the eye.

Out in the courtyard, Blackstone shivered, but that had less to do with the air temperature than with the sight of the police van – the Black Maria – which would be taking him across the river to Southwark Crown Court, and from there to Wormwood Scrubs prison.

It was as the sergeant was half assisting, half pushing Blackstone into the back of the Black Maria that he finally broke his silence.

'I never thought that I'd live to see this day come, sir,' he said bitterly. 'I've always looked up to you, you know. You were a bit of a hero to me, if the truth be told.'

'So you're assuming that I'm guilty as charged, are you, Sergeant?' Blackstone asked.

The question seemed to quite stump the other man.

'Well, they have arrested you, haven't they, sir?' he said finally.

Yes, they've arrested me, Blackstone agreed silently. *They've arrested me – and that means I must have done it.*

Once Blackstone was inside the van, the sergeant locked the doors and he and the constable climbed into the cab.

Blackstone looked around him at the four metal walls and the one tiny barred window.

It was, to all intents and purposes, a cell on wheels, he thought, and he'd do well to get used to this feeling of confinement, because – until they led him to the big drop from which no man returned – a box not unlike this would be his 'home'.

The Black Maria pulled out on to the Embankment. If he'd wished to, Blackstone could have stood up and peered through the small window, taking in a last view of his beloved London. But the pain would have been too great, and he remained on the bench.

Not that it made much difference whether he gazed out of the window or not, he soon realized fatalistically. He knew the city so well that he didn't have to *look* at it to *see* it, and as the van bounced over the cobbles, pictures of the buildings it was passing were being played out in his mind.

The van turned. They were crossing Southwark Bridge now, and soon they would arrive at the magistrate's court, where, after a brief hearing, the duty magistrate would order the prisoner in the dock to be taken down and bound over.

Blackstone found himself wishing that Max had hit him harder – had crushed his skull so that he would have been spared the humiliation he would suffer in the coming days.

But Max had *wanted* him humiliated.

Max had hit him just hard enough so that he would lose consciousness for a few hours and come round again on the Embankment.

The Black Maria came to a sudden screeching, skidding halt. Blackstone was not prepared for it and found himself being catapulted across the van and slammed into the opposite wall, before losing his balance and ending up on the floor.

As he picked himself up, he could hear a banging coming from the front of the van, followed by loud, urgent, *demanding* voices.

The back doors of the Black Maria were suddenly flung open, and light streamed in.

Blackstone blinked – temporarily blinded – then, as his eyes learned to focus again, he saw a hooded man with a pistol in his hand.

'Get out of the van!' the man shouted.

'Who are you?' Blackstone asked.

'Don't ask stupid questions – just get out of the bloody van,' the man bellowed.

The man's accent located him as coming from somewhere in south London, the policeman part of Blackstone's brain thought automatically; the timbre of his voice indicated he was in his thirties, the fact that he had a revolver suggested he was a criminal of some kind, and . . .

'Now!' the man screamed.

It was never wise to argue with someone carrying a weapon. Blackstone went to back of the van and stepped down into the road.

'Hold out your hands,' the man ordered.

And when Blackstone did, he produced a set of keys and unlocked the handcuffs, pulled them free,and let them clatter to the ground.

'You've got about five minutes to get away, so if I was you, I'd make the most of it,' the man said.

Blackstone took a sidestep closer to the centre of the bridge. From there, he could see the lorry that had been deliberately slewed across the road, blocking the Black Maria's passage.

And from there, too, he could also see – with mounting horror – what was happening at the front of the van.

The sergeant and the constable were no longer in the cab but were standing beside it, with their arms held in the air. And a few feet from them was another hooded figure – this one a portly man in a grey overcoat – who was pointing his pistol right at them.

'That isn't . . . it can't be . . .' Blackstone gasped.

'It's nobody you know,' the man who'd released him said unconvincingly, 'and you've already used up a minute of that five minutes I told you you'd got.'

There was nothing he could do at that moment to save his fat sergeant from the position he'd got himself into, Blackstone thought, and if he didn't make a break soon, then Archie's insane – heroic – gesture would have been pointless.

'Three and a half minutes,' the man next to him said.

A small crowd had gathered to watch the unfolding drama, but it was the two policemen and the hooded man who had their attention, and they took no notice at all of the middle-aged man in the second-hand brown suit who had started to run towards the Southwark side of the bridge.

As he passed Patterson, Blackstone tried to signal with his eyes that once he had ensured his own escape, he would do anything he could to help.

But the stout man had his eyes firmly on the constable and the sergeant, and didn't seem to notice him at all.

It was just after eight in the evening, and Archie Patterson was propping himself up against the bar in the Royal Oak when the two men sidled up and stood one each side of him.

'What are you doing?' one of them asked.

'What am I doing?' Patterson repeated, slurring his words. 'I'm getting drunk.'

'Getting drunk – or already *are* drunk?' the second man asked him.

Patterson blinked. 'I suppose I'm *already* drunk,' he admitted. 'Yes, I must be. Getting drunk is what you do when your world collapses around you, when all the cert . . . all the certainties . . . that you've lived your whole life by have suddenly turned to shit.'

'That's a nice overcoat you're wearing,' the first man said. 'How would you describe it?'

'' S an overcoat,' Patterson replied. 'A grey one.'

'And have you been wearing it all day?'

'Mos' certainly – it's brass monkey weather out there.'

The man on Patterson's left produced his warrant card. 'We're from Special Branch,' he said.

'Good for you,' Patterson told him.

'Are you carrying a weapon on your person, Sergeant Patterson?' the man on the right asked.

Patterson giggled. 'Certainly am,' he said. 'I've got a knuckle-duster in my right pocket, a blunderbuss in my left pocket, and a sword down my trouser leg. Why do you ask?'

'This is serious, Sergeant Patterson,' the man on the right said. 'Do you have your pistol on you?'

'Certainly have,' Patterson replied, patting his shoulder holster. He frowned and patted it again. 'It 'pears I don't,' he corrected himself.

'Then where is it?'

'If it's . . . if it's not next to my left tit, it must be back at the Yard, safely locked up. Why? Where did you imagine it was? Did you think I'd thrown it in the river?'

'That's certainly a possibility we've considered,' the man on the left said. 'Now the next thing we need to ask you is where—'

'Tired of answering questions,' Patterson said. 'Getting very bored with them, if the truth be told.'

'Just one more question,' the man on the left coaxed.

'And then will you leave me alone?'

'That will depend on your answer.'

Patterson nodded and nearly lost his balance.

'All right,' he agreed.

'Where were you at half past five this afternoon?'

Patterson blinked and then gazed blearily into the mirror behind the bar, as if he thought he would find an answer there.

'We're waiting, Sergeant Patterson,' the man on the left said.

'I was . . .' Patterson began. Then he stopped and shook his head. 'I was . . . do you know, I haven't got a bleeding clue *where* I was.'

FIVE

16th December 1916

Once the costermonger at the outdoor market had recognized him, there had been no choice but to put some distance between himself and the New Cut, Blackstone thought – but it had been foolish to come so far, because after a week of living on the streets and eating practically nothing, he had no reserves to draw on.

He looked up and down Tooley Street, which was still shrouded in swirling fog. It was not the street that he had known only three years earlier. Back then, the pubs would have been doing a roaring trade at that time of night. There would have been all manner of customers in them, too – cabbies and costermongers, shopkeepers and prostitutes, off-duty policemen and off-duty criminals – each of them knocking back as much drink as they could afford before the landlord called time. But time was called much earlier these days – the Emergency Powers Act had seen to that – and all the pubs sat silent and lonely, their engraved windows in darkness, their doors firmly shut.

'You can't afford to walk much further, Sam,' he muttered to himself. 'You've got to save your strength.'

For what? asked the voice in his head, which had once issued warnings but now seemed content merely to unceasingly mock him. *What are you saving your strength for?*

'To fight back,' Blackstone said. 'To save Archie Patterson and prove my own innocence.'

And of the two, he thought, saving his fat sergeant was by far the most important.

'*You're storing up trouble for both of us,*' Patterson had said to him that day in the Goldsmiths' Arms – and Patterson had been right.

Of course, it was possible that Archie wasn't in trouble at all – that nobody had made the connection between the bulky man in the grey overcoat who had sprung Blackstone – at gunpoint – from the Black Maria, and the bulky man in the grey overcoat who had been Blackstone's sergeant for nearly two decades.

It was possible – but it wasn't at all likely.

So how *will you save Archie?* asked the malevolent voice. *Do you have a plan?*

No, Blackstone admitted, he didn't have a plan. And, indeed, what plan *could* an exhausted, half-starved man come up with which would save the sergeant from the grip of the powerful Metropolitan Police?

It was the carriage, standing majestically just beyond the corner of Battle Bridge Lane, that brought him to a halt. Carriages were no longer a common sight in London – the rich had shifted their allegiance to chauffeur-driven automobiles years earlier – and even when they were spotted, it was rare to find one driven by a coachman in full livery, as this one was.

Why have you stopped? asked the voice in Blackstone's head.

'I'm looking at the carriage,' Blackstone replied.

No, you're not – you're looking at the coachman.

'And why would I do that?'

Because you know that coachmen are at the whim of their masters. They can never be sure when their day's work will finally end, or even when they'll be allowed to eat.

'That's true, but . . .'

So they always carry food with them, don't they? And perhaps this particular coachman can be persuaded to give a little of that food to a poor wretch who's eaten almost nothing all week.

'I won't beg,' Blackstone said, firmly and angrily. 'However bad things get, I won't beg.'

And then – perhaps because he was afraid the coachman might have magically read his thoughts and would look down on him with contempt as he passed by – he turned off Tooley Street and on to Battle Bridge Lane.

He was halfway between the main street and the river when he saw the shape lying in the road. He thought at first that it was just a load of old discarded sacking, but as he got closer to it, he could see that it was a man.

And not just *any* man, but a gentleman.

A toff!

The supine man was wearing an expensive-looking frock coat, and though he was bareheaded, there was a top hat – which must also belong to him – on the ground a few feet away.

For a moment, Blackstone thought of stepping around him – the man was probably drunk and so had no one to blame but himself – but then he relented and knelt down beside him.

The man groaned. 'Where am I?'

He certainly did not smell of alcohol, Blackstone noted.

'You're just near the river,' he said. 'Do you remember how you got here?'

'I was in my carriage, going along Tooley Street,' the man replied, his voice steadier now, but still confused. 'I started to feel a little peculiar and thought a walk down to the river might clear my head. I told my coachman to wait for me, and set off down Battle Bridge Lane . . .'

'That's where you are now.'

'. . . and then, I suppose, I must have fainted.'

'Do you think you can stand up?' Blackstone asked.

'Perhaps – if you help me.'

'Of course,' Blackstone agreed.

There'd been a time – only days earlier – when hauling the man to his feet would have been no trouble at all, but Blackstone was so weak now that even offering a little assistance took a great deal of effort.

Even when he was standing, the man held on to his rescuer for at least half a minute before finally relinquishing his grip.

'Still feel peculiar,' he admitted, 'but I think I'll be all right now.'

'Is there anything else I can do for you?' Blackstone asked.

'You might retrieve my top hat for me, if you don't mind,'

the man said, smiling. 'And then I would appreciate it if you could give me your support until I reach my carriage.'

'It will be my pleasure,' Blackstone said, picking up the hat and offering the man his arm.

The walk back up Battle Bridge Lane put a strain on both of them, but eventually they reached Tooley Street and the carriage.

As the coachman climbed down from his box to assist his master, the gentleman turned to Blackstone.

'Look here, my good man, I'd like to give you a little something for your trouble,' he said.

Blackstone shook his head. 'That won't be necessary. What I've done for you, I'd have done for any man.'

'Perhaps *you* would, but there are many people who would not,' the gentleman countered. 'You might have robbed me as I lay there, and – God knows – you look as if you could use the money. But instead, you behaved like a Christian, and that is surely worthy of some small reward.'

'I don't . . .' Blackstone began.

The man reached into his waistcoat pocket and produced a coin. It was a golden guinea.

'Take this,' he said, holding out the coin. 'Come on, man, you can tell from the way I'm dressed that I won't miss it, and it could do a great deal for you.'

It could indeed, Blackstone agreed silently.

'Thank you,' he said, taking the guinea and pocketing it.

'No, thank *you*,' the gentleman said.

An hour earlier, he had been hoping desperately for a turnip, and now he had a guinea in his pocket, Blackstone thought, as he watched the coach drive away.

And yet, though he had wanted the turnip, he had not wanted the guinea, and he wondered why that was.

You know *why it was,* said the malevolent voice.

'Do I?' Blackstone asked.

Of course. What have you spent most of last week thinking about?

'Surviving.'

Just so. And now you have a guinea which will buy you decent food and a roof over your head at night. Now you have the luxury to think about the future – and you don't want *to think about the future.*

The voice was right, he thought. Just before he had found the toff, he had been thinking about the future – and it had been agony. The guinea would buy him weeks in which he would have nothing to do but contemplate what lay ahead – and that was just unbearable.

End it now, Sam, said the voice. *Accept that you'll never be able to save Archie. Spare yourself the humiliation of the trial. You're already as good as dead – why not go all the way?*

Yes, why not go all the way, Blackstone agreed.

He had always suspected that he might eventually kill himself – on two occasions he had come very close to making that suspicion a certainty – and whenever he had pictured it happening, it had always involved the river.

And how could it not have involved the river? The Thames was the beating heart of the city he loved, and what better way to make himself at one with that city than by drowning himself in the soothing waters?

He turned off Tooley Street and began what he had accepted would be his last walk down Battle Bridge Lane.

Blackstone had almost reached Battle Bridge Steps when he realized he was being followed.

'You're slipping,' he told himself. 'The old Sam would have noticed them long ago.'

But that was just the point! He wasn't the old Sam any longer.

He turned to face his enemies – and even before he'd turned, he was sure that was *exactly* what they were.

There were two of them – young thugs with bad teeth and twisted expressions. They had not volunteered for the army like all the decent lads from the area had. They had stayed behind, like jackals – free, now that the lions had gone, to feed on what-ever looked weak and helpless.

'We saw that toff give you some money,' one of them snarled. 'Why would he go and do that?'

'He'd fainted,' Blackstone said wearily, knowing that this was nothing more than a ritual leading to a demand, but going along with it anyway. 'I helped him back to his carriage.'

'Dropped your trousers and let him have his way with you,

more like,' the young thug said. 'Anyway, we saw him hand you money – and now we're going to take it off you.'

What good was a guinea to a man who was planning to drown himself? Blackstone wondered.

Why not simply hand it over to them?

And yet, he was surprised to discover, he did not *want* to hand it over – in fact, he was willing to fight to the last drop of his blood to keep it.

'Come on, you old bastard,' one of the thugs said impatiently. 'Give us the money.'

He was the leader, Blackstone decided. He was the one who would make the first move.

'Make us work for it, and we'll have to hurt you,' the second thug said. He turned to the other boy. 'Ain't that right, Sid?'

'That's right,' Sid agreed.

Sid was *definitely* the leader – the plan was only the plan when he'd confirmed it.

'Well?' Sid demanded.

Blackstone shrugged. 'I'm not giving you the money. Do what you have to do.'

'Oh, I will,' Sid said. 'Believe me, I will.'

One moment, his open hand was empty, the next it was closed and gripping a knife.

'Get him, Bill!' the young thug shouted.

But Blackstone knew it wouldn't be like that, and that though he was supposed to turn to defend himself against Bill, it was Sid who would want to draw the first blood.

He turned for a split second – as Sid had been expecting him to – then swung round again.

Sid was rushing at him, the knife held high in his hand, ready for a downward stab.

'Amateur!' Blackstone thought in disgust.

Didn't the thug know that, in a knife attack, the blade should go in upwards? Whatever *were* they teaching young criminals these days?

Sid feinted to the right and then switched quickly to the left.

It was his genitals that first learned the plan had gone wrong, though the message quickly spread to the rest of his body, and he screamed and then sank to his knees.

Blackstone's right foot, which had only just returned to the ground, lashed out again and caught him in the chest.

That would hurt – but not as much as if the boot had struck its intended target, which was Sid's face.

He had less than a second in which to deal with Bill, Blackstone told himself, but even before he felt the blackjack strike his skull, he knew that he was not going to make it.

His legs buckled beneath him, and he fell to the ground. He would have to move quickly if he was to survive, but he was already accepting that that would be almost impossible.

Bill was on him, straddling him and pinning him down. Sid was struggling to his feet and looking around for his knife. Blackstone tried to break free, and realized just how hopeless it was.

Sid had found his knife on the ground, and was now kneeling next to Blackstone and Bill.

'I'm not goin' to kill yer,' he said, in a cracked voice. 'That'd be too quick. What I'm goin' to do instead is cut yer eyes out.'

He could find his way to the river with no eyes, Blackstone told himself – and a blind man can drown just as easily as a seeing man.

'If you're going to do it, then get on with it,' he said.

'You'd like that, wouldn't yer?' Sid taunted. 'You'd like it to be over as quick as possible? But I'm goin' to make yer wait. I'm goin' to give yer time to *think* about it.'

'If this is an example of the much-vaunted British sense of fair play, then it is a rather bad one,' said a voice behind them.

They all turned. The speaker was a stocky man of about Blackstone's age. He was wearing an opera cloak which had not been in fashion for at least a decade, and was leaning heavily on a walking stick with a silver handle.

'Are you a foreigner or somefink?' asked Sid.

Oh yes, he was a foreigner all right, thought Blackstone.

Only a few days earlier, he had assumed that Vladimir was dead, but now, hearing the man's voice for the first time in nearly twenty years, he recognized it immediately.

'Yes, I am a foreigner – I would have thought that was obvious when I spoke of your *British* attitude to fair play,' the newcomer said calmly. 'And now that I have made my point, I will leave you to your unpleasant – and, if I may say so, somewhat cowardly – business, and be on my way.'

'Hang on a minute,' Sid said, 'before you go, I want that walking stick and whatever yer've got in yer pocket.'

'I am afraid that will not be possible,' Vladimir told him.

'Give me your stuff, or we'll cut out *your* eyes, as well,' Sid said.

The man in the cloak frowned. 'You should not have threatened me,' he said, with a new, harder edge to his voice. 'I do not like being threatened.'

Sid stood up, waving his knife in front of him. The new arrival lifted his walking stick up, as if he hoped to defend himself with it.

'That won't save you, grandad,' Sid sneered.

'No, that won't save yer,' echoed Bill, still astride Blackstone.

Sid should have been paying more attention, Blackstone thought. He should have noted that Vladimir was standing perfectly comfortably without the support of his stick – and he should have drawn a very worrying conclusion from that.

But he didn't.

'I'll slice you up, you dirty foreign bugger,' Sid boasted. 'First, I'll cut your heart out, and then I'll . . .'

He stopped speaking as the casing of the stick clattered to the ground and the thin naked sword it had held glittered in the moonlight.

'OK, take it easy, mister, none of us wants any trouble,' Sid said.

But he did not sound half as frightened as he should have, because he still thought he could control the situation.

Vladimir took one step forward, the sword flashed, and Sid sank to the ground.

Blackstone felt Bill go rigid on top of him.

'Listen,' the young thug said, in a panic, 'this wasn't never part—'

The sword whistled through the air, slashing across Bill's throat. The young man gurgled, and his blood began to gush from the wound like a fountain.

Blackstone pushed the dying thug off him.

'His lungs will fill in seconds, and he will drown in his own blood,' Vladimir said easily. 'Why do I do these things?' he continued, and now – though he was still speaking in English – he was addressing himself. 'In Russia, I'm a serious man – perhaps even a grave one – but the moment I set foot on these shores, I feel an almost irrepressible urge to behave exactly like a cheap music-hall comedian. And what does that result in? It results in me having to kill two young hooligans *who didn't even get the joke!*'

There was no regret in his voice, Blackstone noted – merely a hint of annoyance at the inconvenience he had caused himself.

Bill was thrashing around on the ground, trying to scream and finding it impossible.

Blackstone raised himself on one elbow but did not feel strong enough yet to struggle back to his feet.

'I have a little business to conduct at the end of this lane, and then I intend to leave the area as quickly as possible,' Vladimir said, leaning forward and wiping the blood off his sword on the dead Sid's jacket, 'and if you are in any state to do so, I would advise you to follow the same course of action yourself.'

Blackstone made no reply. He was ashamed of his present condition – deeply ashamed – and of all the people in the world from whom he might wish to hide his fall, the Russian was at the top of the list.

How could he let this man, above all others – the man who had worked with him to prevent the assassination of Queen Victoria; who, in Russia, had partnered him in solving the case of the missing Fabergé egg – see what he had become?

Bill had stopped writhing, and – with a final desperate gurgle – he died.

'I have probably just saved some young woman from a life of domestic drudgery and violence,' Vladimir said, picking up the sheath of his sword and sliding the sword back into it. 'But, then again, this hypothetical young woman will probably end up married to someone just as bad as this brute.'

Then he turned and began to walk towards the river.

He had to get away before the police arrived, Blackstone told himself. If he didn't, they would probably add these two murders to the list of crimes they were pinning on him. He put both hands on the ground, palms down, and attempted to lever himself up.

And then his brain decided it was all too much of an effort and shut itself down.

Blackstone had no idea how long he had been unconscious, but when he came to again, he was aware of the sound of someone approaching him from the river.

'I was supposed to meet my contact at the foot of the steps, but he was obviously alarmed by my little contretemps with your friends and has rowed away into the night,' Vladimir said. He took a flashlight from his pocket and shone it over Blackstone's trunk. 'Your clothes are covered with blood, but that is hardly surprising,' he continued. 'You need to change out of them, or it will not take even your slow British coppers long to work out that you were involved in all this.'

Go away, Blackstone prayed silently. *Please just go away.*

'We all have to pay for our little idiosyncrasies in the end,' Vladimir said, 'and while it is true, on the one hand, that I undoubtedly saved your life tonight, it could also be argued that I am indirectly the cause of the present state of your wardrobe –' he gave a small sigh – 'so I suppose I had better give you the money for a new outfit.'

He had to speak now, Blackstone told himself. There was simply no choice in the matter.

'I have money,' he croaked.

Vladimir shrugged. 'If you wish to cling to your tattered pride – to your pathetic sense of dignity – then that is up to you.'

He turned away, took a few short steps towards Tooley Street, then spun around again.

'I know you,' he said.

'You're mistaken,' Blackstone told him.

'I am sure I know you,' Vladimir said, squatting down and shining his torch into Blackstone's face. 'Is it . . . could it be you, Sam?' he gasped.

'Please go away,' Blackstone said weakly. 'You're endangering my investigation.'

'Your investigation?' Vladimir repeated, disbelievingly.

'I'm in disguise.'

Vladimir shook his head slowly. 'Of course you are,' he agreed.

He stripped off his cloak and held his hand out to Blackstone. 'Let me help you to your feet,' he suggested.

SIX

The Hansom cabs which were lined up at the rank on Tooley Street had a defeated air about them that was detectable even from a distance. It had not always been thus – when Blackstone had first started working at New Scotland Yard, the Hansoms had been undisputed kings of the streets, and the clip-clop sound of their horses' hooves had seemed as much a part of London life as the yells of the newspaper vendors.

But their glory days were over, and the petrol-driven 'taxis' – so called because they had taximeters which measured the mileage – had been eating away at their business for years. Now, there were only a couple of hundred Hansoms left in the whole of London, and even though they were cheaper than the taxis – six pence a mile in the Hansoms, eight pence a mile in the taxis – the cabmen were finding it harder and harder to make a decent living.

'They're like me,' Blackstone thought, with a bitter whimsy born of hunger and exhaustion. 'They're desperate to keep on going – but they're doomed.'

Vladimir helped Blackstone into the Hansom at the front of line, then looked up at the driver, who was sitting on his box behind the cab.

'The East India Dock Road, cabbie,' he said. 'I'll bang my stick on the roof when I want you to stop.'

'The East India Dock Road,' Blackstone repeated softly to himself. 'Little Russia.'

He knew it well. It was home to countless Russian revolutionaries and members of the tsarist court who had fallen out of favour. Former peasants from the Ukraine lived there, and rubbed shoulders with horse traders from Siberia and tailors from Minsk. And, for the moment at least, it appeared to be where Vladimir had established his base.

As the cab pulled away from the curb, the Russian said, 'So tell me, Sam, however did you come to be in this pitiful condition?'

'It's quite a long story,' Blackstone said.

'It's quite a long way to our destination,' Vladimir replied.

And there was a commanding edge to his voice that said he would have the story, one way or the other.

Despite his exhaustion and his pain, a grin came to Blackstone's face. It was typical of Vladimir to want to know the full story, he thought, because the Russian had a thirst for information – *any* information.

It was always possible that, one day, some of that information might come in useful – just as a collector of string might, one day, suddenly need to wrap a large and complex parcel that required miles of the stuff. But that was not why the string collector collected string, nor why Vladimir collected information.

It was an obsession, and Vladimir could no more resist it than some of his compatriots could resist a bottle of vodka. He was – and always had been – an addict.

'Whether a story is long or short, it is always best to start at the beginning,' Vladimir nudged.

Blackstone sighed. There was no getting round it, he decided.

He began by telling Vladimir of his first meeting with the head of the Special Branch.

He was only halfway through when the Russian interrupted him.

'I don't think that I much like the sound of this Superintendent Brigham of yours,' Vladimir said. 'He is just the sort of man I would take great pleasure in crushing, and – don't misunderstand me, Sam – I do not mean that in any metaphorical sense.'

When Blackstone got on to Max, Vladimir found it impossible to restrain his amusement.

'He didn't know the man's name, and yet he was prepared to hand over twenty-five thousand pounds to him,' the Russian said, between chuckles. 'For that amount of money, I would demand – as a minimum – that he gave me his first-born child as a hostage.'

'But then maybe you're not as desperate as Brigham – and the British government,' Blackstone pointed out.

'Desperation is a weakness,' Vladimir said, 'but when combined with foolishness, it is nothing less than a capital crime – and Brigham clearly *is* a fool. Why did you agree to go along with his plan?'

'I was ordered to.'

'I would not have obeyed that order, even if it had come as a direct instruction from His Imperial Majesty Nicholas the Second, Emperor and Autocrat of All the Russias,' Vladimir said.

Blackstone laughed – it seemed to him to be a long time since he had done that.

'Have I said something funny?' the Russian asked.

'I know you too well to believe what you just said, Vladimir,' Blackstone replied. 'If His Imperial Majesty Nicholas the Second – Emperor and Autocrat of All the Russias – had told you to saw off your arm with a teaspoon, you would have tried your hardest to comply.'

'True,' Vladimir agreed, rather uncomfortably, 'but I still don't think you should have obeyed the instructions of a jumped-up bureaucrat like Superintendent Brigham.' He paused. 'Of course! How foolish I'm being! It was not Brigham's order that made you decide to accept the mission. That wasn't it at all. So why don't you tell me your real reason?'

'I couldn't bring myself to get my neck free of a noose by putting another man's neck in its place,' Blackstone said.

Vladimir nodded, as if Blackstone had simply confirmed what he already knew.

'That has always been your greatest weakness,' he said ponderously, 'although, admittedly, it has also always been your greatest strength. What happened next?'

Blackstone told Vladimir about the meeting at the Western Dock and waking up on the park bench with a thousand pounds in his pocket.

'What do you think was Max's motive in "fitting you up", Sam?' Vladimir asked.

'I'm still not sure,' Blackstone admitted. 'The only answer I can come up with is that it bought him some time.'

'You mean that as long as the police were devoting all their energy to questioning you, they wouldn't really be looking for him?'

'That's right.'

Vladimir shook his head.

'That doesn't make sense,' he said. 'Carrying your unconscious body from the docks to the embankment must have both taken quite some time and been very risky. And the thousand pounds he put in your pocket means a thousand pounds less for him. So it seems to me that, on balance, the advantages he gained from framing you were far outweighed by the disadvantages.'

'It seems that way to me, too,' Blackstone said.

'Still, life is full of unsolved mysteries,' Vladimir said philosophically, 'and there is no doubt that he did frame you. But what surprises me, to be honest, is that Superintendent Brigham took the bait quite so easily.'

'It was the only way he could make it seem like my mistake, instead of his,' Blackstone said. 'And then, of course, it was also what Assistant Commissioner Todd wanted.'

'I remember Todd from Russia,' Vladimir said. 'If there was such a thing as the king of fools, he would be wearing the crown.' He glanced out of the window, to see where they were. 'And now we come to the best part of your narrative,' he continued.

'The best part?'

'Your escape! I am eager to learn what devilish trickery you used to break free.'

'It was nothing to do with me,' Blackstone said, and he told Vladimir what had happened on Southwark Bridge.

'I wish I'd met this Sergeant Patterson of yours,' Vladimir said. 'He seems like a remarkable man.'

'He is,' Blackstone agreed.

'And what of his accomplice – the man who released you from the handcuffs? Do you think that he was a policeman, too?'

'No,' Blackstone said. 'Archie would never have asked another officer to take the same risk as he was taking.'

'So who *was* the second man?'

'He was probably some criminal who owed Archie a favour.'

'Yes, that is more than likely,' Vladimir agreed.

He glanced out of the window, then lifted his cane and banged once on the roof of the Hansom. The cab slowed, and then came to a halt.

Looking out himself, Blackstone saw that they had pulled up in front of a house that was only distinguished by its ordinariness.

'We have arrived,' Vladimir announced.

The bed on which Archie Patterson lay was far too narrow for a man of his girth, and the room that contained the bed was so cramped that it was almost impossible to avoid banging into one of the walls. Still, that was only to be expected, he thought. After all, this wasn't the Ritz – it was Pentonville Prison.

He shifted slightly – in search of a more comfortable position, even though he already knew there wasn't one – and, looking up the ceiling, cast his mind back to his brief appearance in the magistrates' court.

The press have not been informed about what happened at the docks, nor been given the name of the man whom Patterson is accused of helping to escape, but the very fact that a detective sergeant from Scotland Yard should be involved in holding up a Black Maria is more than enough for them – and they have gone to town on it. So when Patterson is brought up from the cells and emerges in the dock, he is not surprised to see that both the press gallery and the public gallery are just about as full as they possibly could be.

The magistrate's clerk looks down at the paper in his hand, then up at the dock in which Patterson is standing.

'How do you plead?' he asks. 'Guilty or not guilty?'

Patterson is not sure how he is going to respond, because he still doesn't know whether he did it or not.

He remembers being in the Goldsmith's Arms with Ellie Carr, and he remembers being arrested in the Royal Oak by the two officers from Special Branch, but he can recall nothing in between.

So did he hold up the Black Maria, or didn't he?

All the evidence would suggest that he did, and he knows that he would have laid down his life for Sam Blackstone without a second's thought, so the chances are he is guilty as charged.

'Guilty or not guilty?' the clerk repeats impatiently.

'Not guilty,' Patterson says.

And he's thinking, 'If they're going to lock me up and throw away the key, the least I can do is make them work for it.'

Ellie Carr has managed to scrape together a little money to pay for Patterson's solicitor, and now that solicitor stands up.

'My client is a married man with three small children, and he would like to request bail so that he can set his affairs in order before he comes to trial,' the solicitor says.

'Because we all know I won't be able to set my affairs in order after the trial,' Patterson thinks.

The magistrate glances in the direction of the inspector in charge of the case. The inspector nods.

'Bail is set at twenty-five pounds,' the magistrate says.

There is an explosion of coughing from the back of the court-room, and when Patterson turns his head towards it, he sees that the person causing the disturbance is Assistant Commissioner Todd, who, between coughs, is glaring first at the magistrate and then at the inspector.

The inspector clears his own throat. 'The police feel that twenty-five pounds is too little, Your Worship,' he says.

The magistrate glances at Todd again. 'Very well,' he agrees. 'Bail is set at two hundred and fifty pounds.'

'Todd will never forgive me for rescuing Sam Blackstone and denying him his revenge,' Patterson thinks.

And then he wonders if he's just admitted to himself that he's guilty.

If I didn't rescue Sam, then I bloody well should *have done,* Patterson thought, still gazing up at the ceiling.

He was going down for a long time, he accepted. It wouldn't be easy for him, but that didn't matter. What *did* matter was that his lovely wife and beautiful kids would suffer, too. The only bright spot in his increasingly darkening sky, he told himself, was that at least Sam seemed to have escaped.

The woman who answered Vladimir's knock was plump, middle-aged and had a welcoming half-sincere smile on her face.

'Good evening, Mr Hoskinson,' she said, in a cultivated accent which didn't quite come off, 'and good evening to you, too, sir,' she continued, looking at Blackstone.

'Good evening, Mrs Collins,' Vladimir replied affably. 'My friend has had an accident. He will require a hot bath as soon as possible.'

The woman nodded. 'You take him up to your apartment, sir, and I'll put the copper on.'

Mrs Collins looked just like a landlady was supposed to, Blackstone thought, as Vladimir assisted him up the stairs. In fact, there was not a theatre producer in the whole of London who wouldn't immediately cast her as one. But even without a stage to perform on, she was only *playing* the role, because no real

landlady could ever have looked at her unexpected visitor – dishev-
elled, dirty, and with his bloodstained suit not quite entirely hidden
by Vladimir's cloak – and acted with such equanimity.

'Is Mrs Collins . . .' he began.

'She's half-Russian,' Vladimir said, as if that was all the answer
Blackstone needed.

And, in fact, it was.

SEVEN

Vladimir's apartment continued the illusion of ordinariness
that Mrs Collins had created on the doorstep. It was well
furnished – though not extravagantly so – but had the
slightly uncared-for feel with which many confirmed bachelors
seem to imbue their residences.

Blackstone wondered how the *real* Vladimir would have
furnished his apartment – and then realized that, after years of
spying, it was possible there *was* no real Vladimir any more.

The Russian gestured that he should sit in the best armchair.

'Would you care for a glass of vodka, Sam?' he asked.

It was tempting, but after days of near starvation, Blackstone
didn't think he could risk it.

'No vodka, but I wouldn't mind a cup of tea,' he said, looking
across at the large samovar – the only real hint of Russia in the
room – which was sitting in the corner.

'Tea, it shall be,' Vladimir agreed, immediately busying himself
with the samovar.

'I've told you all about me,' Blackstone said. 'Now it's your
turn. What are you doing here in London?'

'I am just passing through,' the Russian replied, far too casually.
'I arrived two days ago, and by tomorrow evening I will be gone.'

'And what was the purpose of your short trip?'

'There were some people here who I needed to talk to.'

Vladimir crossed the room, handed Blackstone a glass of tea,
then sat down opposite him. The tea was hot and very sweet,
and as he sipped at it, Blackstone started to feel a little better.

'And what was it you needed to talk to these people *about*?' Blackstone asked.

'Naval movements, arms production – matters of that nature,' Vladimir replied, squiggling in his chair to make himself comfortable. 'I was doing what I have always done, Sam – I was spying.'

'On us?'

'Naturally, I am spying on *you*. Why else would I be in England at all?'

'But we're your allies – we're fighting Germany on the Western Front, and you're fighting it in the east,' Blackstone protested.

Vladimir laughed. 'Of course you're our allies – that is precisely why I am here. You can always trust your enemies' intentions, Sam. They have one aim, which is to destroy you. And so, in order to prevent that, you try to discover what their plans are – which divisions they will move to where, on which front they intend to concentrate their attack.' He waved his hand expansively through the air. 'These are purely mechanical matters, which any competent spy could deal with, and they hold no interest for me.'

'But spying on your friends *does* interest you?' Blackstone suggested.

'It fascinates me,' Vladimir admitted. 'Your friends, you see, have part of their minds on the present conflict, and the other part on the future. If they lose the war, then half their effort will have been wasted. But what if they win? The old threat will have been vanquished, but there is a new threat – and that comes from those who were formerly your allies. Everyone has plans to be top dog, Sam, but, by the very nature of things, there can only be *one* top dog.'

'So you're here to find out what Britain intends to do once the war is finally over?'

'That – and whether you have the *capacity* to do it.'

'And have you learned anything of interest?'

'I have learned more than any other man in my position would have done,' Vladimir said. He grinned. 'I am very good at my job, you know.'

'You haven't answered my question,' Blackstone pointed out.

'Indeed, I have not,' Vladimir agreed.

Blackstone lit up a cigarette from a packet that Vladimir had given him earlier. He hadn't smoked for a whole week, and it felt almost as if he was inhaling opium.

'Aren't you taking a bit of a chance by telling me all this, Vladimir?' he wondered.

The Russian laughed again. 'I don't think so. Who would you tell, and why would they listen to you? By your own account, you're a wanted man – a criminal, and possibly a traitor. And even if they would listen, you'd never be able to prove that I was actually here. Last night I was at a party given by Grand Duke Dimitri in Moscow. Tonight, even as we speak, I am at the ballet, watching a rather bravely experimental revival of *Don Quixote*. And I can produce a score of witnesses, of the most reputable kind, to verify those claims.'

'I'm sure you can,' Blackstone agreed.

There was a knock on the door and two of Mrs Collins's servants entered with a tin bath. They half bowed to both Vladimir and Blackstone, and – like Mrs Collins – seemed to find nothing extraordinary about Blackstone's condition.

The servants placed the bath in front of the blazing fire, then left the room, only to return a couple of minutes later with four large pails of hot water.

As they headed for the door a second time, Vladimir said, 'Wait! When my friend has stripped off his clothes, you may take them away and burn them.'

Blackstone undressed, and lowered himself gently into the bath. He found the hot water soothing, but also a reminder of how many parts of his body *needed* to be soothed.

'Would you like me to scrub your back for you, Sam?' Vladimir asked.

'I'd appreciate it,' Blackstone replied.

Vladimir picked up the scrubbing brush and – with surprising gentleness – began to massage Blackstone's back with it.

'Before I leave, I'd like to give you some money, Sam,' the Russian said as he worked. 'I regret I cannot spare you more than one hundred pounds – this is a very expensive war, and even our secret service is feeling the squeeze – but with that amount of money, you could at least escape from London.'

'I won't leave London,' Blackstone said firmly.

'Why not?'

'It would be like running away.'

'And what are you doing while you are *in* London – what

would you be doing in London even with a hundred pounds in
your pocket – but running away?' Vladimir wondered. 'No, I'm
wrong. What you are doing here is much worse than running
away – you are hiding like a frightened rabbit.'

It was true, Blackstone thought. Money wouldn't change his
circumstances. Whether it was the guinea the old gentleman had
given him on Battle Bridge Lane or the hundred pounds that
Vladimir was offering him now, he would still be a wanted man.

'As long as I'm here, there's a chance I can clear my name,'
he said stubbornly.

'You can only do that by getting this Max to confess,' Vladimir
pointed out. 'And how will you find him when you don't even
know what he looks like? You have to face the fact that even if
you passed him in the street, you would not recognize him. And
you *won't* pass him in the street, because he will have left London
even before you were arrested.'

There was no disputing that argument, Blackstone acknow-
ledged silently.

So maybe he would drown himself, after all.

Blackstone was back in the armchair, facing Vladimir. He was
wearing a thick dressing gown and had just consumed a mound
of sandwiches that Mrs Collins had made for him. Now, finally,
his body felt able to accept the Russian's offer of a glass of
excellent vodka.

'I have an idea,' Vladimir said, out of the blue.

'An idea about how to find Max?'

'No, not that, though I will certainly instruct my agents to do
whatever they can in that respect,' Vladimir said. 'The idea that
has just come to me, however, is of an entirely different nature.'
He took a sip of his vodka. 'Isn't there an English expression
that runs along the lines of a change being as good as a holiday?'

'Something like that,' Blackstone agreed.

'Well then, why don't you have a change? Why don't you
come back to Russia with me?'

'I couldn't get out of the country,' Blackstone said. 'The police
will be watching for me at the ports.'

'My dear friend, you surely don't imagine we'd be leaving
through a port, do you?' Vladimir asked.

'Why would you want me to go back with you?' Blackstone asked suspiciously.

'I don't, particularly,' Vladimir answered offhandedly. 'The suggestion was purely unselfish. Consider it, if you wish, a token of my gratitude for the help you have given me in the past.'

Blackstone didn't believe any of it for a minute.

What he *did* believe was that, somewhere between Battle Bridge Lane and this apartment, Vladimir's quick brain had come up with a way in which he could use his old English comrade in Russia.

'Think about it, Sam,' Vladimir urged. 'If you are ever to triumph over your current difficulties, you will need to be strong. And you are not strong at this moment. In fact, you are a wreck. In Russia, you could rebuild both your strength and your confidence, and when you returned to England, you would again be the man you once were.'

It had to be a big job Vladimir had in mind for him, or he wouldn't be pushing quite so hard, Blackstone thought.

'Would I be of any help to you in Russia?' he asked innocently.

Vladimir shrugged. 'Who can say? I might, perhaps, be able to come up with some minor task you could help me with – purely for your own amusement, you understand.'

'Where in Russia would we be going? To Moscow?'

'No, we would be going to St Petersburg – or rather, Petrograd, as we're supposed to call it these days, since Petersburg sounds too German.'

'Is Agnes in Petrograd?' Blackstone heard himself say.

Now, where had that question come from? he wondered. She was not a carriage in a logical train of thought which had detached itself prematurely. In fact, he was not conscious of having been thinking about Agnes at all.

The explanation, he supposed, was that it was impossible to think of Russia without thinking of the woman who – for a few short days – he had thought would be his forever.

Vladimir had still said nothing.

'Well, is she there or not?' Blackstone asked, giving up all pretence that it was merely a casual question.

'Agnes is . . .' Vladimir began.

'Agnes is what?'

'Agnes is dead. She died of the fever, twelve years ago.'

'You were considering lying to me, weren't you?' Blackstone asked.

'On the one hand, you were once in love with Agnes, and possibly a little of that love still remains,' Vladimir said. 'On the other hand, you probably think that since she was working for me all along – and got you to work for me, without you even realizing it – she was actually unworthy of your love.'

'And the point of that little speech is . . .?' Blackstone asked.

'I was weighing up whether the thought of seeing Agnes again would make you more inclined – or less inclined – to come with me.'

'You were thinking of lying,' Blackstone repeated.

'In a manner of speaking,' Vladimir agreed.

He didn't want to go to Russia, Blackstone thought. In Russia, there would be bitter-sweet memories of Agnes in the air. In Russia, he would be completely in Vladimir's power. No, he didn't want to go to Russia – but there was something he *did* want, very badly.

'I think I'd rather stay here and take my chances,' he said.

For the briefest of moments, he thought he saw a hint of panic in the Russian's eyes. Then it was gone again.

'What we're really doing at the moment is negotiating, isn't it, Sam?' Vladimir asked.

'If you say so,' Blackstone replied blandly.

'So tell me what it is you want,' Vladimir suggested.

'I want you to save Archie Patterson.'

Vladimir frowned. 'That might be difficult. I have considerable resources at my command here in England, but even I would think twice before organizing a prison escape.'

'I didn't say that I wanted you to get him out of prison. I want you to *save* him.'

'I'm afraid I don't understand what you mean.'

'I want you to find a way to clear his name.'

'You want me to prove him innocent, even though you – and everyone else – seem to know he's guilty?'

'Yes.'

'But that is an impossible task.'

'Not impossible – just very difficult,' Blackstone said. 'And if anyone can do it, you are that man.'

Vladimir knocked back his glass of vodka and immediately poured himself another one.

He sat in complete silence for five minutes – not moving, seemingly hardly aware of where he was – and then a smile came to his face.

'I can offer no guarantee it will work, but I think I have devised a scheme that might do the trick,' he told the other man.

'You're not just saying that, are you?' Blackstone asked.

'Of course not,' Vladimir replied, and if he had taken offence, he certainly didn't show it.

'I need your word,' Blackstone said. 'Your solemn promise.'

'You have it,' Vladimir told him. 'I give you my solemn promise that I will do everything in my power to get you what you want. Is that good enough to fulfil my part of the bargain?'

'It's good enough,' Blackstone agreed.

He wondered what upholding *his* part of the bargain would entail. It would probably be something difficult, he thought; it would probably be dangerous, and there was a good chance that he would lose his own life in the process. But if it got Archie Patterson out the mess he was in, then it would all be worth it.

Vladimir stood up. 'Well, now that that is all settled, we must get ready to leave,' he said.

'We're going *now*?' Blackstone asked.

'Not this very second – I need time to pack a few things – but certainly within the hour.'

'When we first arrived here, you told me you were leaving tomorrow night,' Blackstone said.

'I said no such thing,' Vladimir contradicted him. 'My exact words were "By tomorrow night I will be gone". And so I will.'

He was a tricky bugger, Blackstone thought – as slippery as a snake.

And then he began to wonder just how many loopholes there were in the bargain they had just struck.

PART TWO
Development

EIGHT

The first time he had taken a walk from Vladimir's apartment to Nevsky Prospekt, Blackstone had been convinced he'd never make it back again, but it was getting easier every day, and that morning he'd even got as far as the Winter Palace.

He calculated that it was the twenty-second of December in England, which meant that even though there was a war going on, decorative bunting would be hanging across the streets, and shops would be staying open late so that shoppers could buy presents and Christmas cards.

There were no signs of festivities in Petrograd. It wasn't even the twenty-second of December in Petrograd, because while most of Europe had switched from the Julian calendar to the Gregorian calendar more than three hundred years earlier, Russia had clung stubbornly to the former, so it was still only the ninth of December there.

'Which means that I arrived here several days before I left England,' Blackstone thought whimsically.

He was pleased that he was starting to find things funny again, and delighted that the voice in his head seemed to have grown tired – for the moment – of taunting him.

Even so, he had not left all his anxieties behind in England. He was still worried about what would happen to Archie Patterson, and even thinking about the plans that Vladimir had for him was enough to bring him out in a cold sweat.

He had reached the tea shop that had become his favourite place to take a short rest. He stepped inside, walked over to his usual table – which was next to a large potted fern – and sat down.

The waitress – who had a pretty face that said nothing of her origins, though the broad hips and stout legs clearly marked her out as an ex-peasant – brought him his customary glass of tea without him even asking.

Blackstone smiled at her. 'Thank you,' he said automatically, then added, *'Bol'shoe spasibo.'*

She smiled back. *'Pozhalusta.'*

The waitress placed the glass on the table, then stood back to watch what her customer did next. Blackstone picked up his lump of sugar and, instead of putting it in his tea, raised it to his mouth and clamped it firmly between his teeth.

The waitress's smiled broadened.

'Ochyen kharasho,' she said – which, but for the signs of congratulation and encouragement, could have meant anything at all.

'Bol'shoe spasibo,' he said, making full use of his entire Russian vocabulary for the second time in less than a minute.

The waitress turned and walked away. Blackstone raised the glass to his lips and swilled the hot liquid around in his mouth, allowing it to absorb some of the sugar before he swallowed it.

Teaching him to drink in this way had been an elaborate joke, he realized, because none of the other customers were doing it. But it was the peasant way of drinking, according to Vladimir, and perhaps it was her way of saying that, like her, he was a peasant himself.

And so he was.

Vladimir looked out of his office, across the dull waters of the Fontanka Canal. He loved St Petersburg (and it was always Petersburg – never Petrograd – to him). But his love of the city had nothing to do with its fine buildings or sweeping boulevards, and when people described it as a monumental city – meaning a city full of monuments – they were missing the point, as far as he was concerned.

As he saw it, the *whole* of the city – the very existence of the city – was a monument to an iron will. And it was that iron will that always had – and always would – inspire him.

There had only been marshland where Petersburg now stood when Peter the Great had decided that Russia needed a new capital – and one that looked towards the west, over the Gulf of Finland, rather than gazing into the navel of its own Slavic heritage.

What a man Peter had been – a giant, in every sense of the word. Once he had decided to relocate his capital to the very edge of his empire, he had allowed nothing to stand in his way.

He had virtually banned any building with stone in the rest of his vast empire, so that there would be enough masons available to work on his new project.

He had drafted in forty thousand serfs annually – one man from every ten or twelve households – to work on the city, and these men were marched hundreds of kilometres from their homes, often in chains.

The serfs drained the swamp and built the city. Labouring under harsh conditions, tens of thousands of them had died, but that had not halted the progress, because if Russia was rich in one thing, it was rich in expendable manpower.

In just ten years, the city was finished. It was a magnificent achievement and one that would only have been possible in Russia – and, even then, only under a strong tsar.

As his mind shifted from the glories of the past to the present realities, Vladimir sighed. The war was in its third year. At least three million Russian soldiers had already been killed, and a million more had deserted and were roaming the countryside, scavenging what they could. There was a shortage of rifles and shells, which meant that men went into battle without a covering barrage or a weapon of their own. And the supply lines, which had never been very good, had almost completely broken down.

What Russia needed was a new Peter the Great, Vladimir thought. With Peter in charge, they might still have lost three million men, but their sacrifice would have brought at least a few real victories. With Peter running the war, the men working in the munitions factories would never have dared to go on strike as they did now, for fear that the tsar himself would descend on the factory and personally rip their heads from their shoulders.

Yes, they needed Peter, and all they had was Nicholas – a weak man sustained only by his belief that God had chosen him to lead Russia.

And my own personal tragedy, Vladimir thought, as he felt a tear run down his cheek, is that I can know all this and yet still be devoted to the tsar we have.

He heard the door open behind him and whirled round.

'Don't you ever knock?' he demanded.

The pretty girl in the doorway froze.

'I did knock,' she protested.

'Then knock harder next time,' Vladimir said harshly.

'I'm sorry,' the girl said.

Vladimir wiped the back of his hand across his eyes.

'No, I'm the one who's sorry,' he said. 'Of course you knocked, and if I didn't hear you, it was because I was thinking of something else.'

'Are you all right?' the girl asked worriedly.

'I'm fine, Tanya,' Vladimir replied unconvincingly.

'Are you sure?' the girl said.

'I've never been better,' Vladimir told her – and this time there was more fire in his words.

As the tea began to warm him, Blackstone found himself thinking back to his epic journey from London to Petrograd, a journey which – due to a fever-induced haze – he now only retained fragments of.

They are in a small motor boat in the middle of the English Channel, lashed by the wind and the rain, rocked by waves that seem as high as small mountains. Blackstone, lying on the floor, knows they will never make it to France – that they have nothing to look forward to but a watery grave. Vladimir, on the other hand, seems as calm as if he was boating across a mill pond.

The waves grow higher and higher; the boat is awash with salt water. And then a set of lights – which at first Blackstone thinks exist only in his imagination – suddenly appear, bobbing up and down in the darkness.

'Ah,' Vladimir says, seeing the Russian trawler himself and shouting to make his voice heard above the wind. 'Our taxi has arrived.'

After that, everything was a blank, and the next time he was conscious of anything, they were back on dry land.

They are on a train. Blackstone knows this because he can hear the click-click-click of the wheels below him, but he has no idea how they got there. They have the whole carriage to themselves, but Vladimir is standing in the doorway, talking to someone in the corridor.

'How sick is he?' asks the other man.

'It is a bad fever, but he will survive,' Vladimir answers.
'Are you sure of that?' the other man says.
'He will survive,' Vladimir repeats firmly. 'He will survive because I need him to survive.'

Blackstone put his glass of tea back on its saucer.

'I *need* him to survive,' he said softly.

Had he really heard Vladimir say that?

And *if* he had said it, what did it mean?

Vladimir looked across his desk at the young woman who had been the subject of his wrath – and then his contrition – minutes earlier.

He had nurtured many protégés over the years, he reflected. Some of them – through weakness, greed or treachery – had been a disappointment to him, and he'd been forced to deal with them accordingly. But there had been others who had developed the ability to navigate their way around the complex and all-encompassing web that he had spun over so much of Russian life.

Yes, some of them had been very good indeed, but none of them – not even Agnes – had come close to being as accomplished as this girl. Tanya was both intelligent and fearless, and though she had her weaknesses, he knew exactly what they were and was sure he could keep them under control.

'How is your visitor?' the girl asked.

'Need you sound so disdainful whenever you refer to him?' Vladimir wondered.

'I don't like him,' Tanya said.

'How can you possibly say that you do not like him when you don't even know him?' Vladimir said sharply.

Tanya opened her mouth to say something, then changed her mind and clamped it closed again.

'Well?' Vladimir demanded.

'I know that he's English – and that's enough.'

'That wasn't what you were *going* to say, was it?'

'No.'

'So instead of saying what you really feel, you fall back – for reasons of your own – on simple prejudice. And we cannot afford prejudice in our line of work, Tanya. If we do not see things as they really are, we are doomed.'

The girl looked down at her hands.

'I'm sorry,' she said.

'You must meet him,' Vladimir told her. 'Perhaps we will all go out to dinner together.'

'Do we have to?' Tanya asked.

Vladimir scowled. 'I am not used to having my instructions questioned,' he said.

'I didn't mean to . . .'

'We will start the conversation again, and this time you will be the woman I trained – the woman I know you can be.'

Tanya took a deep breath.

'How is your visitor?' she asked for a second time, and though there was no particular warmth in her question, her previous antagonism had quite vanished.

'He is making an excellent recovery from the fever,' Vladimir said. 'He told me that yesterday he walked almost as far as the Admiralty Arch.'

The girl frowned. 'He *told* you?'

'He told me,' Vladimir repeated.

'And you didn't know that already?'

'No.'

Once more, Tanya's eyes became riveted on her hands.

'Tell me what you're thinking,' Vladimir said.

The girl looked up. 'I don't want to incur your displeasure three times in a morning,' she said.

'You have no choice in the matter,' Vladimir said.

Tanya nodded, acknowledging the truth of the statement.

'If you don't know what he's done until he tells you himself, that can only mean that you're not having him watched,' she said.

'You're quite right – I'm not.'

'And is that wise?'

Vladimir shrugged. 'Perhaps not – but what choice do I have? His value to me is that he is an unknown quantity to everyone but the two of us, and how could he remain unknown if I had men following him?'

'Does he have any idea why he is here?'

'No, but he is aware that I have brought him to Russia so that I can use him for "my own peculiar end".'

'You're quoting from Shakespeare,' Tanya pronounced. 'That's part of Iago's speech in Act One, Scene One, of *Othello*. You used to read it to me when I was younger.'

'So I did,' Vladimir agreed, delighted that she'd remembered. 'I chose that particular play precisely *because* of Iago. I wanted you to learn from his example – but also to become wary of developing his flaws.'

'And are you upholding your side of the bargain with the Englishman?' Tanya asked, changing the subject slightly. 'Are you doing all you can for this sergeant of his?'

'I am,' Vladimir said, 'though not in a way that Sam Blackstone could possibly have imagined.'

Ellie Carr looked down at the man on the marble slab in the mortuary.

The inspector who'd brought him had wanted only one question answered: was it murder, or was it suicide?

But while the question was straightforward enough, finding the answer might prove much more complicated, because the man had been hit head-on by an express train and was now spread out in front of her like a bloodied and unfinished jigsaw puzzle.

Despite an extensive search of the area around the track, parts of him were *still* missing and might never be found, but if he had been killed before the train hit him – if he'd been shot or strangled – then it still might be possible to uncover evidence of that among the mangled remains.

'Where are you, Sam? Are you safe?' she heard herself say, and she realized that though she'd thought she'd be able to banish Blackstone from her mind while she was working, she'd obviously fallen at the first fence.

Someone coughed directly behind her, and she turned to find herself looking at a tall thin man. He was, in fact, almost as tall and thin as Blackstone, but whereas Blackstone bought his suits from the second-hand stalls in the markets, this man had clearly had his made by one of the best tailors on Savile Row.

'Dr Carr?' the man asked.

'If I find out that you got in here by bribing my clerk, I'll tear the rascal's balls off,' Ellie Carr said.

'I'm sorry, I don't understand,' the man replied.

'Balls,' Ellie repeated. 'Testicles! The twin sacs that dangle between men's legs – and which they all seem so inordinately proud of.'

'I know what balls are. What I haven't quite grasped—'

'Let me ask you a question,' Ellie interrupted him. 'Are you one of those toffs who sometimes think it might be a jolly jape to take a peek at all the blood and gore in my mortuary?'

'Certainly not!' the man replied. 'My name is Courtney Hartington, and I represent the firm of Hartington, Hartington and Blythe, solicitors.'

'And which one are you?'

'I've already said . . .'

'Are you Hartington? Or are you Hartington?'

The solicitor gave her thin smile. 'Since I am the senior partner, I suppose I am the first Hartington,' he said.

'Well, now that's cleared that up, but you still haven't explained why you're in my mortuary,' Ellie Carr said, 'because neither I nor the bloke lying in bits on the slab need your services.'

'Perhaps *you* don't need my services,' Hartington agreed, 'but your friend Sergeant Patterson most certainly does.'

'He's already got a solicitor,' Ellie pointed out.

'Yes, he has,' Hartington agreed, 'and while it would be quite unprofessional of me to say he's not a very good one, I feel it my duty to point out that, in this world, you get what you pay for.'

'And, from the way you're dressed, Archie can't afford to pay for you,' Ellie said.

'He doesn't need to,' Hartington replied. 'I have already been satisfactorily recompensed.'

'Who by?'

'The gentleman – or lady – has made it clear to me that he – or she – would prefer to remain anonymous.'

'And why have you come to me?' Ellie Carr asked suspiciously. 'Why aren't you saying all this to Archie's wife?'

'My instructions are that I'm to deal directly with you.'

'So are you saying that this gentleman . . .'

'Or lady.'

'. . . knows me?'

'I'm afraid I can neither confirm nor deny your acquaintance-ship with the client in question.'

'All right, then, another question,' Ellie said. 'What can you do for Archie that his cut-price solicitor couldn't do?'

'Well, for a start, I could post his bail,' Hartington said.

On his previous excursion, Blackstone had settled for just one glass of tea, but he had pushed himself harder that day than he ever had before, and when his body told him that it would be wise to order another tea and rest a little more, he did not argue with it.

Even when he'd finished this second glass, he didn't leave immediately, but remained in his seat and watched the world of Petrograd pass him by, and, as a result, he'd been in the tea shop for over an hour when he finally stood up.

As he reached the door, the waitress smiled at him again.

'*Mne kazhet saya vy,*' she said.

Blackstone shrugged apologetically. 'I'm sorry, I just don't understand,' he said.

'*Mne kazhet saya vy,*' the waitress repeated, more slowly this time.

'*Bol'shoe spasibo,*' Blackstone said helplessly.

As he stepped out on to the pavement, a woman strode past, and even the brief glance he caught of her face was enough to make his heart miss a beat.

The woman kept on walking, heading in the direction of Kazan Cathedral, and Blackstone just stood and watched her, unable to move.

It couldn't be her, he told himself.

Vladimir said she was dead.

But then, he thought, Vladimir lied a lot.

He found his legs and set off in pursuit, though catching her up wouldn't be easy, because Agnes had always been a good walker, and he was still a little weak from the fever.

How long had it been since he had last seen her, he asked himself, as the effort to reach her made him struggle for breath.

Jesus – it had been eighteen years!

They are sitting in a tiny railway carriage in the middle of the vast steppes. They have declared their love for each other and had intended to go back to England to start a new life together. But the evidence has been mounting up, and now Blackstone can

*no longer fight off the conclusion the evidence so clearly points
to: that all the time their love had been growing, Agnes had been
Vladimir's agent and had been using him for Vladimir's ends.*

*'It was Vladimir's decision that you should come back to
England with me, wasn't it?' he asks.*

*'I want to come back with you, Sam, my darling,' Agnes says.
'I know you don't believe me now when I say that I love you, but
you will in time – because I'll find ways to prove it to you.'*

*'Nevertheless, it was Vladimir's decision,' Blackstone says
unyieldingly.*

'Nevertheless, it was Vladimir's decision,' Agnes agrees.

'Why? So you can spy on me as you did on the Count?'

'He asked me to report to him if I discovered anything interesting.'

'Of course he did!'

*'But he did not have high expectations that I would have anything
to report. When you return to your humdrum work in Scotland
Yard, you'll be of no further use to Vladimir – because he has no
interest in the doings of London pickpockets and bank robbers.'*

*'So what is in it for him? Why does he want you to go back
to London with me?'*

*'I am Vladimir's gift to you. He believes that I can make you
happy, and I know that I could. But let's forget Vladimir, Sam. Let's
pretend that he never existed and we're starting afresh. Neither of
us has to be anybody's gift. We could be a gift to each other!'*

'It won't work,' Blackstone says.

*'Why?' Agnes asks, almost hysterical now. 'Because of your
foolish pride? Because Vladimir found me before you did?'*

*'Because if I accept his gift now, he'll have a hold over me
for ever – and I can't allow that.'*

*Agnes takes a handkerchief out of her bag and dries her
eyes.*

*'You're right, of course,' she admits. 'Vladimir is hard enough
to resist even if you're not in his debt.'*

He was gaining ground on the woman, but only because she was
slowing down as she approached the tram stop.

He wondered why he was doing this – wondered, if he did
catch her up, what they would find to say to each other after all
those years.

A tram came rattling down the street and pulled up at the stop. The woman climbed on board, and the tram moved off again.

Perhaps it had been Agnes, and perhaps it hadn't. He was no longer sure. But the one thing he was *almost* certain of was that she was in Petersburg, for though he was by no means a fanciful man, he could sense her presence in the air.

NINE

Vladimir's apartment was on the first floor (or the second floor, as the Americans would call it, Blackstone reminded himself) of a prosperous-looking building not far from Nevsky Prospekt. It was rather a large apartment for a single man with only one servant, but then it needed to be large to accommodate the railway.

Vladimir's study, at the front of the house, was where the railway had its nerve centre. From there, tracks ran off in all directions: to Moscow (Vladimir's bedroom), to Baku (the guest bedroom), to Warsaw (the dining room), to Kiev (the small parlour) and to Vladivostok (which was sited in the lumber room overlooking the Neva, at the back of the apartment). Walls did not impede the network – if a wall was in the way, it had simply been tunnelled through.

And along each line were stations – some the sort of grandiose monuments that provincial towns with pretensions opted for, others like the tumbledown shack at which Blackstone had said his last farewells to Agnes.

The apartment was otherwise sparsely furnished – furniture was, on the whole, incompatible with the efficient running of a railway – but what little he had bought was functional and betrayed nothing of its owner's personality.

The locomotives themselves were truly exquisite, and there were no two of them alike.

'This one was owned by the Great Russian Railway Company and is painted in its colours,' Vladimir explained as they sat in the study, waiting for dinner to be served, 'whereas this model was not brought into service until after the state took over the company in the 1880s, which is why it is in imperial colours.'

And though they drew their power from the electrified track – which Vladimir controlled from a panel on his desk – each had a small boiler which produced steam as the locomotives ran along the rails.

Blackstone found it slightly disturbing that the railway existed *at all*. It seemed wrong that a man whose work was so grounded in the harsh realities of life should yet be able to sustain a fantasy world in his own apartment.

It was disturbing, too, that Vladimir had chosen to share this secret world with him – had exposed so much of his inner self.

But, of course, it was always possible that the railway was no more than a prop in Vladimir's game – a camouflage behind which the real Vladimir was lurking, unseen.

'What do you get out of your rail network, Vladimir?' he asked, testing out this latter theory.

'I find it soothing,' the Russian replied. 'In a country where nothing works – where I am forced to *employ* chaos in order to *control* chaos – it is pleasant to spend a little of my time with something orderly, something that always runs as it is supposed to.'

'So it exists purely to give you pleasure?'

'Yes.'

'I don't believe you,' Blackstone said. 'You're not a man to waste effort, and if you can't achieve at least two objectives with a single course of action, then you'll find another way to do things.'

'What do you mean?' Vladimir asked, suddenly cautious.

'There are two reasons you brought me to Russia. One was to protect me, but the other was so that you could use me.'

Vladimir laughed. 'You are right, of course,' he admitted.

'So the model railway does have a second purpose?'

'Yes.'

'And what is it?' Blackstone wondered.

'You don't need to know that now,' Vladimir replied, 'and let us pray that you never find yourself in a position where you *do* need to know.'

The study door flew open – almost as if they were under attack – and Vladimir's massive servant, Yuri, entered the room and grunted something that was probably incomprehensible even to most Russians.

'Dinner is served,' Vladimir said grandly. 'Let us go and see what culinary delights my master chef has prepared for us this evening.'

Most visitors to the Patterson household would have been ushered into the hardly used front parlour, but Ellie Carr was almost a part of the family, and Maggie took her into the kitchen, instead.

It was a cosy room. It smelled of baking and stews, and it was dominated by a large table at which the Patterson clan ate all their meals. A large copper kettle, permanently just off the boil, sat on the hob next to the fire, and two canaries – known to the family alone as Sam and Ellie – chirped cheerfully in a cage that rested on top of the Singer sewing machine.

The two women sat down at the table, and Ellie told Maggie about Mr Hartington.

'Why should a big lawyer like him want to represent my Archie?' Maggie asked when Ellie had finished.

'I suspect the answer is that he's getting a hell of a lot of money for it,' Ellie said.

'But who'd be willing to pay?' Maggie fretted. 'We all think the world of Archie, of course, but he's not really an important man in anybody else's eyes.'

'I don't know who's footing the bill,' Ellie admitted, 'and frankly, as long as he *keeps* footing it, I don't give a damn.'

A light, which could almost have been hope, appeared in Maggie's eyes. 'Do you think he can get my Archie off?' she asked.

'He didn't promise that,' Ellie said cautiously.

'But he might, mightn't he?'

'I think Archie has more chance with him than he would have with any other solicitor,' Ellie said, still treading a thin line.

Tears appeared in Maggie's eyes. 'Archie's going to gaol, isn't he?' she asked. 'Whatever happens, he's going to gaol.'

'It seems likely,' Ellie agreed.

Maggie sniffed and forced her lips into a tight smile. 'Still, it looks as if this Mr Hartington can get him out on bail for Christmas at least, and that's something, isn't it?' she said.

'I think you're being amazingly brave,' Ellie said softly.

'Oh, don't be so nice,' Maggie pleaded. 'If you're nice, I'll start blubbering, and once I've started, I won't be able to stop.'

'A good cry might make you feel better,' Ellie said.

'It probably would, but there's still the kids' suppers to prepare and their clothes to wash, and you can't do that when you're sobbing your heart out,' Maggie said.

'Perhaps I could do all that,' Ellie suggested.

Maggie smiled. 'That's what I needed,' she said. 'A bit of humour to cheer me up!'

'I don't know what you mean,' Ellie told her.

'You're a very clever woman,' Maggie said, 'and I think it's marvellous the way you cut up all them bodies – I wouldn't have a clue where to start, myself. But if you think you can look after my three kids properly – even for a few hours – then you're living in a dream world.'

Ellie grinned. 'Well, you've really put me in my place, haven't you?' she said. 'And quite right, too.'

Yuri had prepared wild boar for dinner that night, though, with his massive hands, he looked better equipped to strangle the beast than to cook it. Still, Blackstone had eaten worse – though he was pushed to remember when – and Vladimir, who seemed to regard food as no more than fuel, cleared his plate without comment.

When the meal was over, Vladimir suggested that they return to his study for a chat and a few vodkas, but once they were there, the Russian went straight to his desk and switched on his railway control panel.

'It relaxes me,' he said.

Blackstone looked around the network of tracks, and at the engine shed which covered all the space along the front wall that was not occupied by the double doors leading on to the small balcony.

'How many locomotives have you got?' he asked.

'Fifty-seven,' Vladimir said automatically.

'And are they all different?'

'Of course.'

Shaking his head in wonder, Blackstone opened the French doors and stepped out on to the balcony for a breath of air. It had only recently stopped snowing, so except for the tram lines that ran down the centre of it – and which were cleared by the wheels every time a tram passed over them – the street below was covered in a gentle white carpet.

It was not a majestic street, like Nevsky Prospekt, Blackstone thought – it was nowhere near as wide for a start – but it was pleasant enough, and he was sure that most of the people who occupied the apartments beside and across from Vladimir's considered themselves quite fortunate to live there.

A little of Petrograd's chill night air was more than enough, but before he stepped back inside, Blackstone took another gulp of it, in preparation for what he was sure was going to be a very difficult conversation.

'I'd like to know exactly what you're doing to clear Archie Patterson's name,' he said, as he closed the balcony doors behind him.

Vladimir, bent over his controls, flicked another switch. 'It's complicated.'

'I'd still like to know.'

'You must learn to be patient, Sam,' Vladimir said. 'Like my locomotives, my schemes criss-cross each other, and to an outsider there seems to be no pattern to them, until, of course, the final rail switching is completed and each element of the scheme approaches its intended destination.'

'Which is a fancy way of saying you're not going to tell me?' Blackstone suggested.

Vladimir nodded. 'I would trust you with my life, Sam, but I will never be willing to let you – or anyone else – see the workings inside my head.'

He flicked another switch on the control panel, and one of the trains – which had seemed to be on an inevitable collision course with another – swiftly changed tracks.

There was another question – an important question – that Blackstone wanted to ask his host, but before he could pose it, it would be necessary to throw Vladimir off guard.

'There's a small Russian phrase that I'd like you to translate for me,' he said.

'Oh yes?' Vladimir asked, glancing up from his panel.

'*Mne kazhet saya vy*,' Blackstone said, pronouncing the words slowly and carefully.

'Who said that?' Vladimir wondered.

'A waitress in a tea shop on Nevsky Prospekt.'

'And who did she say it to?'

'She said it to me.'

Vladimir laughed – a great deep belly laugh that seemed to fill the whole room.

'What's so funny?' Blackstone said.

'I must keep a closer watch on you, my friend, or you will get into trouble,' Vladimir told him. '"*Mne kazhet saya vy*" means "I really fancy you"!'

He was clearly expecting Blackstone to laugh, too – to join in his merriment with embarrassed good humour.

'I thought I saw Agnes on Nevsky Prospekt this morning,' Blackstone said bluntly.

For a second, Vladimir froze. Then he said, 'At what *time* this morning?'

'Why should it matter what time it was?' Blackstone wondered.

'Please answer the question.'

'It must have been about noon.'

Vladimir laughed again – though this time there seemed to be little genuine amusement behind it.

'Ah, then, if it was noon, you must have been blinded by the noonday sun,' he said.

'This isn't a joke,' Blackstone said angrily.

'Of course it isn't,' Vladimir agreed, growing more serious. 'But you didn't see her, Sam. You only *imagined* that you saw her – because you're still in love with her!'

'I'm not,' Blackstone said.

'You can say what you like, but you can't fool me,' Vladimir told him.

'Perhaps I was still a little in love with her when I came to Petrograd,' Blackstone admitted. 'She's been like a ghost walking through my life, and you can't easily fall *out of* love with a ghost. But when I saw her today . . .'

'When you *thought* you saw her today.'

'. . . I realized that what's past is past. And I realized something else, too – that I love Ellie Carr more than I ever imagined I could, and that if I ever get out of this mess, I'm going to ask her to marry me.'

'Then congratulations are in order – assuming the lady will have you,' Vladimir said.

'But I still want to talk to Agnes,' Blackstone said. 'I want finally to lay the ghost to rest.'

Vladimir sighed. 'As I've already told you several times, Agnes is dead.'

'When I knew her, she was a healthy young woman, who had a good chance of living into her seventies – or even her eighties,' Blackstone said. 'So it seems rather convenient for you that she should have died.'

'Convenient for me?' Vladimir said quizzically. 'How could it have been convenient for me?'

'I'm not sure – but I have a theory.'

'Then, by all means, outline it for me.'

'You were afraid that, once I was in Russia, I would want to see her. And that might upset the delicate balance of your plan – it might prove an obstacle to the pattern you've already laid out for each of us to follow. So you told me she was dead, and you instructed her to keep away from me.'

'If Agnes was still alive, she could do the job I have in mind for you – and much better than you ever could,' Vladimir said, with brutal frankness. 'If she was still alive, I wouldn't need you at all.' He reached into his desk drawer and took out a series of photographs. 'I was hoping to spare you these, but since you are inclined to doubt my word . . .'

Vladimir laid the pictures on the table, and though he didn't want to, Blackstone forced himself to look.

Each photograph was taken from a different angle, but in all of them Agnes was lying in her coffin.

Looking at them, Blackstone felt sadness wash over him – but it was the sadness over the death of someone he had known, not the sadness that came from the loss of a loved one.

Of course, the photographs actually proved nothing in themselves. With good make-up and a good photographer, anyone could turn a living person into a convincing corpse.

'I could show you her death certificate, but you wouldn't be able to understand it,' Vladimir said, reading his mind. 'I could have her body disinterred, but after all these years I doubt there would be much left of the Agnes you knew.' He paused. 'It is very important to me that you accept the truth about her death, Sam,' he continued urgently.

'Why?' Blackstone asked.

'Because as long as you have even the vaguest suspicion that she is still alive, you will not be effective in the role I have selected for you.'

'A role you've still not explained to me,' Blackstone pointed out.

'The time is not yet right,' Vladimir said. He looked down at his control panel. 'Let me tell you a little more about my railway.'

TEN

10th December 1916 – Julian calendar; 23rd December 1916 – Gregorian calendar

Blackstone was out on his regular morning walk when he saw the poster for the first time. It was on the wall of a dress shop in Nevsky Prospekt. It had clearly been pasted up in a great hurry – the fact it was not straight was evidence of that, as were the air bubbles under the surface – but, given its nature, it was hardly surprising that the man who had put it up had not wanted to hang around.

Three cartoon figures were depicted in the poster. The middle one – drawn to a much larger scale than the others – was a man with a long untidy beard. He had his hands stretched out in front of him, and a woman was kneeling on his left hand, while a man knelt on his right. Both of them were looking up at him – like devoted pets trying to be on their very best behaviour.

The man on the right hand was wearing an elaborate military uniform. He had a splendid crown on his head, yet the face below the crown was that of a village idiot. The woman on the left hand was dressed in a ball gown, and *her* face seemed to be suffused with maliciousness and cunning.

On the whole, the smaller of the two men had emerged as the least savaged of the artist's subjects, Blackstone decided. True, there was a good deal of contempt in the broad strokes of his caricature, but it was possible to detect an element of pity, too, whereas, when drawing the other two, the artist had been inspired by nothing but blind hatred.

A policeman appeared on the scene, blowing his whistle and swinging his arms up and down in front of him as he shooed the onlookers away from the offending poster. Once he had it to himself, he took a scraper out of his pocket and began to attack the poster, starting in the middle, with the bearded man's mouth, and working his way down over the two kneeling figures.

And that was how it went, Blackstone thought. Whatever else there was a wartime shortage of in Petersburg, there seemed to be no lack of paper, ink and paste. Every night, under the cover of darkness, anti-government protestors would stick their posters to the walls, and every morning the police would remove them – but not before half the population of the city had had a chance to see them.

He turned and looked up and down Nevsky Prospekt. Ladies in fine silk dresses were striding majestically towards their waiting carriages, followed by liveried servants weighed down by elaborately wrapped purchases. Government officials, dressed in impressive uniforms, bustled self-importantly from one ministry to another. Students, also in uniform – Russia seemed to be obsessed with dressing up in uniform – walked by him, debating weighty issues (or perhaps – for all he knew – merely discussing their chances of losing their virginity). Trams rattled along the middle of the wide boulevard, and taxi drivers blew their horns furiously at pedestrians and at each other.

Standing there – observing the pageant – it was difficult to believe that Russia was still caught up in a war that had already cost millions of its young men their lives, Blackstone thought. It seemed almost incredible, too, that in other – less prosperous – parts of the city, women began queuing up for bread at three o'clock in the morning – and often came away empty-handed. And there was no indication at all that, on the other side of the Kalinkinski Bridge, there were factories where the workers toiled under almost unbearable conditions and were more often on strike than they were manning their machines.

But Vladimir had said that all this was true – and Vladimir knew about such things.

*   *   *

'They've switched magistrates on us,' Hartington told Ellie, as they – and Hartington's clerk – entered the magistrates' court.

'They've done what?' Ellie asked.

'They've switched magistrates on us,' Hartington repeated. 'The one you saw at Archie Patterson's first appearance – Jenkins – is an affable old soul, who would have been more than willing, under any normal circumstances, to have released him on a twenty-five pound bond.'

'But they weren't normal circumstances, because he saw the way that Assistant Commissioner Todd was looking at him,' Ellie said bitterly.

'Exactly,' Hartington agreed. 'Jenkins will always bend with the wind, and the dark powers that are ranged against you believe that whatever Todd and his ilk might do, I could tie him in knots. And, of course, they're right – I could – which is why they've given us a man called Lambert Charnley, instead.'

'And what's Lambert Charnley like?' Ellie asked gloomily.

'I believe that the technical term for his kind of person is "a right proper bastard",' Hartington said.

When the magistrate entered the courtroom, the court rose, and it was only when she sat down again that Ellie Carr got a proper look at him.

He was in his mid-forties, she guessed. He had an angular face and thin lips that seemed to have been specifically created to express contempt. But it was his eyes that really unsettled her. They were humourless and pitiless, and burned with cold determination to prevail – at whatever the cost to others or to justice.

They were as good as done for, Ellie thought, and though she did not know exactly where the torpedo would hit them – or even what kind of explosive it might be carrying – she was certain that they were going down.

When he was called on by the clerk of the court to speak, Hartington stood up. He was an impressive figure, Ellie conceded – cool and authoritative – but even before he spoke, he was fighting a losing battle.

'There has been a very strange occurrence, Your Worship,' Hartington said, in a rich, round voice. 'So strange, in fact, that

I can't remember another example of it in all the time I have been practising law.'

'And what might this strange occurrence have been, Mr Hartington?' the magistrate asked.

'I sent my clerk to post my client's bail – some two hundred and fifty pounds. That would normally have been sufficient to ensure his release, but my clerk was told that, on this occasion, I must make a second petition to the court.'

The magistrate nodded. 'It is a little unusual,' he agreed, 'but then it is also rather unusual for a serving police officer to be charged with such a heinous offence, is it not?'

'I hadn't thought of it quite like that,' Hartington said, bowing his head slightly. 'I thank Your Worship for enlightening me.'

'I'm glad to be of service to you, Mr Hartington,' the magistrate said complacently. 'Shall we move on to the question of bail now?'

'If Your Worship pleases,' Hartington said, 'I wish to make a formal application—'

'I have been giving the matter my careful consideration and have decided to raise it to five hundred pounds,' the magistrate interrupted him.

Hartington looked crestfallen. 'But . . . but, as already stated, Mr Jenkins set it at two hundred and fifty,' he stuttered.

'He did indeed,' the magistrate agreed. 'But, since then, new evidence has come to light . . .'

'What new evidence?'

'. . . which, though I am not prepared to reveal it to counsel at this time, has inclined me to raise the amount of bail required to five hundred pounds.'

'Your Worship, my client, as you can see for yourself, is a poor man,' Hartington said pleadingly.

'He seems to have had no trouble in raising the money to pay for an expensive solicitor,' the magistrate sneered.

'A poor man,' Hartington repeated. 'How can he be expected to come up with five hundred pounds?'

'I don't know,' the magistrate admitted. 'But that is his problem, rather than mine, and if he can't come up with the money, he must remain in gaol.'

'You might as well set it at a thousand pounds,' Hartington said, with a sudden flash of anger.

The magistrate scowled. 'Very well, that is just what I'll do,' he said. 'Bail is set at one thousand pounds.'

'And if my client – by some miracle – did manage to raise that amount, would he then find that the bar had been magically raised again, and he was now required to find one thousand five hundred pounds – or perhaps two thousand pounds?' Hartington demanded, the anger still evident in his voice.

'I don't like your tone, Mr Hartington,' the magistrate said sternly.

'I'm sorry, Your Worship,' Hartington said in a broken voice. His shoulders slumped, and he bowed his head again. 'But it all seems so unfair,' he muttered to himself.

'What was that?' the magistrate said.

'Nothing, Your Worship.'

'I insist on knowing what it was that you just said!'

'I . . . I said, it all seems so unfair.'

'By which you mean that you consider *me* to be unfair! Or is there some other interpretation that can be put on the remark?'

'No, Your Worship,' Hartington said miserably.

'In that case, you will apologize immediately!' the magistrate instructed him.

'Gladly, Your Worship,' Hartington agreed. 'I . . . I simply don't know what came over me.'

The magistrate nodded. 'And now that you have apologized, I *will* answer the question that you put to me a few moments ago.'

'There's no need, Your Worship,' Hartington said.

'But there *is* a need,' Charnley contradicted him. 'You asked me if, when you came to pay the bail, the bar would have been "magically" raised to one thousand five hundred pounds, didn't you?'

'Yes, Your Worship – and that was quite wrong of me,' Hartington said meekly.

'Yes, we have already established that,' Charnley agreed. 'But to return to the point – you will find, when you know me better, Mr Hartington, that all my rulings are based on both the law of the land and solid common sense, and, thus, when I set bail at one thousand pounds, it will remain at one thousand pounds.'

Hartington was suddenly straighter and more confident again.

'Since my practice mostly concerns commercial matters at the highest possible level, I do not normally appear in magistrates' courts myself,' he said, 'and, as a result of that, my knowledge of how they operate is perhaps a little rusty, so I would beg Your Worship's indulgence . . .'

'You have already apologized for your behaviour once, Mr Hartington,' the magistrate interrupted. 'There is no need to do it again.'

'With the greatest respect, Your Worship, you seem to have misunderstood me,' Hartington said. 'It is advice on a procedural matter for which I wish to beg your indulgence.'

'A procedural matter?' the magistrate repeated.

Hartington's clerk opened his briefcase, and Ellie saw that it was bulging with banknotes.

'Yes, a procedural matter,' Hartington said. 'To whom should we pay the bail money?'

Hartington and Ellie were sitting in a workmen's café, close to the Southwark Magistrates' Court.

Some of the workers gave the solicitor puzzled looks – as if to ask what the hell he thought he was doing there – but if Hartington noticed the looks, he gave no sign of it and seemed perfectly at home with a large mug of steaming tea in his slim, delicate hands.

'You were brilliant in court,' Ellie said, full of admiration.

'Yes, I was rather,' Hartington agreed complacently.

'But you had me really worried for a while. Why didn't you tell me what you were going to do?'

'Yes, I suppose I could have explained my strategy to you beforehand,' Hartington said, 'but then, you see, you wouldn't have looked worried at all – and your genuine concern was a necessary part of the act.'

'A necessary part of the act?'

'I needed the magistrate to feel that he was totally in control of the situation, and that we were losing ground every time I opened my mouth. I needed him to feel confident enough to set a figure for bail that he couldn't amend without losing face. And that is just what I got him to do.'

'How much money did your clerk actually have in that briefcase of his?' Ellie wondered.

'One thousand pounds,' Hartington said.

'So even before you walked into the court, you knew exactly how much it would be!'

Hartington smiled. 'I am costing my client – whoever he or she might be – a great deal of money,' he said. 'But I think you'll agree, having seen me in action yourself, that I'm worth every penny of it.'

ELEVEN

It was snowing again, Blackstone noted, looking out of Vladimir's study window on to the street below. And it would keep on snowing relentlessly for months to come.

He wondered whether he would still be in Petrograd when the snows melted – and then, realistically, he wondered if he would even be *alive* when the spring finally came.

He turned around to face Vladimir, who was – as usual – manipulating the small world that was his railway.

'As I was walking along Nevsky Prospekt this morning, I noticed a cartoon,' Blackstone said. 'There were two small figures in it, who, I think, were meant to be the tsar and tsarina, and one much larger one – a wild-looking man with a long scraggly beard.'

'The man's name is Grigori Rasputin, and he is a semi-literate Siberian peasant, with an unquenchable thirst for both alcohol and debauchery,' Vladimir said with disgust. 'He is also considered by some people to be a *starets* – a holy man – and two of his most devoted followers are the tsar and tsarina.'

'It's hard to imagine the tsar of all the Russias and his wife being under the sway of a semi-literate peasant,' Blackstone said sceptically.

'That is because you do not understand what makes them tick,' Vladimir said. He paused again. 'Have I got that right – "makes them tick"?'

'You've got it right.'

'The Romanov dynasty has ruled this country for over three hundred years. The tsar considers he has a divine right to govern, and when you see him performing one of the great ceremonies of state – drinking the holy water from the Neva River at the start of spring, for example – it is hard not to believe that God is looking down approvingly.'

'But . . .?'

'But the home life of the tsar and tsarina has little of the imperial splendour about it. Their private apartments contain just the kind of furniture that you would find in the home of any senior clerk living in Peckham.'

'You're exaggerating,' Blackstone said.

'They have at their command the finest craftsmen in Russia – which is to say some of the finest craftsmen in the whole world – but they choose to buy mass-produced furniture from a catalogue provided by Maples of London. It is what they feel comfortable with,' Vladimir said firmly. 'They are a very domestic family. At home – and in their letters to each other – the tsar and tsarina use the terms "Hubby" and "Wifey". They dress all four of their daughters in exactly the same way – even though there are six years between the youngest and the oldest – and smother them in the kind of love that would only be appropriate with much younger children. And, of course, they dote on their son, the tsarevich Alexei.'

'How does Rasputin fit into all this?' Blackstone asked.

'I was coming to that,' Vladimir told him. 'The tsarevich is a haemophiliac – a curse that he inherited through his mother.'

'Is she a haemophiliac herself?' Blackstone wondered.

'No, it is very rare for women to suffer from the disease, though they have proved most efficient at carrying it and passing it on to their male children,' Vladimir explained.

'I see.'

'Much of the time, Alexei is not even allowed to walk, but instead is carried around like a baby, by a huge sailor. Even a slight jolt – one which you or I would probably not even notice – is enough to start him haemorrhaging, and a small cut could lead to disaster. And since, as the tsar and tsarina see it, the future of Russia and the Romanov dynasty rests on his thin shoulders, his health is of paramount importance to the whole family.'

'The family think that this holy man – Rasputin – has the power to heal him,' Blackstone guessed.

'Once, when Alexei was little more than a year old, he was bleeding for days. The physicians had all but given up on him, and even the family thought he would die,' Vladimir said. 'Then, in desperation, they summoned the so-called *starets*, who had already acquired something of a reputation as a healer. Rasputin spoke soothingly to the tsarevich, and the bleeding stopped. And that is not the only time he is supposed to have cured him. It's said that he once cured Alexei by merely speaking to him over the telephone.'

'I still don't see . . .' Blackstone began.

'It is only a small step from guiding them in the care of their son to guiding them on how to rule the country. Rasputin told the tsar that he should dismiss his cousin as head of the army and take charge himself. And that is what he has done, so now the tsar is at army headquarters in Mogilev, which is over five hundred miles from Petersburg. And the tsarina – or rather her mentor Rasputin – is left running a country that covers one-sixth of the earth's surface and has a population of over one hundred million.'

'Now that *has* to be an exaggeration,' Blackstone said sceptically.

'That Russia is so big?'

'That Rasputin's running the country.'

'I assure you, he is running it as much as anybody can be said to be running it,' Vladimir replied. 'Even so, things would not be quite so bad if the tsarina was popular. Catherine the Great made some terrible mistakes and caused immense suffering – but the people liked her.'

'And they don't like Alexandra?'

'They do not – and that is partly her fault. The people expect their monarch and his wife to appear in public, but Alexandra is painfully shy and rarely does so. I have heard stories of provincial aristocrats who have stood on railway platforms for hours on end, waiting for the royal train to pass through the station. They don't expect to meet her personally. They don't even expect her to wave at them – though they hope she will. It is enough for them to catch a brief glimpse of her as the train rushes through. And what do they see when the train finally arrives at the station? That she has pulled down the blinds!'

Vladimir flicked more switches on the control panel, and more trains began to move.

'And now we are at war with Germany, and she is a German herself,' he continued. 'So was Catherine the Great, for that matter, but – as I said – she was popular. The people think Alexandra is betraying us to the Kaiser and that Rasputin is her lover. Neither of those things is true. She is deeply in love with her husband and, like many converts, fanatical about her adopted country.'

'Does *no one* like her?' Blackstone asked.

'Aside from Rasputin, she has only two real friends,' Vladimir said. 'The first is Anna Vyroubova, the daughter of one the tsar's bureaucrats. The other is General Kornilov.'

'A general!' Blackstone said, surprised.

'Ah, now we stray into the realms of the romantic novel,' Vladimir said. 'Alexandra's mother died when she was quite young, and she was brought up mostly at the court of her grandmother, your Queen Victoria. It was there that the tsar first saw her and started to fall in love with her. His mother and father were opposed to any idea of them marrying – they wanted a better match for their son than a mere provincial princess – but Nicholas was determined to have his own way in the end.' Vladimir shuddered. 'I wish he had shown half as much determination in ruling Russia.'

'And how does this General Kornilov come into the picture?' Blackstone asked.

'He was a young officer serving under our military attaché at the Court of St James. Nicholas arranged for him to meet her. It was not difficult – she was, after all, very low in the royal hierarchy. It was Kornilov's job to prepare her for her life in Russia. They became friends – to the extent that a junior officer *can* become friends with a future tsarina of Russia. And now he is like a faithful old dog, whose only aim in life is to serve her.'

'I see what you mean about the realms of the romantic novel,' Blackstone admitted.

'But we are straying far from our subject, which is that, to the extent to which *anyone* can run this chaotic country, it is being run by Rasputin.'

'But surely the tsarina can't really believe that a peasant would know how—' Blackstone began.

'The Minister of the Interior has rented an apartment in which some of his officials hold secret meetings with Rasputin,' Vladimir interrupted him. 'The officials carry two things with them when

they go to those meetings. The first is a list of actions that the
Minister would like to see taken, and the second is a bag of
money. They hand the money and the list over to Rasputin. He
goes back to his own apartment and, over five or six bottles of
sweet Madeira wine – never less – he considers the Minister's
request. Then, the following morning, he will ring up the tsarina
and tell her what she should do. And there is no guarantee – even
though he's already been paid – that Rasputin will ask her to do
whatever it is the Minister wants her to do.'

'That seems incredible,' Blackstone said.

'A man with no education – no grasp of geography, economics
or warfare – has the power to appoint or dismiss ministers at will,'
Vladimir said, with rising anger. 'And he does so regularly.'

'Can't anyone do anything about it?'

'The dowager empress presented the tsarina – her daughter-
in-law – with an ultimatum. She said quite plainly that either
Rasputin must be banished from court or she would herself leave.
She never thought for a moment that she would be the one to
go, but she was – and her son, the tsar, did nothing to prevent
it. After that, there are few who would even dare to think of
trying to change things.'

Archie Patterson had lost weight during his time in gaol, but it
was weight he could well afford to lose. Now, being handed his
first pint of bitter in over a week, he emptied it in three quick
gulps, then signalled to the waiter to bring him another one.

'Is your client paying for this, as well?' he asked the tall thin
man in the Savile Row suit.

'My client is paying for *everything* as long as you are willing
to follow instructions,' Hartington said.

'What kind of instructions?' Patterson asked suspiciously.

'Instructions which, I can assure you, Mr Patterson, will only
serve your own best interests.'

'Would you care to be a little more forthcoming than that, Mr
Hartington?' Ellie Carr asked.

'Certainly,' the solicitor agreed. 'If the sergeant is, in fact,
guilty of the crime of which he's been accused—'

'He doesn't know whether he's guilty or not,' Ellie Carr interrupted. 'I've been reading up on what the head-shrinkers in Vienna

have got to say on the subject, and I think he's probably suffering from something called repressed memory syndrome.'

'You will concede, however, that even if he is innocent, the weight of evidence against him is so strong that he's likely to be convicted anyway?' Hartington asked.

'We shouldn't start out with the assumption that Archie . . .' Ellie began.

'Yes, I'll be convicted anyway,' Archie Patterson said gloomily. 'There's no doubt at all about that.'

'In which case, I suggest that we change the plea from innocent to guilty, and ask for the mitigating circumstances to be taken into account when the sentence is passed.'

'And just what mitigating circumstances might they be?' Archie Patterson wondered.

'That though you broke the law, you only did it to prevent a greater injustice being done.'

'I did it to save an innocent man – Sam Blackstone – from false imprisonment?' Patterson guessed.

'Precisely.'

'That would only work if everybody thought Sam was innocent,' Ellie said. 'But they don't. And there's almost as strong a case against him as there is against Archie.'

'Then the case against Inspector Blackstone will have to be weakened to the point at which it collapses completely,' Hartington said.

'And how would we go about doing that?' Patterson wondered.

'We – by which I mean specifically you, Sergeant – will have to track Max down and get him to confess.'

'Hang on,' Ellie said, 'there's been nothing in the papers about Max, so how do you even know his name?'

'I know a great many things that the general public are kept in ignorance of,' Hartington said.

'I might have a slight chance of finding Max if he was still in London – but he won't be,' Patterson said. 'He'll be long gone. He was probably gone even before Sam was arrested.'

'Leaving London would indeed have been the logical course of action for him to have followed,' Hartington agreed. 'Nevertheless, my sources are adamant that he is still here.'

'And do your sources know *exactly* where he is?' Ellie asked.

'Unfortunately, they do not,' Hartington admitted. 'That is where the "tracking down" part comes into it.'

'And how would we go about that, exactly, Mr Hartington?' Ellie Carr wondered.

'Sergeant Patterson is the professional in these matters, and I wouldn't presume to advise him.' Hartington paused. 'Or maybe there is *one* small piece of advice I might give him,' he continued. 'When I am representing a company that is suing another company over some kind of financial malfeasance, I usually begin by looking through the ledgers for the paper trail, and once I have found it, I follow it doggedly, wherever it takes me.'

'And I'm sure that works out just beautifully for you when you're dealing with gentlemanly crimes such as fraud and embezzlement,' Ellie Carr said sarcastically. 'But you see, Mr Hartington, Max doesn't have a silk top hat and doesn't belong to some exclusive West End club. He's a common robber and a con man – and he won't have *left* a paper trail.'

'Actually, he might have,' Patterson said. 'But even if there is a trail for me to follow, and even if – against all the odds – I manage to find him, there's no guarantee he'll confess.'

'No, there are no guarantees in anything of what I said,' Hartington agreed. 'But what I am offering you, Sergeant Patterson, is the chance to clear your friend's good name and improve your chances of a plea for mercy. Are you willing to grasp that chance?'

'Yes, I am,' Patterson said.

'There is . . . er . . . one slight complication,' Hartington said, and – to Patterson's and Ellie's amazement – he looked a little embarrassed.

'What kind of "slight complication"?' Ellie asked.

'The magistrate can't go back on the amount of bail required – I boxed him into a corner over that – but he can tinker with the other terms, and the spiteful hound has done just that.'

'Whatever you've got to say, just spit it out,' Ellie told him.

'Sergeant Patterson must surrender himself on the thirty-first and make a fresh application for bail.'

'He has to surrender himself on *New Year's Eve*!' Ellie exclaimed. 'And will there even be any magistrates on duty on New Year's Eve?'

'Oh yes, there will be *one*,' Hartington said. 'But he'll have a great many cases to deal with – and I'm sure Lambert Charnley will have asked the clerk to put Sergeant Patterson at the bottom of his list.'

'So once he's inside again, he'll stay inside,' Ellie said.

'I suspect so,' Hartington agreed.

'In other words, Archie not only has to find a needle in haystack, but he's got just seven days to do it?' Ellie asked.

Hartington smiled encouragingly. 'I have the greatest confidence in Sergeant Patterson's detecting skills,' he said.

It was ten fifteen when the doorbell rang, and Blackstone heard Yuri's heavy footfalls as he made his way up the hall.

'Now, I wonder who could possibly be visiting us at this time of night?' Vladimir said.

Did he wonder? Or did he know *exactly* who it was? That was the problem with Vladimir, Blackstone thought – it was almost impossible to distinguish between when he was lying and when he was telling the truth.

There was the sound of the door bolts being drawn, followed by an urgent clattering of heels in the corridor, then the study door suddenly flew open, and a girl entered the room.

She was quite tall and quite slim. But it was her hair that immediately drew Blackstone's attention. It was almost jet black and was not cut short – as was the fashion – but instead spilled over her shoulders and covered half her face.

She was carrying a poster in her hand, and she marched straight over to Vladimir's desk, slammed it down hard in front of him and spoke very rapidly in Russian.

'In case you haven't noticed, we have a guest, Tanya, and I think it would only be courteous for us to speak in a language he can understand,' Vladimir said in English.

'Have you seen this, Vladimir?' Tanya asked, switching languages with ease.

'And I also think it would be polite of you to say hello to our guest,' Vladimir said.

Tanya turned her head towards Blackstone very slowly, as if she had a stiff neck.

'Good evening, Mr Blackstone,' she said, in a flat, dull tone. Then she turned back to Vladimir, again with slowness and care.

'You have to do something about it,' she said.

'Come and look at this, Sam,' Vladimir suggested. 'You might find it interesting.'

Blackstone walked over to the desk and looked down at the poster that Tanya had brought.

It was much cruder than the one he had seen that morning – in every sense of the word. There were only two figures in it – the tsarina and Rasputin – and both were naked. The tsarina was lying on her back, with her legs spread. Rasputin was on top of her, his spotty backside the focal point of the whole drawing.

'It's an insult to the monarchy, and that makes it an insult to Russia,' Tanya said. 'You *have* to do something about it.'

Vladimir shrugged. 'What *can* I do?' he wondered. 'I could track down the artist . . .'

'Artist!' Tanya snorted. 'You call the man who produced this abomination an *artist*?'

'Yes, I do,' Vladimir said mildly. 'Art, as I understand it, is anything that engenders an emotional response in the viewer – and this has certainly done that with you.'

'It's nothing but filth!' Tanya protested.

'Yes, that's just what it is,' Vladimir agreed. 'But it's *effective* filth.'

Blackstone listened to the whole exchange with growing amazement. He was sure there was not another person in the whole of Russia – except, of course, for the royal family – who would have dared to talk to Vladimir as the girl was doing now, and yet Vladimir seemed quite happy to let her get away with it.

'As I was saying, I could track down the artist and have him imprisoned – or even send him on the long walk from which there is no return – but some other cartoonist would only spring up to take his place,' Vladimir said.

'When I said you had to do something about, I was not referring to the vile creature who drew this – and you know that,' Tanya said furiously. 'I meant that you must do something about Rasputin.'

'I have tried, through my agents, to bribe him to return to his family's village in Siberia,' Vladimir said, his tone still mild. 'I have been most generous – in fact, I have offered him considerably more than my poor department can really afford – but he simply refuses to go.'

'You have access to the tsarina, don't you?' Tanya asked.

'I have limited access – and then only when she's feeling in the mood to see me.'

'Then you must go and see her, and tell her all about his scandalous behaviour.'

'She's already been told about it. She refuses to believe anything bad about him.'

'She would believe *you*.'

'She would not. And by trying to tell her, I would lose what little influence I have.'

'In that case, you must have the bastard killed.'

'I will not go against the tsar's explicit wishes,' Vladimir said.

'Is that meant to be a joke?' Tanya demanded. 'You know yourself that you *constantly* go against his wishes!'

'That isn't quite true,' Vladimir said firmly. 'I do things that I suspect his majesty would disapprove of if he knew about them – but since he has not specifically instructed me *not* to do them, that is not the same thing at all.'

'You're splitting hairs,' Tanya said.

'Yes,' Vladimir agreed heavily. 'That is what a man in my position is sometimes forced to do.'

'So you'll stand by and let Rasputin destroy Russia?'

'The tsar is my absolute master – I have no choice but to obey him,' Vladimir said.

'There are times when you make me so angry that I almost hate you,' Tanya said, shaking her head furiously from side to side.

And as she shook her head, her hair swirled – and Blackstone saw what it was that she'd been hiding.

The ugly scar ran from the top of her right cheekbone to her jaw and was almost a quarter of an inch wide. It had puckered, angry edges and made the right side of her face look twisted and disproportionate.

A look of horror swept across the girl's face when she realized what had happened. Her anger evaporated, and she reached up and clawed the hair back into place with all the desperation of a drowning man clutching at a straw.

'Thank you for bringing this poster to me. You may now leave us,' Vladimir said softly.

Tanya nodded – but very carefully.

'Yes, thank you,' she said in a tiny voice.

And then she turned and left the room.

'Who is she?' Blackstone asked when she had gone.

'She's my best agent.'

'But she can't be more than seventeen or eighteen!'

'She's older than she looks, but her apparent youthfulness is an advantage I've exploited on many occasions. Besides, her age is unimportant. She comes from good stock, and she was born to do this work.'

'Do her parents – this good stock she comes from – approve of the work she is doing?' Blackstone asked.

'She is a young woman, not a child,' Vladimir replied. 'She does not need their approval.'

'But *do* they approve?' Blackstone insisted.

'They do not know,' Vladimir admitted, 'but speculating on their approval or disapproval is pointless. Tanya is doing work that needs to be done – and that is all that matters.'

'How did she get that scar?' Blackstone asked. 'Was it through working for you?'

'That is as pointless a question as the one you asked previously,' Vladimir said.

'Did she get that scar working for you?' Blackstone persisted.

'I think that I will run my trains for a little while before I go to bed,' Vladimir said.

He flicked a number of switches in rapid succession. Several locomotives backed out of the engine sheds, and others began their journey to different parts of the apartment.

Blackstone looked on, fascinated by the intricacy of the layout, and as he watched, he noticed that two locomotives – one that emerged from the parlour and another that had been in his bedroom – were approaching each other on the same piece of track.

Soon, he thought, Vladimir would switch one of the trains on to a spur.

But then both trains passed the last point at which they could possibly be diverted.

Blackstone glanced across at Vladimir. The Russian was staring at the wall, with an intensity strong enough to burn a hole in it.

'Look out for your trains!' Blackstone said.

But Vladimir paid no attention.

The collision, when it came, could not have been at more than two or three miles an hour, but, on two such small objects, it had a devastating effect. The locomotives buckled and twisted through the air – dragging their carriages behind them – then crashed down on to the floor.

Now, when it was too late, Vladimir came out of his trance and looked down impassively at the wreckage.

'What happened there?' Blackstone asked.

'I was distracted for a moment,' Vladimir admitted, 'and in my line of work, that can be fatal.'

'And what was distracting you?'

'I was thinking that, for the general good, it is sometimes necessary to destroy the things we love – and that there are even occasions when one of those things we must destroy is ourselves.'

'It's a little late at night for riddles,' Blackstone said.

But he could tell that Vladimir was not really listening.

'I have no desire to destroy myself unnecessarily, Sam,' the Russian continued, 'and that is why I have been considering just how *finely* I could split a hair.'

TWELVE

11th December 1916 – Julian calendar; 24th December 1916 – Gregorian calendar

I t seemed to Patterson as if all the clocks in London were conspiring to remind him of how little time he had to accomplish his almost impossible task.

'Bong!' said the clock in his local church tower, as he left home that morning. *Only six days and twenty-two hours left.*

'Bong!' said Big Ben, as he passed the Palace of Westminster. *Another hour gone, and you're still no closer to finding Max.*

And now this caretaker – this insignificant little runt in charge of the small government warehouse in Wapping – was wasting even more of his precious time by refusing to let him go inside.

'They're only dusty old records,' he told the man. 'Nobody gives a tuppenny damn about them.'

'If nobody gives a tuppenny damn then why are *you* interested in them?' the caretaker countered.

It was a fair point, Patterson agreed silently, but he couldn't help wishing that the cantankerous bugger hadn't been bright enough to make it.

If only he had his warrant card, he thought. A warrant card was the magic key that opened most doors.

But he didn't have his warrant card. It had been taken from him when he was arrested – and since no one at the Yard believed that there was even the remotest possibility it would ever be given back to him, it had probably already been destroyed.

'We wouldn't be more than a half an hour, would we?' Patterson said, looking for support from Ellie Carr, who had insisted on accompanying him.

'You've got to have an official pink form,' the caretaker said stubbornly. 'You can't get in the warehouse without an official pink form. And don't you try offering me any money,' he added, seeing Patterson's hand reaching in the general direction of his wallet, 'because that won't work.'

'For Gawd's sake, mister, give us a break!' said Ellie Carr, lapsing into the cockney that she had once spoken naturally, but now only resurrected for her own amusement.

'Give you a break?' the caretaker repeated.

'We 'aven't been entirely honest wiv you, mister,' Ellie said. 'Me an' my friend here . . .' She looked up at Patterson. 'What did you say your name was, dearie?'

'Archie,' Patterson said.

'Me and my friend Archie just want a bit of time alone together,' Ellie continued. 'And since he don't have the money for a hotel, we're just looking for somewhere what's nice and dry.'

'I didn't realize that you were on the game,' the caretaker said, surprised. 'I'd never have guessed.'

'Yeah, well, I try not to look too obvious,' Ellie told him. 'But you do see my problem, don't ya?'

'You could always go to the park,' the caretaker suggested. 'It's not that far from here.'

'Go to the park!' Ellie repeated. 'In this weather! It's cold enough to freeze the tits off me – and the balls off him.' She paused for a moment. 'Look, a girl's got to make a livin', ain't she? And if you was to let us go inside, I might be willing to provide the same service for you as I'm about to provide for Arnold here.'

'Archie,' Patterson said.

'Archie,' Ellie corrected herself. 'Same service – only, in your case, it'll be for free.'

The caretaker licked his lips, which were cracked and covered with a white slime.

'How long would you need?' he asked.

'Well, now you're asking somefink,' Ellie said. 'Some of my gentlemen friends are in and out again in no time at all – you'd fink they was competing in a speed championship – but there's others what need a lot of encouragement before they can perform, and I ravver fink –' she lowered her voice – 'that Albert here might be one of the second kind.'

'Archie,' Patterson said.

'Anyway, what do you care how long it takes, as long as you get your share in the end?' Ellie wondered.

The caretaker licked his lips again. 'If I let you in, you will be careful not to mess the place up, won't you?' he asked.

'We'll treat it like it was our own home,' Ellie promised.

'There are times when you make me so angry that I almost hate you,' Tanya had said to Vladimir, and that had sent him into a mood from which he had still not recovered the following morning.

In fact, he barely spoke at the breakfast table, and it was only as he was about to leave the apartment that he said, 'By the way, you should not make any plans for tomorrow, because Tanya wants you to go with her to one of the mills on the other side of the river.'

'She *wants* me to go with her?' Blackstone said questioningly.

'Or, if you prefer it, I have instructed her to take you with her as a bodyguard,' Vladimir amended.

'Why would she need a bodyguard?'

'She will need one because, tomorrow, she will not be Tanya the government agent. Instead, she will be Natasha the revolutionary.'

'I don't understand,' Blackstone admitted.

'This is a country that is largely indifferent to the loss of

human life on a grand scale,' Vladimir said, 'which makes it all
the stranger that it should be so unreasonably tolerant of its
revolutionaries.'

'You're still not making sense,' Blackstone said.

Vladimir sighed. 'No, I don't suppose I am,' he admitted. 'Listen
and learn. From Russia's viewpoint, the most dangerous revolutionary alive today is a man called Lenin. He is beyond our reach
at the moment because he is living in Switzerland, but once – in
1895 – the authorities did get their hands on him. And what did
they do with him? Did they lock him up and throw away the key?
No! Instead, they sent him into exile in Siberia – for *three years*.'

'I have to admit that doesn't seem like a particularly harsh
penalty,' Blackstone replied.

'It was softer than you could ever imagine,' Vladimir said.
'When you think of men being exiled to Siberia, do you picture
them being taken there in chains and under guard?'

'Well, yes, I suppose I do.'

'If you are a peasant, sentenced to *katorga* – which means
hard labour – then that *is* what happens to you. But if you are
middle class – and Lenin's father was an inspector of schools
– you are meted out much gentler treatment. Lenin was not taken
to Siberia – he was told to make his own way there. And from
what I've heard, he had a pleasant time during his exile – he
even went duck shooting a few times.'

'And what has this got to do with Tanya?' Blackstone asked.

'The point is that in this country we do not *eliminate* the
revolutionary groups – we *watch* them. And, more importantly,
we *infiltrate* them. But, of course, if our agents are to gather
important information on the revolutionaries, they must give them
information on us in return.'

'Is the information that your agents give to the revolutionary
groups genuine information?'

'Yes – for the agents to be credible in the eyes of the revolutionaries, the information they supply *must* be genuine.'

'That's insane,' Blackstone said.

Vladimir laughed bitterly. 'You have no idea quite how insane
it is,' he said. 'We once had an agent named Evno Azef, who
rose to a high level in the Social Revolutionary Party. Based on
the information he gave us, we were able to arrest the head of

the Combat Organization, which was the military wing of the SRP, responsible for bank robberies and general acts of terrorism.'

'So that operation was a great success,' Blackstone said.

'Indeed, it was,' Vladimir agreed. 'But, of course, it left a vacancy at the top of the Combat Organization, and Azef – our agent – was appointed to the post.'

'And, as head of the Combat Organization, he had to pretend to be involved in terrorist activities?' Blackstone guessed.

'You have still not got the idea, have you?' Vladimir asked. 'He couldn't *pretend* to be involved in terrorist activities – he actually had to *be* involved in them. We know now – though we did not know it then – that he not only helped to plan the assassination of Grand Duke Sergei, the Governor-General of Moscow, but that he was behind the murder of Plehve, the Minister of the Interior, who was – strictly speaking – his boss. Naturally, the revolutionaries thought he was wonderful and trusted him completely, so the information he was able to feed us on them was absolutely first-class.'

'So, ultimately, you gained more from having him as your agent than you lost?'

Vladimir shrugged. 'I would say so, but I have no doubt that Grand Duke Sergei and Minister Plehve would disagree with me.' He paused. 'At any rate, you now understand what Tanya is doing when she becomes Natasha, and why she needs a bodyguard.'

Ever since Vladimir had decided, back in London, that he could find a use for Blackstone – and thus offered him passage to Russia – Blackstone had been waiting to find out what that use would be. But this wasn't it, he decided. Being Tanya's bodyguard just wasn't a big enough job – an important enough job – to justify all Vladimir's efforts.

'Why couldn't one of your men be Tanya's bodyguard?' he asked suspiciously.

'There is a chance that one of my men will be recognized by the revolutionaries,' Vladimir replied. 'You, on the other hand, are new to Petersburg. Tanya will tell everybody that you are a comrade from England – perhaps a member of a radical group which once tried to assassinate the prime minister – and they will believe it, because you look as if you could be such a man.'

Blackstone shook his head in disbelief.

'You're just filling in my time until you need me for the big job, aren't you?' he asked.

A wisp of a smile crossed Vladimir's lips.

'Perhaps,' he said.

Ellie Carr looked around the warehouse, which was rectangular and about the size of a small chapel. The place was positively crammed with shelving, and on each shelf sat a stack of documents covered with two years' accumulated dust.

'Well, now I've used all my feminine wiles to get us inside, would you mind telling me why we're here?' she said to Patterson.

'When the government declared war on Germany, one of the first things it did was round up all the Germans living in Britain,' Patterson replied, walking over to the nearest shelf and picking up a file. 'There were thousands of Germans in London alone. There were shopkeepers, printers and lawyers, maids and mechanics – think of any job or trade, and the chances are you'd find a few Germans who were involved in it.'

'I can believe that,' Ellie said, recalling the number of Germans she'd come across over the years.

Patterson put down the file and moved to another shelf.

'Some of the Germans – especially the older ones – were deported straight away,' he continued, 'but the government didn't want the younger men going back to the fatherland, because the chances were that they'd join the army as soon as they got home. So what they did was they locked them in prison camps on the Isle of Wight or the Isle of Man. If the men who'd been arrested had young families, those families were allowed to stay – if they wanted to, and if they could afford to – but, otherwise, it was a clean sweep.'

'I know you enjoy spinning a yarn, but I wish you'd get to the point,' Ellie Carr said.

'So last night, when Mr Hartington was talking about paper trails, I started wondering what had happened to all the records that those Germans had left behind them.'

'Records? What kind of records?'

'All kinds of records. The Germans are buggers for keeping them. As far as they're concerned, if it's not written down, it hasn't happened – so there had to be mountains of the bloody things. Anyway, I got on the phone to a few blokes I know, to see if I could find out what had happened to them.'

Ellie smiled. One of the things that Sam Blackstone most valued in his sergeant was that he knew 'a few blokes'. In fact, Archie seemed to know *hundreds* of blokes, from newspaper editors to street sweepers, from jockeys and prize fighters to the butlers at some of the grandest houses in the country.

'And I take it that one of these blokes was some help,' she said.

'He was a lot of help,' Archie confirmed. 'He told me that the government had no idea what to do with all that paperwork, which all looked harmless enough, and they were about to burn it when some bright spark in the Ministry of War pointed out that the Germans were a tricky lot, and some of the documents might contain secret codes hidden in them, which could help the war effort. That was complete and utter rubbish, of course, but war fever had reached such a pitch that people were kicking dachshunds in the street – just because they happened to be German – so there was no limit to the idiocy.'

'I saw a man kick a dachshund once,' Ellie Carr said 'He was a big man, and it was such a little dog.'

'And what did you do?'

'I thought of trying to discuss the matter with him in a logical way, but I could see that would never work, so I showed my disapproval through a more physical manifestation.'

'You hit a *big* man?' Patterson asked, surprised – although he told himself he should never be surprised at anything Ellie did.

'I caused him a certain amount of discomfort,' Ellie said vaguely. 'I may be small, but I'm very sneaky.' She grinned. 'Tell me more about the records.'

'The government decided to buy this warehouse to store the documents in,' Patterson continued. 'It was always the plan that, when there was time available to do it, somebody would go through all the records looking for hidden secrets, but, of course, that's never happened.'

'So all the records are here,' Ellie Carr said. 'Are we looking for anything specific?'

'Yes,' Patterson replied. 'We're looking for the records from some of the *Vereins*.'

'And what in Gawd's name is a *Verein*?'

'It's a bit like a club and a bit like a union, but it's much more than both of them. It's said that if you get twelve Germans in one place, they'll always form a *Verein*.'

'How do you happen to know all this?' Ellie wondered.

'Sam and I worked on a case once where I got to know all about the *Vereins*,' Patterson said. 'One of the bigger ones, if I remember rightly, was called the German Industrial and Theatre Club. It held dances and concerts every week, but it also served as a base for the typographers', bicyclists' and chess players' *Vereins*, which were much smaller. And it ran its own benefit societies – all the *Vereins* did – so if any member got sick or lost his job, they'd look after him. They'd also bury him if his family couldn't afford to.'

'All very admirable, in its way, but I still don't see . . .' Ellie began.

'The *Vereins* kept meticulous records on all their members, and since it would be unthinkable for a German in London not to join at least one . . .'

'There's a chance that there's some record of Max,' Ellie said.

'Yes,' Patterson agreed, 'especially if he went on the *Wanderschaft*.'

'The what?'

'It means "the wandering" and it's an old German tradition. Young men used to pack their belongings in a knapsack and wander around Germany, taking a variety of jobs just for the experience, but in the last fifty years or so they've expanded their horizons and started wandering in other countries.'

'And since Max seems to know his way around London, you think he may have come *here* on a wandering?'

'Exactly.'

'But you've no idea whether Max is his real name or not, or how long ago he might have visited London,' Ellie pointed out.

'That's true,' Patterson agreed, 'but I think we can narrow down the possibilities.'

'How?'

'We know he's in the navy, don't we?'

'Yes – otherwise, he'd never have had access to the documents.'

'And we know he's not very high-ranking.'

'Yes again, because he could only ever get his hands on one small piece of information.'

'So the chances are he's not been in the navy long, which

probably means he was here sometime between 1911 and 1913, and only left because he was called up to do his military service.'

'That's brilliant – but it's still a long shot,' Ellie said.

'Of course it's a long shot,' said Patterson, a hint of irritation in his voice. 'But if we're ever going to save Sam's reputation, following long shots is all we've got.'

'You're right,' Ellie said, suitably chastened. 'Let's get to work.'

It took them half an hour to find the files of the German Industrial and Theatre Club, and another fifteen minutes to find a membership file that fitted their profile – but when they did find it, it was worth the effort.

Reading through the record – and guessing at most of the words – they learned that Max Schneider had been born in Hamburg in 1894, had joined the *Verein* in 1912 and had left in 1913. While he had been in England, he had lodged at a house in Hooper Street, which was just off Commercial Road and right in the centre of what had been pre-war Little Germany.

The reason for his departure in 1913 was clear by a cutting from the *Londoner Zeitung*, the German newspaper published in London.

The cutting read:

Max Schneider wurde von der Marine eingezogen. Er wird auf einem U-Boot dienen. Wir wünschen ihm alles Gute.

'"Marine" is probably German for the navy, and "U-Boot" just has to be U-boat, doesn't it?' Patterson asked.

'Definitely,' Ellie Carr agreed. 'Is there anything else in the file?'

There was.

And it was something they'd never even dared to hope for.

A photograph!

The picture was of three young men sitting at a table, with steins of German beer in front of them; according to the writing on the back of the photograph, Max was the one in the middle.

He was a pale, intense young man, with a haughty expression and hard eyes, and it was not hard to believe that when he decided to sell his country's secrets, he had been too arrogant to use any first name but his own.

'It's starting to look like less of a long shot now,' Patterson said excitedly.

'Yes, it is,' Ellie replied, without a great deal of enthusiasm.

'What's the matter?' Patterson asked.

'Don't you think it was all a little *too* easy?' Ellie replied. Then she shook her head angrily. 'I'm being far too negative,' she said, 'and we can't afford to be negative.'

'No,' Patterson agreed, 'we can't.' He copied down Max's address and slipped the photograph into his pocket. 'Well, it's time for you to pay the piper, who's waiting breathless at the door,' he said.

'I'm looking forward to it,' Ellie replied.

The caretaker was standing in the doorway, blocking their exit.

'You've been a long time,' he complained.

'Well, like I said, it takes some blokes a long time to build up steam in their engines,' Ellie replied.

'But it's my turn now?' the caretaker asked hopefully.

'Course it is, dearie,' Ellie agreed. She paused. 'Listen, you don't mind a bit of dampness, do you?'

'Dampness?' the caretaker repeated.

'Only, me steak and kidney pie's been losing a bit of gravy recently – if you know what I mean,' Ellie said.

'No, I don't know what you mean,' the caretaker said.

Ellie sighed. 'Me hairy clam's a bit off-colour,' she said. 'Me Blackwall Tunnel's sprung a leak.'

'You've got the clap!' the caretaker said.

Ellie shook her head. 'I can't have, dearie. I'm always most particular about the gentlemen what I go wiv.'

The caretaker stepped quickly to one side. 'Get out of here – the pair of you!' he said.

'Listen, I'm more than willing to uphold my side of the bargain,' Ellie said reasonably.

'Now!' the caretaker shouted, making sweeping gestures with his arm. 'Leave right now.'

Ellie shrugged. 'There's just no pleasing some people, is there, Arthur?' she asked.

'Archie,' Patterson replied.

*   *   *

It was already dark by the time Patterson and Ellie Carr reached Hooper Street, a road lined with substantial terraced houses that had seen better days but which had not yet slid far enough down the scale to be categorized as slums.

Several of the houses had a large sign in their front windows which said 'Vacancies' and number eleven was one of them.

Patterson knocked on the door, and the knock was answered by an unshaven man in his shirtsleeves.

'Yes?' he said.

'We'd like to speak to the landlady or landlord,' Patterson said.

'She's not in,' the man told him.

'Do you know when she'll be back?'

The man shrugged. 'She's probably out on the razzle, so Gawd knows when she'll come home. But I'll tell you this much for nothing – she won't be sober when she does.'

And then he closed the door on them.

Another hour wasted, Patterson thought.

Tick-tock. Tick-bloody-tock.

'We can come back tomorrow,' Ellie said encouragingly.

'Yes, we can,' Patterson agreed bitterly. 'I've always said there are very few better ways of enjoying Christmas Day than inter-rogating a drunken landlady.'

They started to walk back down the street and had not gone more than a few yards when the door of number seven opened and a middle-aged woman with fiery red hair stepped on to the pavement, effectively blocking their way.

'Are you a copper?' she asked Patterson.

'What makes you think that?' Archie replied.

'Well, you look like a copper,' the woman said.

'As a matter of fact, that's just what he is,' Ellie said. 'But why is that of any interest to you?'

The woman sniffed. 'If you ask me, it's about time that Elsie Wilson got a visit from the police.'

'How long has she lived there?' Patterson asked.

'Must be ten years now since she moved in with her husband – or rather the man she *said* was her husband. Poor soul!'

'Poor soul?'

'He hanged himself in the outside lavatory, about eight years ago. Living with that woman, it's a miracle he lasted

that long without topping himself. I could tell you stories
about her that would make your hair curl.'

'Then please feel free to do so,' Patterson suggested.

THIRTEEN

*12th December 1916 – Julian calendar; 25th December 1916
– Gregorian calendar*

M aggie Patterson lay in the big double bed, next to her
husband. She was pretending to be asleep, though in
truth, with all the worry, she'd hardly slept at all.

This was the first Christmas Day in years that she wouldn't
be up at six o'clock, waiting at the front door for Sam Blackstone
to arrive with a plump goose, she thought. It would be the first
Christmas in years that Archie wouldn't spend most of the
morning rearranging the furniture, so that when Sam came back
again at noon, with Ellie and half a dozen orphans from Dr
Barnardo's in tow, there'd be space to fit them all in.

What happy Christmases they'd been, with the kids eating their
tangerines, and then – when they thought the grown-ups weren't
looking – playfully throwing the peel at each other. How contented
Sam and Archie had looked, sitting at one end of the room and
supping more bottles of brown ale than were strictly good for them.

They'd played games – pin-the-tail-on-the-donkey and blind-
man's-buff – and everybody had ended up laughing so much that
they were almost in tears. And then Sam had produced gifts for
everyone, and though it always seemed as if the orphans got the
best presents, nobody had complained, because that seemed only
fair.

It wouldn't be like that this Christmas. Archie wouldn't be
there – he had to go out searching for this Max bloke. And even
if he had been there, there wouldn't have been any goose, because
when there was no wage coming in and what little savings you'd
had were shrunk almost to nothing, you couldn't afford to splash
out on luxuries.

She wondered how long Archie would be in prison, and if she would be able to stand it.

'You'll *have to* stand it,' she told herself. 'You've got to hold yourself together for the sake of the kids.'

But if she got ill, the kids would have to go into an orphanage – there was nowhere else they *could* go. And she couldn't even rely on their Uncle Sam to help her out, because whatever they all said about clearing his name, none of them really believed he was ever coming back.

'You're not asleep, are you?' she heard Archie ask.

'No,' she admitted, 'I'm not.'

'Have you been to sleep at all?'

'Maybe for a short time.'

Archie laughed. 'So all night long we've both just been lying there, each trying to fool the other,' he said. 'If we'd known that, we could at least have got up and made a cup of tea. And I could use a cup now – I'm spitting feathers.'

'I'll make you one right away,' Maggie said, starting to get out of bed.

'You'll stay where you are,' Archie replied, laying his big beefy arm over her. 'I'll make it.'

'I *want* to make it,' Maggie said, lifting the arm off her.

And it was not quite a lie, because she *did* want to make it. But the more urgent reason for going downstairs was that she wanted to be as far as possible from Archie when the inevitable tears came.

When Tanya appeared at the door of the Vladimir's apartment, she was dressed in the typical peasant costume of a heavy sheepskin coat (a *shooba*) and felt boots (*valenki*), and she had a scarf on her head, which she'd tied in such a way as to hide her scar completely.

'Vladimir has told me he wants you to come with me,' she said from the doorway.

'Would you like to come inside for a few minutes first and drink a glass of tea to warm you up?' Blackstone asked.

Tanya shook her head. 'We have to go now,' she said firmly.

'As you wish,' Blackstone agreed, and as he followed her down the stairs, he was thinking, 'This time last year, Maggie would already have started cooking the goose.'

They caught the number fourteen tram, which rattled along Sadovya Street and soon reached a large square which had a church on one side and a large covered market on the other.

'What's that market called?' Blackstone asked.

'Why should you be interested?' Tanya asked sullenly.

'Why shouldn't I be interested?' Blackstone countered.

'It's called the Haymarket,' Tanya snapped. 'There! Are you any the wiser for knowing its name?'

'Dostoyevsky thought of it as the stinking heart of the city,' Blackstone said, 'and it's here that his central character, Raskolnikov, kisses the ground before turning himself in to the police.'

'You've read *Crime and Punishment*?' Tanya asked, astonished.

'Yes.'

'And am I supposed to be impressed?' Tanya said, rapidly converting her astonishment into something close to contempt.

'Tell me, do you resent the British as a whole, or is it just me that you have an objection to?' Blackstone asked.

'Let me answer that question with one of my own,' Tanya said. 'How big are the factories in England?'

'It depends.'

'Do they have more than a thousand workers?'

'Some may do, perhaps, but not very many.'

'In Petrograd, a factory with only a thousand workers is considered small,' Tanya said.

'I don't see the point,' Blackstone admitted.

'Russia could never have built those factories without the help of British capital. But in return for that help, you require rates of interest that are almost ruinous.'

'Without those huge factories, which you say we helped you to build, your troops would have even less equipment and supplies than they've got now,' Blackstone pointed out.

'And how can we meet these interest rates?' Tanya asked, as if he had never spoken. 'By paying our workers low wages and by housing them in filthy dormitories where whole families sleep in one bed!'

'And you blame us for that?' Blackstone asked.

'Tanya doesn't blame you,' the girl said. 'Tanya thinks that if the mighty Russian Empire is to be preserved, such evils must be tolerated – but then she would think like that, because she is the product of a privileged upbringing and has never really known hunger and cold.'

'But *you're* Tanya,' Blackstone said.

'No,' the girl replied firmly, 'today I am Natasha, and I know that *nothing* – not a vainglorious empire, not a bloody war – can excuse the way the proletariat are treated in this country.'

Before an important interview – and this might turn out to be a *very* important one – Archie Patterson liked to clear his head, which was why, even though it would swallow up a few minutes of the precious time he had left, he told the taxi driver to drop them on Leman Street.

It was as they were getting out of the cab that he first noticed that Ellie Carr was carrying her black leather medical bag in her right hand.

'Are you planning to do a little bit of doctoring on the side?' he asked, looking down at the bag.

Ellie grinned. 'Not if I can help it. I don't like live patients – they complain too much.'

'Then I don't understand why you've brought your doctor's bag with you,' Patterson said.

'I brought it because you couldn't bring your warrant card,' Ellie replied enigmatically.

The road itself was almost deserted, although – it being Christmas Day – all the pubs in the area were full of men, just as all the kitchens in the houses were full of women.

They walked in silence down Leman Street, where there had once been German bakers and confectioners, butchers, boot makers, tailors and cigarette manufacturers – all of them now long gone.

If the Germans themselves had been employed to wipe out the evidence that they had once had a colony on this spot, Patterson thought, there would not have been a trace of them left. But the task had fallen, instead, to men who lacked Teutonic thoroughness, so although someone had chipped away the raised letters that said *Deutsche Bäckerei* from the front of one of the shops, that same someone had failed to paint over the space those letters had occupied, so the words were still there in a sort of ghostly transfer.

'Sloppy,' Ellie Carr said.

'What's sloppy?' Patterson asked.

'That,' Ellie replied, pointing to the words *Drücken Sie einmal* over the bell-push of what had once been a German tailor's shop.

'Yes, it is,' Patterson agreed, and he hoped that on the battle-fields of the Western Front, the Germans were being somewhat less efficient than their reputation would indicate, and the British rather more so.

They turned left on to Hooper Street. As they passed number seven, Patterson noticed that the red-haired woman – who'd told them her name was Mrs Stanton – was looking through her front window and had a malicious smile on her face.

The woman who answered their knock at number eleven was probably in her middle fifties. She had a pinched face and a peevish expression – and, looking at her bloodshot eyes and veined cheeks, Patterson had no doubt that she had indeed been out on the razzle the day before.

'What do you want?' she asked.

'Are you Mrs Elsie Wilson, the landlady of this boarding house?' Patterson replied.

'Yes.'

'Well, I'm from the police – Detective Sergeant Patterson – and I'd like to ask you a few questions.'

'On Christmas Day?' the woman asked.

'It won't take more than a few minutes of your time, Mrs Wilson,' Patterson reassured her.

And perhaps he had been too reassuring – too lacking in the confidence of authority – because the woman's eyes narrowed, and she said, 'Have you got a warrant card?'

Patterson made an elaborate show of patting down all his pockets.

'I seem to have left it at home,' he admitted finally.

The landlady smirked. 'Well, if you haven't got a warrant card, you can just piss off.'

'Actually, we can't,' Ellie Carr said firmly.

'You what?' the woman asked.

'I'm a physician working for the public health department,' Ellie said, holding up her doctor's bag, 'and under legislative order seven hundred and thirty-one stroke eight – better known, as I'm sure you're aware, as the Blackstone Act – I have the right to enter any premises, at any time and without any warning.'

It was plain from the look on the woman's face that she believed Ellie, Patterson thought – and he was not surprised, because though he knew she was talking absolute bollocks, even he *almost* believed her.

'I keep a nice clean house,' Mrs Wilson whined. 'I'm most scrupulous about it.'

'Perhaps you are, and perhaps you're not,' Ellie said crisply. 'We'll see for ourselves, once we're inside.'

On this special day of the year, they should have smelled the aroma of cooking fowl the moment they entered the house, but there was only cold air wafting down the corridor of number eleven, Hooper Street.

'Haven't you started your lodgers' Christmas dinner yet?' Patterson asked, surprised.

'On what they pay me, I'm not cooking them a special Christmas dinner,' Mrs Wilson said sourly. 'Besides, I've got a gentleman caller coming round later, and I have to get myself ready for him.'

'Before I begin my inspection, we'd like to ask you about this man,' Ellie said, showing her the picture of Max.

'I've never seen that bloke before in my life,' Mrs Wilson said, barely looking at the photograph.

Ellie sighed. 'I really don't want to close this boarding house down,' she said, 'but if you refuse to cooperate, you'd be surprised how many things I can find wrong with it.'

'Why do you want to know about him?' Mrs Wilson asked.

'We suspect he may recently have become a typhoid carrier, and we need to track him down in order to test him,' Ellie said.

'But he's back in Ger . . .' Mrs Wilson began, before she realized she'd made a mistake.

'What was that?' Patterson asked.

'Nothing.'

'You were about to say he's back in Germany,' Patterson told her. 'If you've never seen him in your life, how do you know he's German?'

'You said so.'

'No, we didn't.'

'All right,' Mrs Wilson conceded. 'He did lodge here a few years ago – but if I'd known then that the Kaiser was going to declare war on us, I'd never have let him through the door.'

'Tell us about him,' Patterson said.

'What do you want to know?'

'Anything you can remember,' Ellie Carr said. 'Anything that you think might incline me to take a more favourable view of your kitchen when I get around to inspecting it.'

'He was a waiter in one of them German restaurants.'

'And?' Patterson said.

'And he was a nice boy – for a German, I mean.'

'So you have no complaints about him?'

'None at all.'

'And nobody else complained, either?'

'Not as far as I can remember.'

'I've got this new chemical test I'm just bursting to try out,' Ellie told Patterson. 'It can find the most horrible bacteria even in places that have been thoroughly scrubbed.'

'All right, when he had his friends round, he was a bit noisy,' Mrs Wilson admitted.

'You allowed him to entertain his friends in his room?' Patterson asked. 'That's not normal, is it?'

'Well, no,' Mrs Wilson admitted. 'But like I said, apart from the noise, he was a very nice boy.'

'And what *sort* of noise did they make?'

'They had a gramophone.'

'A big one?'

'It was quite large.'

'And he played it half the night, didn't he?' Patterson asked.

Mrs Wilson's eyes narrowed. 'Who's been talking?' she demanded. 'If it was that spiteful ginger bitch, Gertie Stanton, from number seven . . .'

'Actually, it wasn't her,' Patterson lied. 'But where we got the information from is neither here nor there, now is it? Did he play the gramophone half the night or not?'

'Sometimes.'

'And how did your other lodgers feel about that?'

'Some of them didn't mind so much.'

'They all minded – and they all moved out.'

'Well, yes, they all moved out eventually, but people do move on – that's the nature of the business.'

'You allowed him to do something that made all your other lodgers leave,' Patterson said.

'Well, yes, I suppose I was bit soft on him,' Mrs Wilson admitted. 'He wasn't my type at all, but he did have a very nice bottom.'

'And what happened as each of your lodgers left?'

'I rented out his room again. It's what landladies do.'

'Presumably, you let out all the rooms to people who didn't mind Max's noise?'

'Yes.'

Patterson sighed. 'Getting a straight answer out of you is harder than pulling teeth,' he said. 'It was Max's friends – the ones who'd been making the noise with him – who rented the rooms, wasn't it?'

'I forget.'

Ellie sniffed loudly. 'I can smell the mould in here,' she said. 'It's almost overpowering. I think we'll have to have this whole place fumigated.'

'All right, yes, they were all Max's friends,' Mrs Wilson admitted.

'And were they Germans, too?'

'No, they were as English as you and me. Max was the only foreigner in the place.'

'It sounds to me as if you drove all your old lodgers out just so Max's friends could move in,' Patterson mused. 'From a business point of view, that seems to make no sense at all.'

'Oh, you've run a boarding house yourself, have you?' Mrs Wilson asked tartly.

'No, I haven't,' Patterson said, 'but I do know that when you've got good, reliable lodgers, you want to hold on to them, not drive them out and take in new ones who might only stay for a week.'

'What makes you think the lodgers who left were reliable?' Mrs Wilson challenged.

'Weren't they?'

'As a matter of fact, they weren't. They were a right shower – they hardly ever washed, and they were always behind with their rent.'

'Funnily enough, Mr Thomas – who lodged with you for three years, until Max's gramophone drove him out, and has been lodging at number seven ever since – has quite a different story to tell,' Patterson said. 'He told me that all the lodgers who left were quiet, respectable people.'

'He's lying,' Mrs Wilson said. 'Anyway, the people who replaced them were just as quiet and respectable – and Max personally vouched for their good character and stability.'

'And how many of those quiet, respectable lodgers are still here?' Patterson demanded.

'None of them,' Mrs Wilson muttered.

'I'll give you one last chance to tell the truth, and then we're closing this place down,' Patterson said.

'All right,' Mrs Wilson replied, defeated. 'When the first of the old lodgers threatened to leave, I told Max he'd have to quieten down a bit, but he said I shouldn't worry, because he could fill every room in the house with his waiter friends, and I could charge them double what I'd been charging before.'

'Double?' Patterson repeated. '*Double!*'

'That's right.'

'How could simple waiters have afforded to pay you double the rent your old lodgers had been paying?' Patterson asked.

Mrs Wilson shrugged. 'I never asked, and Max never told me.'

He was building a clear picture now, Patterson thought.

Max comes to Britain ostensibly to work in a restaurant. And perhaps he *does* actually work in a restaurant, but his real job – which just has to be something criminal – pays him far more than being a waiter ever could.

He's living high on the hog – having the best time of his life. And then his call-up papers arrive, and he has to go back to Germany. He doesn't like living on the wages of a very junior officer at all, and then one day he comes across a piece of information which, if handled right, can make him a fortune. And the real beauty of it is that it's the British who'll be willing to pay the most for it – and he knows parts of London like the back of his hand.

'He got an official-looking letter from Germany and then he left, didn't he?' Patterson asked.

'How did you know that?' Mrs Wilson wondered.

'Just answer the question!' Patterson barked.

'Yes, he got a letter, and the next day he was gone. And all his pals went at the same time, leaving me to build up my business again from scratch. It just goes to show, doesn't it?'

'Just goes to show what?'

'It goes to show that, even if they seem pleasant enough on the surface, you can never trust a Hun.'

FOURTEEN

The tram's terminus was at a large arch, which might have looked majestic but for the poisonous yellow sky that framed it.

'Before you ask, that's the Narva Triumphal Arch,' Tanya said skittishly. 'Alexander the First had it built at the end of the Napoleonic Wars. His idea was that it was the first thing the soldiers would see when they returned to the city. It was their reward – and the only one they got – for risking their own lives and seeing so many of their comrades die.'

'Natasha really does despise the tsars and all they stand for, doesn't she?' Blackstone asked.

'Natasha doesn't know any better,' Tanya said ambiguously.

Beyond the arch, there were half a dozen factories, each with several tall chimney-stacks pumping out filth into the atmosphere.

'That's where we're going,' Tanya said, pointing to a long, rectangular building with very tiny windows.

'A dark, satanic mill,' Blackstone murmured, almost to himself.

'What did you say?' Tanya asked.

'A dark satanic mill,' Blackstone repeated. 'It's from a poem by—'

'William Blake,' Tanya interrupted. 'I know.'

'Must be a hell of a place to work in,' Blackstone mused.

'No doubt it would be,' Tanya replied. 'But it is not where the poor souls employed by the Narva Cotton Company *work* – it is where they *live*.'

An old man in a shabby uniform, which included an ancient

cutlass, was standing guard at the entrance to the dormitory block. When he saw Tanya, he smiled and gestured that they should go inside.

'A member of the party?' Blackstone asked.

'A sympathizer,' Tanya replied.

The inside was indeed a vision of hell. It seemed to be one large room, and it was crammed with row after row of narrow bunk beds. There was little light and virtually no air, and the whole place stank of stale cabbage and human sweat.

Four men were standing at the end of the nearest row. From their clothes, it was clear that three of them were workers in the mill. They had careworn faces and were old before their time. The fourth man was wearing a suit and looked shabbily respectable. He was perhaps twenty-six or twenty-seven, and his eyes burned with the fire of a true fanatic.

Tanya greeted them all, then pointed to Blackstone and gave a short speech. When she'd finished, the men all nodded sagely.

'I've just told them you're a comrade who's part of the revolutionary struggle in England,' she said. 'For some reason, that seems to impress them.'

'Maybe not everyone in Russia is quite as anti-British as you are,' Blackstone suggested.

'We are going to discuss our strategy,' Tanya told him. 'From time to time, I will translate what has been said. I don't want to, but since you are supposed to be a fellow revolutionary, my comrades will expect it – so please try to act as if you are interested.'

'I *am* interested,' Blackstone said.

The strategy 'discussion' went on for half an hour. Most of the talking was done by the man in the shabby suit, and when one of the workers tried to interrupt him, he would wave his hands extravagantly in the air.

'It has been decided that the strike will not end until the workers' demands are met,' Tanya told Blackstone at the end of it.

'And what *are* their demands?' Blackstone asked.

'A fifty per cent increase in wages and a twenty per cent decrease in hours,' Tanya said.

'No, that's not *their* demands – that's what your mate in the suit wants them to ask for,' Blackstone said. 'What do they want for themselves?'

Tanya looked at him suspiciously. 'Vladimir did not tell me you could speak Russian,' she said.

'Nor can I,' Blackstone replied. 'But I can read men, and I've been reading this lot for the last half-hour. So what is it they *actually* want?'

'We will talk about it on the way to the factory, when my comrade is not reading you in the way that you appear to have read him,' Tanya said.

'I take that to mean that he's not coming to the factory himself,' Blackstone said.

'No, he is far too valuable to the party – and to the workers' movement in general – to be put at risk over such a minor skirmish.'

'Or, to put it another way, it'll all be left up to the poor bloody infantry, as it always is,' Blackstone said.

'I'm afraid I don't understand what you just said,' Tanya told him.

But she did – he could see that she did.

The pub had been heaving when they'd walked in, ten minutes earlier, but now most of the men had drifted off for their Christmas dinners, and they virtually had the place to themselves.

Patterson looked down at the pint of best bitter he was holding in his big hand. Knowing, as he did, that the chances were he'd soon be back in prison, it was tempting to drink as much beer as he could force down himself. But there was still work to be done, and he needed a clear head to do it. So, with a sigh, he put the glass back on the table, untouched.

'We've reached a dead end, haven't we?' Ellie Carr asked.

'Were you expecting to find Max had gone back to his old lodgings?' Patterson asked.

'No, but . . .'

'Then what were you expecting?'

Ellie shrugged helplessly. 'I don't know what I was expecting.'

'Just by establishing that Max did live there once, we've taken a big step towards finding him,' Patterson said.

'Have we? I don't see how.'

'We started this investigation in the belief that what Hartington said about Max still being in London is true, didn't we?'

'Yes, we did, but now I've started asking myself *why* we should believe him. What does he know? He's a posh solicitor. He's probably never brushed shoulders with a criminal in his life.'

'No, he probably hasn't,' Patterson agreed, 'but he most likely got the information from whoever's paying him.'

'If the man who's paying him knows that Max is still in London, why doesn't he simply tell us where to find him?'

'I've no idea,' Patterson admitted, 'but if Hartington's convinced that he's still here, then so am I.'

'And I suppose I am, too,' Ellie conceded. 'So what's our next step?'

'The next step is based on our knowledge that Max once lived in Hooper Street and that he was probably involved in some sort of criminal activity,' Patterson said.

'Go on.'

'In some ways, criminals are a lot like animals – they're never really comfortable away from the places they know. So if Max *is* in London, he won't be *too* far from Hooper Street.'

'Not *too* far?' Ellie said quizzically.

'That's right,' Patterson agreed. 'He won't have gone to ground anywhere he's likely to run into Mrs Wilson, of course, but I'd be surprised if he's more than half a mile away from Commercial Road. So that's the area we'll concentrate our search on.'

'So we show Max's photograph to people on the street and in the shops and pubs, and see if anyone recognizes him?' Ellie asked.

'That's right.'

'It's one of the most crowded areas of this very crowded city,' Ellie said. 'How many people do you think there are living there?'

'Quite a lot,' Patterson admitted.

'The strike started when a group of mothers arrived half an hour late for work because their children were sick,' Tanya said, as they walked towards the mill. 'That was nothing unusual – children are always getting sick in that place, and once one comes down with something, it is not long before a lot of the others catch it. But what was different this time was that it was the older children who had caught the fever, and that made things especially difficult.'

'Why?' Blackstone asked.

Tanya snorted with contempt at his ignorance. 'The older children can look after the babies when they are sick, but the babies cannot look after the older children,' she said.

'Of course – I should have seen that,' Blackstone agreed humbly.

'The mothers asked if one of them could go back to the dormitory in the middle of the morning, to check on the sick children,' Tanya said. 'The foreman told them they were employed as cotton spinners, not nurses. The women accepted that. They knew that perhaps one or more of the children would be dead by the time their shift was over, but there was no guarantee that a visit would save them – and if they lost their jobs by disobeying the foreman, they would have no money to feed *any* of their children, and they would *all* starve to death.'

'I hope that sometime during this strike I meet that bastard,' Blackstone growled. 'I'll teach him how to be compassionate, even if it kills him.'

'There was worse yet to come,' Tanya said. 'The foreman told them that since they were half an hour late, they would be fined half a day's pay. That was too much for even the downtrodden to take, and they walked out.'

'So, at the start of their meeting with your mate . . .'

'Josef. His name is Josef.'

'At the start of their meeting with Josef, what were they demanding as a condition for returning to work?' Blackstone asked.

'They wanted the half-day's pay that the women had been docked reinstated, and the right for at least one of them to go back to the dormitory when children were sick.'

'They weren't asking for a fifty per cent increase in wages and a twenty per cent decrease in hours?'

'No.'

'But your comrade talked them into it?'

'Josef can be very persuasive – and the workers look up to him. They know nothing beyond the villages they came from and the mill in which they now work. But he is an educated man, wise to the ways of the world, and if he tells them something, they believe it to be correct.'

'And what *did* he tell them?'

'He said that we have the owners over a barrel and that they are bound to concede.'

'Was he telling the truth?'

'No, of course not.'

'So why did he lie to them?'

'It was *unlikely* that the employer would agree to their first demand – withdrawing the fines and allowing one woman to visit the dormitory – but there was always a slight possibility that he would.'

'And wouldn't that be a good thing?'

Tanya snorted again. 'The important thing is not that matters are resolved, but that there is a strike. Real change does not come through gradualism; it comes through confrontation.'

'And to hell with the mill workers?' Blackstone asked.

'Josef says that you cannot make an omelette without first breaking a few heads,' Tanya said.

'You mean "eggs",' Blackstone corrected her.

'I mean *heads*,' Tanya said firmly. 'Or to put it another way, Josef believes that there can be no victory if there is not some suffering first. And he is not alone in this belief – Vladimir, who is his antithesis, believes exactly the same thing.'

There was a large square in front of the mill, and as they approached it, they could see that a crowd of several hundred people – men, women and children – had gathered in front of its gates.

'They're all worried that the owner will try to bring in new workers from the outside to replace them,' Tanya explained.

'Should the children be here, when there's a chance of things turning violent?' Blackstone asked.

'The hope is that there will be no violence *because* the children are here,' Tanya said. 'It is a tactic that has often been used in the past.'

'And does it always work?'

Tanya shrugged. 'It *usually* works,' she said cautiously.

The people in the crowd were cold – and probably hungry – but they were in the sort of good spirits that people often are when – after one humiliation too many – they have finally decided to take a stand.

Tanya walked up and down the line, shaking the men's hands, kissing the women and rubbing the children's heads.

She was a very different character from the one he was getting to know, Blackstone thought. This Tanya – or perhaps he should start thinking of her as Natasha – was both liked and respected by the people she was talking to.

She *had* to be convincing in this role, he realized – she would never be given important information to pass on to Vladimir if she wasn't. Yet he still marvelled at the way she could compartmentalize her mind so completely.

Two days earlier, she had been the staunch defender of tsardom who had demanded that Rasputin be killed before he could tarnish the image of the monarchy any further. Yet here she was, encouraging people to take a stand against that same tsardom even if a few heads were broken in the process.

He wondered which side she was really on – and then wondered if she even knew that herself.

The crowd had been quite loud up until that moment, but now a sudden hush descended over it, and in the near distance, there was the sound of horses' hooves on cobblestones.

Clip-clop-clip. Clip-clop-clip.

It would have been impossible to distinguish the hooves over the noise, Blackstone thought, so the people hadn't fallen silent because of what they'd heard; they'd done it because of what they *felt*.

The sound of the hooves grew louder – CLIP-CLOP-CLIP, CLIP-CLOP-CLIP – and then the horsemen appeared from around the corner.

There were twelve of them, and it was not horses they were riding on, but shaggy ponies.

Each man wore a fur hat and carried an evil-looking, short, weighted whip in his hand.

'Cossacks,' Tanya gasped. 'They are Cossacks. We . . . we should have been expecting that.'

The horsemen had arrived in single file, but now they fanned out until they were in a straight line, facing the crowd.

It was a textbook manoeuvre that was both fluid and confident, Blackstone thought. Each rider seemed to understand his mount, and each mount seemed instinctively to know what its rider required of it. The Cossacks used neither stirrups nor spurs to guide their ponies, and the whips they carried had probably never been used on the animals.

But I think I know what they do *use them on,* Blackstone told himself, remembering Tanya's scar.

One of the Cossacks – perhaps their captain – said a few words.

'What was that?' Blackstone asked Tanya.

'He said this is an illegal meeting, and we should disperse immediately,' Tanya replied.

'*Is* it illegal?'

'He seems to think so – and he is the one with the whip.'

Although no apparent order had been given, the ponies began to advance slowly towards the crowd.

Tanya shouted something, first to her left and then to her right, and all the people on the front line of the crowd linked arms.

The ponies drew ever closer. They did not seem to be in the least intimidated by the fact that there was a solid wall of people ahead of them.

Another few steps and they were so close to the front line of the crowd that Blackstone could smell the breath of the pony closest to him.

When the animals were perhaps a foot away, the people on the front line dropped their arms to their sides, and when the ponies pierced the line, they pushed their way either to the left or the right to create a passage for them.

The progress continued, the Cossacks bobbing up and down amongst the sea of humanity like the masts on sailing boats. The horsemen did not speak or look around them. It was almost possible to believe they did not even know that the crowd was there.

When they reached the factory gates, the Cossacks executed a turn, and since this required more space than simply going forwards, there was a great deal of scrambling among the strikers.

Once they had turned, they retraced their steps, and when they were finally clear of the crowd, they formed a single file again and trotted off.

Several of the strikers cheered, but when they realized that most of their comrades were not joining in, they fell silent again.

'That was a warning,' Tanya told Blackstone. 'They wanted to show us how helpless we are and how pointless our struggle

is. If the strikers are here again tomorrow, they will not treat
them quite so gently.'

'And will the strikers be here again tomorrow?'

'Yes, if the strike committee – if *Josef* – can breathe the necessary fire into them.'

'And if *they* are here, will *we* be here?' Blackstone asked.

'Oh yes, we will be here,' Tanya replied.

FIFTEEN

Vladimir had been morose – perhaps even troubled – ever
since the night that Tanya had visited the apartment, but
when he arrived home that evening, he seemed to be
altogether in much better spirits.

'There is no problem that can't be overcome by the clever
manipulation of circumstances, Sam,' he said, as he handed his
cloak to the waiting Yuri. 'And there is no belief – however
deeply held – that cannot be preserved once you have learned to
navigate events around it.'

'I have no idea what you're talking about,' Blackstone admitted,
as they walked towards Vladimir's study.

'No, I don't suppose you have,' Vladimir replied cheerfully,
going straight to his desk and reaching for the panel that controlled
his railway. 'Did you have a good day, Sam?'

'Not as good as the one you've obviously had,' Blackstone
replied. 'Tanya took me down to the Narva cotton mill.'

'Ah yes,' Vladimir said, as if he'd forgotten that small detail
– though Blackstone suspected he never forgot anything.

'The owner sent in a dozen Cossacks to intimidate the strikers,'
Blackstone said.

'Then he must think that the strike has a firm foundation and
that starving the workers back to the mill – which is usually the
preferred option – will not work this time,' Vladimir said. 'Who
is running the strike?'

'A man called Josef,' Blackstone said.

'Ah, then the owner has the right to be worried,' Vladimir said. 'Josef is a splendid chap.'

'A *splendid chap*?' Blackstone repeated incredulously. 'He's your enemy, isn't he?'

'Indeed he is,' Vladimir agreed, 'and at some point in the future, it might be necessary to have him killed – or, worse, horribly maimed, as an example to others – but that doesn't mean I can't admire his professionalism, does it?'

'Tanya thinks it's likely that the Cossacks will charge the crowd tomorrow,' Blackstone said.

'She's a smart girl, so if she considers that probable, it's more than likely to happen,' Vladimir replied.

'So wouldn't it be wise of you to order her to stay away from the mill tomorrow?'

'If she was not there, she would lose credibility, and months of painstaking work would be undone.'

'Aren't you worried she might get hurt – or even killed?'

Vladimir laughed. 'Of course not,' he said. 'What harm could possibly come to her with Sam Blackstone as her bodyguard?' He paused. 'How are you and Tanya getting along with each other?'

'She doesn't like me,' Blackstone said. 'In fact, I'd go as far as to say she despises me.'

Vladimir frowned. 'You must find a way to *make* her like you, Sam,' he said. 'It is vital to my plans that you both like and trust each other.'

'And what plans might they be?' Blackstone wondered.

'You will know when the time is right,' Vladimir said airily, his good humour starting to return. 'I have decided that we're spending far too many evenings in the apartment,' he continued, 'so tonight, Sam, my friend, we will go out and have a little fun.'

'I didn't know you allowed yourself to have fun,' Blackstone said.

Vladimir grinned. 'You're right, of course. My pleasure comes from my achievements, not through surrendering to frivolity.'

'So why are we going out?'

'We are going out so that I can begin the process I spoke of earlier – the one that involves navigating events around my deeply held beliefs.'

'And where will this navigation take place?'

'It will take place in a famous Petersburg nightclub called the Aquarium,' Vladimir said.

'It's a strange name for a nightclub,' Blackstone commented.

'On the contrary, it is a very sensible name, as you will see when we get there,' Vladimir said.

It was becoming almost impossible to get good French champagne at any price, Max Schneider thought, but then, he supposed, since the whole of Europe was engaged in a life-and-death struggle in which millions had already perished, it was only right that even *he* should have to sacrifice something.

Leaving a generous tip on the table – and his last glass of champagne barely touched – Max stood up and walked across the dining room.

He was aware of the eyes that were following his progress, but it did not displease him. In fact, he fairly revelled in it.

After all, why *wouldn't* they look at him? He was a handsome man by any standards, and if watching him brought a little light into their humdrum lives, then he was pleased for them.

He crossed the foyer and stepped out of the front door straight on to the promenade.

He loved Brighton, he thought, as he strolled towards the Royal Pavilion, though he would have loved it even more during the Regency period, when the Prince Regent had made it *the* place to be seen.

Somewhere in the distance, two seagulls squawked in angry dispute, and he felt a shiver run down his spine.

He hated the birds with a passion because they reminded him of Hamburg, where he had been brought up – and Hamburg reminded him of his stern, unyielding father who had been responsible for that upbringing.

'When you were born, I had hopes that you would grow into a real man, Max,' he said, in a voice much deeper than his natural one. 'And look at you now – you disgust me!'

'Why don't you die, Father?' he asked in his normal voice. 'Why didn't you die long ago?'

It was dangerous to be a German in Britain – even one posing as a Norwegian – but he would never go back to the country of his birth, he promised himself. He had known from almost the moment he had landed in England that it was his spiritual home, and even when the money ran out – and it would run out eventually – he would stay and get by as best he could.

The seagulls squawked again, and he found himself wondering how difficult it would be to poison every gull in Brighton.

The walls of the Aquarium nightclub were made of thick glass, and, behind that glass, brightly coloured fish swam endlessly up and down.

The centre of the club, in contrast, had much more muted lighting, though it was still possible to see beyond your own table to the three or four that surrounded it.

There were two other people at Blackstone and Vladimir's table – a young officer in a Guards' uniform and a strikingly attractive woman in a long flowing dress that was covered with jewels.

They both seemed to know Vladimir – they gave every indication of having been waiting impatiently for his arrival – but Vladimir did not introduce Blackstone to them, and they seemed totally indifferent to him.

The lights dimmed in the room, and a spotlight appeared on the stage. A woman walked to the centre of it, and there was thunderous applause.

She was very dark-skinned for a Russian, and her hair was jet black. She was wearing a dress with a long gathered skirt and had a shawl over her shoulders. Four more women, dressed in a similar manner, came on to the stage and stood behind her, and then two men, wearing wide-brimmed black hats, followed.

The guitarists began to play a simple tune, the woman began to sing, and even after a few notes, Blackstone felt a catch in his heart and knew that hers was a voice that could weave magic.

She sang five songs, full of melancholy and passion, despair and euphoria, and when she walked off the stage, Blackstone was exhausted.

'She's one of the most famous gypsy singers in the whole of Petersburg,' Vladimir told him.

The striking woman at their table had been watching the door for the whole of the gypsy woman's performance, and now she turned to Vladimir and said, in an anxious voice, 'He hasn't come.'

The fact that she was speaking in English was not, Blackstone realized, for his benefit, but simply because the aristocracy only ever spoke Russian to their servants, preferring to converse with each other in either English or French.

The woman reached across the table and grabbed Vladimir's arm with her hand.

'You assured me, Count, that he would be here,' she said.

Vladimir looked down at the hand with some distaste and then removed it – none too graciously – with his own.

'I am not accustomed to having my word doubted,' he growled. 'I told you he will be here, and so he will. His policemen – to whom I have paid out a small fortune – will make sure of that.' And then, as if he could bear the sight of the woman no longer, he turned back to Blackstone and said, 'What were we talking about, Sam?'

'You were telling me that the gypsy singer is famous,' Blackstone reminded him.

'Ah, yes. I believe that, in some countries, gypsies are despised, but in that – as in so many other things – Russia is different. The cabarets and theatres are prepared to pay a great deal to engage the services of a gypsy singer.'

'I imagine they are,' Blackstone agreed, his nerves still tingling from the performance.

'And while most actresses – even quite famous ones – accept it as part of their job to sleep with some of their admirers, a gypsy singer will do no such thing. If you wish to bed her, you must first marry her, and you cannot marry her without the consent of her family, which you can only obtain by giving them a small fortune as a gift.' Vladimir took a sip of his wine. 'Do the members of your English aristocracy ever marry gypsies, Sam?'

'Only in romantic fiction,' Blackstone said.

'Here, it is quite common,' Vladimir said. 'Half of the noblest families in Russia have some gypsy blood in them.'

'He's coming,' the striking woman hissed excitedly, though she did not attempt to grab Vladimir's arm again. 'He's coming.'

Blackstone turned towards the door and saw a man weaving his way uncertainly between the tables. The man had a scraggy beard and was dressed simply in a peasant blouse and baggy trousers – though, as he got closer, it was obvious that the blouse was made of shot silk, and the trousers of the finest cloth.

He had not come alone. Following in his wake were six women, three dressed like prostitutes and three wearing gowns that would not have disgraced a society ball.

'Do you recognize him from the cartoon you saw?' Vladimir asked Blackstone.

'Is he Rasputin?' Blackstone said.

'The very same,' Vladimir confirmed.

Rasputin reached the table that had been reserved for him and sat down. His women – the *rasputinki* – stood hovering uncertainly as he first studied them and then glanced at the seats around the table.

A full minute passed before he pointed first to one of the gowned women and then at a chair on the far side of the table. The woman's shoulders slumped, and as she walked slowly to the seat he had assigned her, it seemed as if her whole world had come to an end.

'They worship him,' Vladimir said to Blackstone. 'When he eats hard-boiled eggs, they beg him to let them take the shells away with them, and if he gives his permission – and he doesn't always – they preserve those shells as if they were precious relics.'

Rasputin had decided that another of the women should sit next to him, and her delight was as obvious as the despair of the other woman had been.

'I'm told that one of his favourite tricks is to stick his fingers deep in a dish of jam and then have his disciples lick them clean,' Vladimir said. 'I'm not sure who I despise more – him or his women.'

When the whole party was finally seated, Vladimir stood up and walked over to Rasputin's table. Once there, he bent down and whispered something in the *starets'* ear. Rasputin replied, and Vladimir took a step backwards and made a great show of shaking his head in a disbelieving manner.

Rasputin spoke again, waving his hand agitatedly through the air, and Vladimir laughed.

Rasputin attempted to rise from his chair – perhaps to take a swing at the other man – but Vladimir placed a powerful hand on his shoulder and forced him down again.

One of the gowned women at the table started to speak to Vladimir. Her face was full of rage, and it was obvious – even from a distance – that she was telling him to leave Rasputin alone. Then Vladimir raised his hand in a commanding gesture, and she fell silent.

Blackstone shook his head in silent admiration. It was unlikely that any of the people at Rasputin's table knew who Vladimir was – the very nature of his business dictated that he be unknown – yet, just by his presence alone, he was dominating them all.

Rasputin said something else to him, and Vladimir nodded.

This time, when the *starets* started to stand up, Vladimir did nothing to prevent him.

Rasputin lifted his peasant blouse and held the edge of it in his teeth, so that his chest was bare. Then he took the waistband of his baggy trousers in both hands and pulled them down to his knees.

He was wearing no underwear, and his penis was immediately exposed to anyone who happened to be looking in that direction.

Rasputin took the penis in his right hand and held it up for Vladimir to inspect.

Two waiters suddenly appeared, one of them holding a tablecloth. They wrapped the cloth around him, then began to hustle him across the room, a manoeuvre not made any easier by the fact that his trousers were still at knee level and he could move at no more than a shuffle.

Vladimir returned to his own table.

'Well, that was most satisfactory,' he said to Blackstone.

'What was it you said to Rasputin?' Blackstone asked Vladimir, in the cab back to the apartment.

'I asked him if he was the *starets*, and when he agreed he was, I told him, in a very contemptuous manner, that I needed proof before I would believe him. Of course, he had the proof right there at the table – he was surrounded by people who could vouch for his identity – but he was drunk, and so, instead of appealing to them, he asked me just what sort of proof I would require.'

'And what did you say?'

'I said that I had heard that the real Rasputin had a wart on the end of his prick, which he uses to drive women into ecstasies. I asked him to show it to me – which, of course, he did.'

'You couldn't have *known* he'd do it,' Blackstone said.

'True,' Vladimir agreed, 'but he has certainly exposed himself in nightclubs before, and I had no doubt that, in order to make me look small, he would expose himself again.'

'But I still don't see why you would have *wanted* him to expose himself,' Blackstone said.

'Ah, that was for the benefit of Grand Duke Dimitri and Prince Felix Yusupov,' Vladimir said. 'I thought it might encourage them towards an action that they were already seriously considering taking.'

Vladimir was playing one of his games, Blackstone recognized – dangling tantalizing bits of information before his eyes, and making him jump through hoops before supplying the context that would make sense of them.

Well, he supposed it helped to pass the time.

'Who are Grand Duke Dimitri and Prince Felix Yusupov?' Blackstone asked dutifully.

'Grand Duke Dimitri is the tsar's younger cousin,' Vladimir said. 'The tsar and tsarina are very fond of him, and though the wider imperial family is really quite large, he is the only member of it who is ever invited to spend much time with them. He serves as the tsar's aide-de-camp and is, in some ways, almost a second son to the tsar and tsarina. It is even rumoured that they are considering marrying him to their eldest daughter.'

'And since you put the show on for him, I am assuming that he was at the Aquarium tonight.'

Vladimir laughed. 'Of course he was. He was the young officer who was sitting at our table.'

'And was this Prince Yusupov there, also?'

'Oh yes. Though they have had their occasional disagreements – and even quite long periods of separation – he is still Grand Duke Dimitri's closest friend and constant companion.'

Even by his own standards, Vladimir was making heavy work of this, Blackstone thought.

'Might I have seen him?' he asked.

'You could not have avoided it,' Vladimir said, with a grin, 'because he was sitting at our table, too.'

'The woman!' Blackstone exclaimed in disbelief.

'Felix has enjoyed dressing up in women's clothes since he was twelve or thirteen years old. His parents were naturally concerned about it, and, in an attempt to cure him of the habit, they sent him to Oxford University, which they believed to be both staid and respectable. Unfortunately for them, however, he joined something called the Bullingdon Club while he was there, and that only seems to have made him worse.'

'A woman!' Blackstone repeated, still not quite able to believe that the strikingly attractive figure who had sat opposite him could have been a man.

'You're not the first one to fail to see through Felix's disguise – not by a long way,' Vladimir assured him. 'Once, he appeared on the stage of the Aquarium dressed as a woman, and everyone was taken in. He sang six songs before he was recognized by some of his mother's friends – even then, they didn't really see that it was actually him until they'd recognized his mother's jewellery, with which he'd lavishly draped himself.'

'Jesus!' Blackstone said.

'And it's not just on the stage or in dim lighting that he can get away with it,' Vladimir continued. 'There was another occasion, after a ball at the opera, when he allowed himself to be picked up by four Guards officers, who took him to the Bear nightclub. He told his friends, later, that in order to escape their amorous intentions, he was forced to throw a bottle of champagne into the nearest mirror, switch off all the lights and make a dash for the street. And perhaps he did do that – or perhaps he made no attempt to escape at all and stayed to service all four of them.'

'You have nothing but contempt for him, do you?' Blackstone asked, remembering the way Vladimir had roughly removed Felix Yusupov's hand from his arm.

'The man is scum,' Vladimir declared with a passion. 'While all the other young men of his class are serving in the army – and some are actually dying for their country – he has found a way to gain an exemption. While the poor starve, Felix spends money like a drunken sailor – a very rich drunken sailor. He has no redeeming features, and the world would be better off without him.'

'And yet, knowing all you do about him, it was still important to you that this man – above all others – should see Rasputin behaving disgracefully?' Blackstone asked incredulously.

'Not above all others,' Vladimir said. 'It was important that Grand Duke Dimitri saw it, too, although it is undoubtedly the case that Yusupov is the leader and Dimitri the follower.'

'I still don't see why you went through the whole charade,' Blackstone admitted.

'I did it because I need him,' Vladimir said. 'And while it is true that I find him so disgusting I would rather dive into a bath of shit than shake his hand, it is also true that he is about to help me to navigate events around my deeply held beliefs.'

SIXTEEN

13th December 1916 – Julian calendar; 26th December 1916 – Gregorian calendar

It was snowing when they arrived at the mill, and half the square was covered with a blanket of unbroken whiteness. The other half – the section closest to the Narva cotton mill gates – was a different matter. There – partly to keep warm, partly because they were too nervous to stand still – the workers had been wandering up and down for over an hour, and as quickly as the snow fell, they were turning it to slush.

'None of the children are here today,' Blackstone said, glancing quickly around him.

'No,' Tanya agreed, 'they are not. It was agreed it would be safer for them to remain in the dormitories.'

'It was *agreed*?' Blackstone repeated quizzically.

'Yes,' Tanya said.

'And Josef went along with it?'

'Of course he went along with it. He is our leader – our vanguard. No such decision would have been made without his consent.'

'That doesn't sound like him at all,' Blackstone mused.

'How can you say that about him, when you have only met him once?' Tanya asked, sounding slightly uncomfortable.

Yes, he had only met him once, but once was more than enough, Blackstone thought.

He had seen the ruthlessness in the other man's eyes – the determination to do anything to advance the cause of the revolution. A man like that would not baulk at the slaughter of the innocents – he would relish the prospect.

So if Josef had changed his mind, it must have been under powerful persuasion.

And who could have provided that persuasion?

Certainly not the mill workers, who looked up to him with the same sort of naive trust that the peasants had once bestowed on the tsar, whom they had called their 'Little Father'.

No, it wasn't them – there was only one person who could have made him change his mind.

'What did you say to him?' Blackstone asked.

'To whom?' Tanya replied evasively.

'To Josef.'

'I said nothing.'

That was a lie, Blackstone thought. Somehow, Tanya had found a weakness in Josef that she could exploit – a point at which pressure could be applied.

And, with a sudden flash of insight, he understood exactly what that weakness – that pressure point – was

'You offered to sleep with him, didn't you?' he asked, surprised by how angry he sounded.

Tanya shrugged. 'What if I did? Do you think that my virginity is as precious as the lives of little children? I certainly do not.'

'You *can't* sleep with him!' Blackstone said.

'A girl must lose her cherry at some time, and I might as well lose mine to Josef,' Tanya said.

'So you find him attractive, do you?'

Tanya shuddered slightly. 'He is Natasha's comrade, and comrades share with each other,' she said.

'And where will Tanya be while Natasha is offering him her body?' Blackstone asked.

Another shudder. 'Tanya will be elsewhere,' the girl said.

Well, if he couldn't change Tanya's – or Natasha's – mind about sleeping with Josef, he could certainly make sure that Josef was incapable of sleeping with her, Blackstone decided, settling on a broken leg as the best way to curb the revolutionary's amorous intentions.

A boy – he could not have been more than ten – came running through the snow and spoke to a woman who might well have been his mother. Almost immediately, an excited murmur ran through the crowd.

'The Cossacks are coming, the Cossacks are coming.'

The cry galvanized the strikers, and they quickly formed lines, with Tanya and Blackstone part of the front one.

As if nature had decided to add drama to the Cossacks' arrival, the snow had begun to fall more heavily, and at first they were nothing more than dark shapes in the distance. Then, as they drew closer, it became possible to pick out the individual features – their fur hats, the whips they held in their hands, the rifles in their holsters at the side of the saddles.

They were riding in single file, as they had the day before, and once again they executed a series of faultless manoeuvres which ended when they lined up side by side, facing the strikers.

But it was not an exact replication of the day before, Blackstone thought. Then, they had formed their line no more than ten metres from the strikers. Now, they were at least thirty metres away – and that was not good.

What am I doing here? he asked himself.

But he already knew the answer to that question – he was there to protect Tanya.

He knew why she was there, too – so that she could gain credibility with the revolutionaries, who would give her valuable information about their plans, which she could then pass on to Vladimir.

And he knew why the strikers were there.

But did *they* know?

They probably thought they were there to win concessions from their heartless managers, but that was not the case at all. The Party had put them there to be hurt, to be an example to other workers who would rise up in their anger and be hurt, too – and on and on, until there was so much anger that even pain could not make them retreat, and the regime would crumble.

There was still a chance the day would not turn out too badly, he thought. There was still a possibility that when the workers realized how serious the Cossacks were, they would run – and the horsemen would let them. And then he read the sheer determination in the Cossack captain's bearing, and he knew that was not about to happen.

The Cossacks were vastly outnumbered, but they had two

things in their favour, both related to their ponies. The first was the elevated position that their mounts gave them. The second was the speed at which they could move.

But if they allowed themselves to be hemmed in, neither of those things would count for anything. So when it started, they would come in hard, doing all they could to cut swathes through the mob – giving themselves room to manoeuvre – and that was why they had formed their line so much further away that morning.

The captain gave the signal, the Cossacks began to advance at a canter, and the lines of strikers tightened their grips on each other.

One Cossack hit the front line a couple of yards to Blackstone's left, another a couple of yards to his right. Both were already slashing out on both sides with their leaded whips.

People began to scream – some from pain, some simply from fear. Those strikers who attempted to pull the Cossacks from their mounts felt the full effect of the whips on their hands and wrists – and heard their own bones breaking.

It did not take more than a few seconds for the front line to break up, and the Cossacks ploughed on relentlessly into the second and third lines.

Blackstone had fought in enough battles to recognize a defeat when he saw one.

'It's all over,' he shouted into Tanya's ear. 'There's nothing more that we can do.'

'Josef says that if we can only stand firm, we can win,' Tanya screamed back at him.

'Look around you,' Blackstone said. 'We're not standing firm – and that bastard Josef isn't even here.'

Some people had started to run, and what had once been a sea of strikers was rapidly being reduced to a small number of islands of desperate resistance, standing isolated in the swirling snow.

One group of five strikers had managed to pull a Cossack from his pony, and now that they had him on the ground, they were attempting to kick the life out of him. Then one of his comrades appeared on the scene, his whip whistled through the air in a series of blurs, and the five men were down.

The ground was littered with men and women. Some of them were lying perfectly still, some trying desperately to crawl away to safety. In several places, the grey slush was already deeply stained with red.

And now even the islands of resistance were breaking up, as strikers ran away in every direction and were swallowed up by the snow.

The Cossacks could have let them go – their own victory was beyond dispute – but this was not about breaking a strike, it was about breaking the labour movement, and the captain sent most of his men to hunt them down.

Tanya suddenly began to run towards the mill gates, to join a small group of men armed with bricks, who seemed determined to make their last stand there. And as she did so, one of the two Cossacks who had remained on the square began to bear down on her.

She was halfway between what had once been the front line and the mill gate when the Cossack caught up to her. His whip slashed through the air, and though she tried her best to dodge the blow, it still caught her across the back and she sank to her knees.

The Cossack slowed, wheeled his pony around her and got ready to finish the job.

And it was at that moment that Blackstone, flinging himself through the air, slammed into the Cossack's chest.

Blackstone fell back to the ground on the other side of the pony, but by twisting and grabbing as he did so, he managed to pull the Cossack with him.

They landed on the hard cobbles in a tangled heap, but – unlike the Cossack – Blackstone had been anticipating this and was the first of the two to recover and pull himself free.

Even so, the Cossack was only a second or two away from becoming dangerous again when Blackstone grabbed his head and began banging it against the cobblestones.

The first bang seemed merely to enrage the Cossack, but after the second his eyes began to glaze over and his hands dropped weakly to his sides. And with the third – when his blood began to form a gory halo around the back of his head – he was perfectly still.

Climbing to his feet, Blackstone saw that the second Cossack, who had been at the other end of the square, was galloping towards him.

He looked around for something that might save him and found it in the shape of the first Cossack's pony, which was used to battle and was calmly waiting to see what would happen next.

He ducked behind the pony, and the second Cossack, seeing the manoeuvre, changed course slightly.

Even at a distance – even in the snow – Blackstone could read the rage on the other man's face and recognized that while the Cossack undoubtedly wanted him dead, it was a slow and painful death he was intending to inflict.

It was perhaps two seconds before the Cossack realized that he had made a mistake – understood that, instead of planning how to exact his revenge, he should have been thinking about what his enemy was doing. But by the time he saw the rifle that Blackstone had taken from the other Cossack's saddle holster, it was already too late, and he had little time to curse his own foolishness before Blackstone shot him through the heart.

Tanya was no longer on her knees, but was lying on her stomach.

Blackstone turned her over. Her eyes were closed, but when Blackstone started to untie her headscarf, they quickly opened again.

'Don't look at my face,' she groaned.

'I need to check how badly you're hurt,' Blackstone said softly, 'and for that I need to . . .'

'Don't look at my face!' Tanya said again – and this time it was almost a scream.

'All right,' Blackstone said soothingly. 'I'm going to lift you to your feet. Do you understand?'

Tanya nodded. Blackstone put his hands under her armpits and raised her up. He could tell that it hurt, but she never made a sound.

'Do you think you can stand on your own?' he asked.

'I think so,' Tanya said.

But the moment that he slackened his hold on her, her legs began to buckle.

He picked her up in his arms and looked around him – at the two Cossacks he had killed and at the injured and dead workers who were fanned out beyond them. In the distance, he could hear screams, which told him that other Cossacks were still engaged in their bloody work. But soon they would return, and if he and Tanya were still there when they did, they were both as good as dead.

'I have to take you away from here,' he told the girl. 'It might hurt, but there's no choice.'

'Then bloody well get on with it,' Tanya said through gritted teeth.

SEVENTEEN

16th December 1916 – Julian calendar; 29th December 1916 – Gregorian calendar

Archie Patterson slowly became aware of the gentle but persistent prodding and opened his eyes to find his wife standing over him.

'I've brought you a nice cup of tea, sweetheart,' Maggie said. 'But I don't want you to take too long over drinking it, because you need to get dressed before the doctor arrives.'

Patterson gave her a sleepy grin. 'The doctor?' he repeated. 'Is somebody sick?'

Maggie put both her hands on her substantial hips, something that she always did when displaying mock annoyance – and sometimes even when the annoyance was real.

'You know very well that when I say the doctor's coming, I'm talking about Dr Carr,' she said.

Patterson's grin widened. It would be fair to say that the two women liked each other – that they were, in fact, firm friends. But even after all the years they had known each other – even after Maggie had conferred on Ellie the honour of entertaining her in the kitchen, rather than the parlour – his wife still refused to call Ellie anything but *Dr Carr*, because she *was* a doctor, and Maggie knew what was right.

'How are your feet?' Maggie asked, with a hint of concern.

'They're fine,' Patterson lied.

'Stick them outside the bedclothes, and let's have a look at them,' Maggie said.

'I've told you, they're all right,' Patterson said, trying to sound like the master of the house – and failing miserably.

'Feet!' Maggie commanded.

With a heavy sigh, Patterson shrugged off the sheets and blankets, and held his feet out for inspection.

'They're covered with blisters,' Maggie said.

'Well, I've been doing a lot of walking these last few days,' Patterson replied weakly.

'I'll boil up some water and you can give them a real good soaking,' Maggie said.

Patterson grinned again – but this time it was a forced grin. 'The way you look after me, you're more like a girlfriend than a wife,' he said.

Maggie punched him playfully on the shoulder and then was instantly serious again.

'It will be all right, won't it, Archie?' she asked.

'Of course it will be all right,' Patterson told her.

He was not lying to her, he thought, as he listened to his wife's heavy footsteps on the stairs – at least, not *exactly* lying. It *could* be all right. They *might* find Max and get him to confess that Sam Blackstone had played no part in the swindle. And if all that happened, he himself might be given a light sentence for his part in the escape that he still couldn't even remember.

But even though he and Ellie Carr were spending sixteen hours a day tramping the streets of what had once been Little Germany – and had the blisters to prove it – they had not found a single person who would admit to ever having seen the man they so desperately needed to find.

And time was running out. In two days, he would have to surrender himself at his local police station, and from there it was only a short step to Southwark Crown Court.

How long a sentence would he get for rescuing his friend?

Ten years at least – and possibly even twenty!

He felt a tear run down his cheek.

'What are you – a man or a mouse?' he asked himself angrily. 'Because if you're a mouse, you're the biggest – fattest – bloody rodent that *I've* ever seen.'

He heard Maggie climbing the stairs again, and then she appeared in the doorway holding an enamel bowl full of steaming water.

'I've put some liniment in it,' she said, walking over to the bed and placing the bowl on the floor. 'Soak your feet in it for a few minutes, and it should make all the difference.'

'I'm a very lucky man, you know,' Patterson said.

'Are you?' Maggie asked.

'There's no question about it. I've got the perfect wife and three wonderful kids – and if that's not lucky, then I don't know what is.'

'I'm going to miss you so much,' Maggie said sadly. Then the sadness melted away, to be replaced by a look of sheer horror. 'I . . . I didn't mean that,' she gabbled. 'What I meant was . . . what I meant was . . .'

But they both knew what she'd meant.

Tanya was very pale and looked so tiny lying in the middle of the great feather bed – but even here she was wearing her headscarf.

'I want to thank you for saving my life,' she said.

'Think nothing of it,' Blackstone answered awkwardly. 'That was what I was there for.'

'You were very brave, and I was very foolish,' Tanya said. 'Vladimir didn't send me there to make any heroic gestures, and yet . . . and yet . . .'

'Go on,' Blackstone encouraged.

'When I saw those workers standing in front of the mill gates – armed with nothing but rocks, yet willing to fight to the end – I had to try to join them. I just couldn't help myself.' A look of uncertainty came to her face. 'Do you think I was being disloyal to Vladimir, Mr Blackstone?'

'Call me Sam,' Blackstone said.

Tanya shook her head weakly. 'No, I can't do that. *Do* you think I was being disloyal?'

'A revolution is a very confusing thing,' Blackstone said. 'There are bad people on both sides, and there are good people on both sides – and when you see some of the good people in trouble, it's hard to turn your back on them.'

Tanya smiled. 'Thank you,' she said.

'What has the doctor told you?' Blackstone asked.

'He says that I have some very bad bruising, but he does not think anything is broken. He has ordered me to stay in bed for several more days.'

'That's very wise of him,' Blackstone said. 'Will your family be coming to see you?'

A wary look came into Tanya's eyes. 'Vladimir has forbidden me to talk about my family,' she said.

'Why would he have done that?'

'If I told you the reason it must be kept secret, that would be almost the same as revealing the secret itself,' Tanya said enigmatically.

And perhaps that secret was why she was so torn in her loyalties, Blackstone thought.

'Can't you talk about them because they're members of the aristocracy?' he asked. 'Or is the secret that they're both revolutionaries?'

'Please don't ask,' Tanya begged. 'If Vladimir knew I had said even as much as I have, he would be very angry with me.'

Of course! Blackstone thought.

That was it!

He was a fool not to have seen it before.

Vladimir had told him that her parents didn't know what she was doing, but that had been nothing but a blind. At least one parent *did* know – because that parent was Vladimir!

'Let us talk about something else,' Tanya suggested. 'Why don't you tell me about yourself?'

It was nothing but a ploy to get him off a dangerous subject, Blackstone thought.

'You don't really want to hear about me,' he said.

'I do,' Tanya replied earnestly. 'I promise you, I do.'

Blackstone smiled. 'All right,' he agreed. 'Where would you like me to start?'

'Vladimir always says that the best place to start a story is at the beginning,' Tanya said.

'Vladimir says a lot of things, and if half of them are true, I'm a Chinaman,' Blackstone countered.

'You don't think badly of him, do you?' Tanya asked, suddenly rather worried. 'You like him, don't you?'

The father desperately wanted him to like the daughter, and now the daughter desperately wanted him to like the father, Blackstone thought. Well, the former of those two things was getting easier and easier, but he was still not quite sure about the latter.

'Please say you like him,' Tanya begged.

'There are many things that I admire him for,' Blackstone said cautiously. 'He's clever, he's resourceful, and he's very brave.'

'But do you *like* him?' Tanya pleaded.

'Yes,' Blackstone was surprised to hear himself say. 'It's probably foolish of me – he'll probably exploit it – but I do like him.'

A contented smile came to Tanya's face. 'Good,' she said. 'Now you can tell me your life story.'

He told her about his childhood, about how grinding poverty had sent his mother to an early grave, and how he himself had spent most of his childhood in an orphanage.

He told her about soldiering in India and Afghanistan.

'It sounds fascinating,' she said.

'And sometimes it was,' Blackstone agreed, 'but it could also be the very vision of living hell.'

He described his first meeting with Vladimir, how they had run across the sloping roofs in the East End of London, in a desperate attempt to reach the assassin's hiding place before Queen Victoria's carriage drew level with it, and how Vladimir had lost his footing and fallen into the packed crowd below.

'He didn't really hurt himself, did he?' Tanya asked, concerned about a possible injury that might have happened before she had even been born.

'No, he didn't really hurt himself,' Blackstone assured her.

Tanya giggled. 'If only I'd seen that for myself! I could have teased him with it for ever.'

Blackstone talked about the first time he had come to Russia, and how, never realizing she was Vladimir's agent, he had fallen in love with Agnes.

'It must have hurt you to leave her behind,' Tanya said.

And Blackstone's mind was suddenly back at the tiny railway station in the middle of the vast steppe.

'I'll protect you as far as London,' Blackstone promises. 'Once you're there, I'll give you what little money I have. From that point, you're on your own.'

'Thank you for your kind offer, but it will not be necessary,' Agnes says. She stands up and walks over to the door. 'If I'm not to be with you, then I will stay in Russia.'

'At least stay on the train until we reach St Petersburg,'
Blackstone suggests.

'I would prefer to get off here,' Agnes replies, almost primly.

'But we're in the middle of nowhere. There probably isn't a hotel
here, and God alone knows when the next train will come through.'

'Please don't worry about me, Sam,' Agnes says. 'It will
not be long before Vladimir hears about me and comes to
find me.'

'It *did* hurt me to leave her behind,' he told Tanya. 'It hurt me
more than I'd ever imagined it would.'

'But it was the only thing you *could* do,' Tanya said. 'If you
had stayed with her, Vladimir would have had your soul trapped
in a stoppered jar.'

She seemed to enjoy his tales of working with the New York
police, but she grew more serious when he talked about Ellie
Carr.

'Ellie seems like a good woman,' she said.

'She is.'

'Then you should marry her.'

'I want to.'

'In fact, you should have married her years ago.'

'I know that now,' Blackstone said.

But had he left it too late? Enmeshed as he was in one of
Vladimir's schemes, would he ever leave Russia alive?

'Tell me the rest of the story,' Tanya instructed him.

And so he did, only ending the narrative with his arrival in
Russia.

Tanya smiled.

'His story being done,
She gave him for his pains, a world of sighs.
She swore, in faith, 'twas strange, 'twas passing strange.
'Twas pitiful, 'twas wondrous pitiful,' she said.

'Is that from Shakespeare?' Blackstone asked.

'It is. It's Othello's speech to the senate. I changed it a little
– which Vladimir would say was rather wicked of me – but it
wouldn't have fitted the circumstances if I hadn't.'

'Do you and Vladimir often read Shakespeare together?' Blackstone asked.

'Not since I was a child,' Tanya said. And then, as if she realized she had said too much, she quickly added, 'Even then, we didn't do it much – probably not more than once or twice.'

The door opened, and Vladimir himself stepped into the room.

His eyes swept over both of them, as if he was trying to assess exactly what had gone on before his arrival. Then he said, 'I would like a few minutes alone with Tanya, Sam.'

'Of course,' Blackstone agreed.

'And you yourself should get some rest, because you have a busy night ahead of you,' Vladimir said.

'Have I?' Blackstone asked. 'What will I be doing?'

'You will be watching history being made,' Vladimir said.

On the first day of their search, Patterson's feet had started to ache towards the end of the afternoon. On the second day, it had been the middle of the afternoon when he had become aware of his blisters. Now, on the sixth day – and despite the soothing footbath that Maggie had prepared for him – he was in pain before he had even covered a hundred yards.

'Well, look on the bright side – at least you'll only have to put up with this for another day and a half, Archie,' he said to himself bitterly, as he and Ellie approached a cobbler's shop on Cudworth Street. 'Once you've surrendered yourself at the police station, the day after tomorrow, there'll be no more long walks for you – not for years and bloody years!'

The cobbler's name was Thickett. He was an old man with a bald, shiny head and walrus moustache, and he had a pair of glasses perched on the end of his nose with such thick lenses that Ellie Carr, however much she tried, just couldn't stop herself from staring at them.

'Yes, you're right, darlin', they're like the bottoms of beer bottles,' the cobbler said.

'I'm sorry, Mr Thickett,' Ellie exclaimed remorsefully. 'I didn't mean to be rude.'

'It's the work, you see,' the old man explained. 'People think that blokes like me just hammer the nails into shoes any-old-how.

I sometimes think they must be confusing us with blacksmiths. But a good cobbler, my little love, is just as much of an artist as that Italian geezer from the old days – you know, the one what painted the Moaning Lisa – and that can be a bugger on the eyes.'

'Can you see this all right?' Patterson asked, showing him the photograph of Max.

'Oh yes, I can see that picture clearly enough,' the old man said. A smile of deepest contentment came to his face. 'Cordovan leather,' he murmured softly to himself.

'What was that you just said?' Patterson asked.

'That's another mistake people make – thinking all leather's pretty much the same,' the cobbler said. 'Well, it's not. There's no finer leather than Spanish leather, and Cordovan is the best of the lot.'

'We're not here to talk about leather,' Patterson said, irritated. 'What we want to know . . .'

Then he saw that Ellie was glaring at him, and decided it would be a good idea to shut up.

'What made you mention Cordovan leather just now, Mr Thickett?' Ellie asked the cobbler.

'That's what his boots are made of,' the old man said.

'Whose boots?'

'The geezer in the photograph that you've just showed me. He said he'd brought them to me specially, because he'd heard I was the best in the business – and so I am.'

'When was this?' Patterson asked.

'Must be about two weeks ago. He told me he was in a hurry and he wanted them the next day. And *I* told *him* that I wouldn't even start to work on them before I'd studied them for a couple of days. Well, he knew a craftsman when he saw one, so eventually we settled on a week.'

'Did he leave an address?' Patterson asked.

'Why would he have needed to do anything like that? He paid for the work in advance, you see.'

'Then you've no idea where he lives.'

'Haven't I?' the old man asked, sounding surprised.

'Have you?' Patterson countered.

'As a matter of fact, I have,' the old cobbler said.

'And would you care to tell me?'

'I don't see why not. He lodges with Mrs Downes, on Collingwood Street.'

EIGHTEEN

From the outside at least, it was the best-kept boarding house they had visited so far – and God alone knew how many they'd called at! The windows were gleaming, the paintwork was scrubbed, and the brass door knocker was so beautifully polished that it almost seemed a shame to use it.

But Patterson didn't notice how pristine the windows were or how shiny the doorknob was. His mind was focused on one thing and one thing only, and the same few words kept rattling back and forth across his head like an express train.

Let it be Max, let it be Max, let it be Max . . .

When Ellie Carr knocked on the door, the knock was answered by a solidly built rosy-cheeked woman in early middle age.

'Can I help you?' she asked, favouring them with a broad smile.

'Are you Mrs Downes, the landlady of this boarding house?' Archie Patterson asked.

'Bless you, no, I'm Lizzy Clough, her niece,' the woman said. 'I'm just helping out for a while.' She glanced over her shoulder into the passageway. 'The truth is,' she continued, in almost a whisper, 'it's starting to look as if it'll be *more* than a while, because I don't think Auntie will ever be able to run the place again.'

'How long have you been here?' Patterson asked.

'Let me see . . . it must be three months,' Lizzy Clough said. 'I know that because I arrived just after the big stock market in Faversham.'

'The big stock market in Faversham?' Patterson repeated, mystified.

'We're country people,' Lizzy explained. 'Farmers. And so was Auntie, before she married Harry Downes, who was London born and bred. Anyway, Harry upped and died – he was never very strong, poor soul – and for the past ten years Auntie has been running the place on her own. But now her legs have started to give way, you see.'

'That's very interesting, but—' Patterson began.

'Yes, it *is* very interesting,' Ellie interrupted. 'Do tell us more.'

'Well, Dad said that she should sell up and move in with us,' Lizzy Clough continued, 'but I told him she loved this boarding house, and it would break her heart to leave it, so I'd come down and give her a hand. He got very grumpy about that, did Dad, and said he needed me for the milking, but, as I told him, where we live, you can't kick a bit of cow shit off your boot without hitting a milkmaid. Anyway, Auntie needed me and I wouldn't be talked out of it, so here I am.' She looked up and down the street, as if it still came as a surprise to her that she couldn't see green fields. 'Funny old place, London,' she concluded.

Patterson cleared his throat. 'We're from the police,' he said.

Lizzy Clough frowned. 'Oh dear, oh dear, there's nothing wrong, is there?' she asked.

'Nothing you should be concerned about,' Patterson assured her. He held out the picture of Max for her to look at. 'Do you know this man?'

'Why, bless you, that's Mr Hansen,' Lizzy replied. 'He says he's a Norwegian, but, to tell you the truth, I'm such a big daft country girl that I've no idea where Norweej is.'

'He's a lodger here, is he?' Patterson asked.

'That's right. He's been here for two months now.'

Which would have given him plenty of time to feed the secret submarine plans he'd stolen to the British government and then set up the ambush on the docks, Patterson calculated.

'Is Mr Hansen at home now?' he asked, and when Lizzy shook her head, he added, 'Do you know what time he's expected?'

'I really couldn't tell you that,' Lizzy said apologetically. 'He's away on business, you see.'

Patterson had a sinking feeling in the pit of his stomach. 'Away on business?' he repeated. 'Or gone for good?'

'Away on business,' Lizzy said firmly. 'His rent's paid until the end of the month, and he's left most of his clothes.'

'Have you any idea where he's gone?' Ellie Carr asked.

'Not really,' Lizzy admitted. 'But before he left, he did ask me to press his blazer and white trousers, and I know for a fact that he bought a new straw hat – so doesn't that mean he will have gone to the seaside?'

'Could we see his room?' Patterson asked, expecting, at any moment, that Lizzy would demand to see his warrant card.

'I don't see why not,' the woman replied. 'After all, you are the police, aren't you?'

'Yes,' Patterson replied gratefully, 'we are.'

Max's room felt cramped, but that was only because it contained not one wardrobe, but two.

'He bought the second wardrobe himself,' Lizzy Clough said. 'He had to. He's got so many clothes they simply wouldn't fit in the wardrobe we provided. Now, if you'd like me to show you—'

'I think we can manage on our own, thank you, Mrs Clough,' Patterson interrupted her.

'I'm *Miss* Clough – and probably always will be,' Lizzy told him, 'unless, of course, some suitable man makes me an offer.'

And since she was looking directly at the sergeant as she spoke, she left little doubt as to who she might consider suitable.

'I'm already married,' Patterson said apologetically.

Lizzy Clough sighed. 'The good ones always are,' she said philosophically. 'So I'll leave you to it, shall I?'

'If you wouldn't mind,' Patterson replied.

'Don't you worry yourselves about making a mess, because I'll be glad to clear it up,' Lizzy said. 'When you're brought up on a farm, time hangs heavy when you're not working.'

And then she backed out of the room and disappeared down the corridor.

'He's certainly got a lot of clothes,' said Ellie Carr, who had already opened one of the wardrobes.

'Some men are like that,' Patterson answered, going across to the bed and checking the bedside cabinet.

'All the clothes have English labels,' Ellie said.

There was nothing in the cabinet drawer but a comb, a box of matches and an empty cigarette packet. Wishing he'd got to the wardrobe first – and so left Ellie with the next job – Patterson lowered his substantial frame awkwardly on to the floor and peered under the bed.

'So his clothes are English,' he grunted. 'What does that prove?

Max must have entered this country illegally, which probably means he couldn't bring much luggage with him.'

There was nothing under the bed – not even a speck of dust. Patterson levered himself up again and ran his hands over the mattress.

'The thing is, I don't think all the clothes *are* new,' Ellie said, clearly puzzled. 'Everything's very well looked-after, but I'd say that a couple of the jackets are at least two years old.'

'I've got jackets that are much older than that,' Patterson replied, deciding he'd better turn the mattress over. 'He probably bought some of the stuff from a good second-hand shop.'

'I don't think we can quite equate your clothes with the ones that Max might own,' Ellie said hesitantly.

'What do you mean by that?'

'Well, I don't want to sound rude, but the only time anybody might mistake you for a snappy dresser was if you were standing next to Sam. But it's clear from the photograph that Max takes a real pride in his appearance, and I can't see him ever buying something second-hand.'

'Then maybe the clothes are not as old as you think they are,' Patterson said, grabbing the corners of the mattress.

'I'm a forensic scientist,' Ellie reminded him. 'On one of my better days, I can tell you how old a piece of snot is, so don't you go questioning my judgement on clothes.'

Patterson grinned. Ellie had a rare talent for making you grin, even when it felt that, any second, your head might explode from all the pressure you were under.

'Yes, some of this stuff is definitely at least two years old,' Ellie said, in a tone that was definitely not to be argued with.

Patterson gave the mattress a heave. It was full of flock and was both surprisingly heavy and awkward to handle.

'Some of these clothes just don't belong in the wardrobe of a man who's only been here for a couple of months,' Ellie persisted.

'Then maybe they belong to a friend of his,' Patterson suggested, as he struggled in his efforts to teach the mattress who was in charge.

The mattress fought valiantly, but as so often happens in a battle between the inert and the dynamic, it was eventually forced to capitulate and allow itself be rolled against the wall.

'When your clothes are as important to you as they seem to be to Max, the last thing you're prepared to do is share your wardrobe with anyone else,' Ellie said infuriatingly. 'For someone like him, it would be almost as bad as sharing his wife with another man.'

But Archie was no longer listening, because now that the mattress was out of the way, he could see the spoils of war – and they were greater spoils than he would ever have dared hope for.

'Look!' he said, holding up his prize for Ellie to see. 'What do you think this is?'

'It's an attaché case,' Ellie replied, puzzled.

'It's *the* attaché case,' Patterson said. 'It's the one that Special Branch stuffed full of money and Sam took down to the docks.'

'Are you sure?' Ellie asked dubiously.

'I'm certain,' Patterson replied. 'After he'd bought it from Harrods, Sam made a nick in the leather, just below the handle, so he'd recognize it again. It wasn't a big nick – you'd never notice if you weren't looking for it – but it was distinctive, and this bag is nicked in exactly the same way.'

'Is there anything inside the case?' Ellie asked.

'I haven't looked yet,' Patterson said evasively.

'Why not?'

Patterson sighed. 'Because, I suppose, I'm still summoning up the strength to handle the disappointment when there isn't.'

'Oh, for God's sake, Archie, open the bloody case,' Ellie said.

'All right,' Patterson agreed, 'but I'm warning you now, we've already had more luck today than any two people are entitled to.'

But, as it turned out, fate had decided to throw in a bonus and at the bottom of the case they found a cancelled railway ticket from London to Brighton.

When his friend had phoned from London to say that he couldn't make the rendezvous after all, Max had first put on a display of anger, then rapidly switched to a tone of bitter disappointment. He had not, in truth, really experienced either of these emotions, but it was his policy to put his friends at a guilty disadvantage whenever the possibility presented itself.

In point of fact, he was quite glad that this particular friend – who could be both tiresome and demanding – wouldn't be coming, because that left him free to do exactly what he liked.

And so it was that, after dinner, he set off on a walk along the promenade in search of new friends – who he hoped would be both younger and more amusing than the one who had let him down.

He decided to avoid the Royal Pavilion – he had learned recently that it had been turned into a hospital for limbless soldiers, and that somewhat diminished its charm – and instead headed in the opposite direction, towards a rather amusing cocktail bar, where he was very much in demand.

There was a cold wind that night, and the only people who appeared to be on the promenade were two drunks, who were advancing slowly towards him in an erratic zigzag.

For a moment, Max contemplated crossing the street to avoid them. Then, noticing that the drunks were very well dressed – and probably had fat wallets which could be easily lifted – he changed his mind.

He stopped walking, took out his packet of cigarettes and patted his pockets as if he was searching for his matches.

'Excuse me, do you have a light?' he asked the first drunk.

At first, the man did not seem to understand what he was talking about, but then he said, 'Light . . . wanna light a shigarette?'

'That's right,' Max agreed.

The drunk turned to his companion. 'Man here wants to light a shigarette,' he said.

'Why don't you give him a light, then?' the second drunk asked.

'Good idea,' the first drunk agreed.

He reached into his overcoat pocket, clumsily pulled out its contents and immediately dropped them.

'Fallen on the ground,' he said, bemused.

'I'll pick them up for you,' Max said, bending down.

He quickly surveyed his potential haul. There was a handkerchief, a pocket watch, a penknife, a bunch of keys and – yes – a nice fat wallet.

It would be a mistake to pocket the wallet just then, Max told himself, because the drunk might miss it and demand to search him. A better plan would be to move just a little distance away and collect it later.

He coughed loudly and gave the wallet a good kick. It flew through the air and landed ten feet behind them. Then he swept up the rest of the possessions and handed them to the drunk.

'You don't seem to have a box of matches,' he said.

'Don't seem to have a box of matches,' the drunk told his companion, as he crammed all the objects back into his pocket.

'I've just remembered – you gave up smoking last week,' the second drunk said.

'So I did,' the first drunk agreed. 'Don't have any matches because I gave up smoking last week,' he told Max. 'Sorry about that.'

'Never mind,' Max said. 'If I can't smoke, I think I'll take in some sea air, instead.'

He walked over to the cast-iron railings and looked out to sea, thus putting himself in the clear if the drunk now realized he was missing his wallet and started looking for it.

But the drunk *didn't* seem to realize it. Instead, he and his companion walked on a few yards, before stopping again.

It might be wise to let them get further away before picking up his prize, Max considered.

On the other hand, the more time that elapsed, the more chances the drunk had to remember the wallet.

He glanced over his shoulder. The two men were standing still, but they were looking in the opposite direction. If he swept the wallet up and walked quickly away, he should be perfectly safe.

It did not occur to him, until he was actually bending down to pick up the wallet, to wonder why the drunk had kept it in his overcoat pocket, rather than the inside pocket of his jacket.

But before he could develop that thought further, he felt a couple of strong arms clamping his own arms to his sides and experienced the unpleasant sensation of having a bag pulled over his head.

NINETEEN

Vladimir looked out of his study window on to the dark street below.

'The car has arrived, so it is time for us to go,' he said.

Blackstone, who had been expecting to leave much earlier, glanced at the clock on the mantelpiece.

'The middle of the night is a bloody funny time for history to be made,' he said.

'History happens when it *can* happen,' Vladimir replied. 'And tonight, it cannot happen before midnight.'

'Thank you for explaining that,' Blackstone said. 'As with all your explanations, everything is now perfectly clear.'

'Sarcasm does not become you, Sam,' Vladimir said.

'Neither does going out at ten o'clock at night in the middle of a Russian winter,' Blackstone countered.

'You should put on a warm coat,' Vladimir said, ignoring the comment. 'We may be sitting in the car for quite some time.'

When they reached the street, Vladimir dismissed the driver and climbed behind the wheel himself.

'This car is a Renault Frères,' he said, as they pulled away. 'I am not a great admirer of the French as a nation, but they certainly do know how to make automobiles.'

The streets of Petersburg were all but empty, and Vladimir handled the car with the calm assurance of a man used to driving on snow. They had been going for ten minutes when he pulled up next to a canal. and pointed to the impressive three-storey building on the other side of the road which was bathed in floodlights.

'That is the Moika Palace, so called because it looks out on to the Moika Canal,' he announced. 'It belongs to the Yusupov family.'

Out of a policeman's habit, Blackstone found himself counting the number of windows at the front of the palace, and found that there were seventy-eight with a view over the canal.

'The Yusupov family must be very rich,' he said.

'What makes you reach that conclusion?' Vladimir wondered.

Blackstone grinned. 'I don't really know,' he said, 'though perhaps it might possibly have something to do with the size of their home.'

'You're easily impressed,' Vladimir said dismissively. 'This shack is nothing when compared to their palace on the Fontanka Canal, which has a theatre, three ballrooms and an art gallery. And let us not forget their palace in Moscow.'

'No,' Blackstone agreed, 'let's not forget that.' He paused for a moment. 'Why are we watching this palace, Vladimir?' he asked.

'Because this is where the history I spoke of earlier is about to be made,' Vladimir replied.

'That seems rather vague,' Blackstone pointed out.

'Perhaps it does,' Vladimir agreed. 'But now our young friend is here, I am sure everything will become much clearer.'

He was pointing to a tall, handsome young man who had appeared at the palace gate and now began to cross the road with the obvious intention of talking to them.

'Who's that?' Blackstone asked.

'Ah, of course, you have never seen him without a dress, have you? That, Sam, is Prince Felix Yusupov.'

The prince drew level with the car, and Vladimir opened the door to speak to him.

'I really have been most awfully clever, Count,' Yusupov said enthusiastically. 'You must come and see my preparations.'

'I appreciate your kind offer, but I would prefer to observe matters from a distance,' Vladimir said.

Felix Yusupov's mouth twisted into an expression of disappointment and petulance.

'Well, if you won't take an interest in it, I don't see why I should bother myself,' he said. 'Perhaps I'll just call the whole thing off.'

Vladimir sighed. 'Very well, if that is your wish, I suppose I could take a quick look,' he said.

The petulance was gone, and now Yusupov was beaming with pleasure.

'I really have been *very* clever,' he repeated.

'Rasputin thinks he is coming to the palace to meet my wife, Princess Irina,' Yusupov said, as the three of them crossed the snow-covered courtyard, 'but, in fact, she is staying at our palace in the Crimea.'

'Ah yes,' Vladimir said to Blackstone, 'when we were talking earlier, I forgot to mention their palace in the Crimea.'

'What was that you said?' Yusupov asked.

'I was just briefing my colleague,' Vladimir said. 'Where are your servants tonight?'

'I've given them strict instructions that they are to remain in their quarters at the back of the palace,' Yusupov said. 'The fewer people who have suspicions there might be a conspiracy afoot, the better.'

Blackstone and Vladimir followed Yusupov down into a two-roomed basement.

'This is where Rasputin will spend his final moments,' the prince said, with some relish.

So that was what it was all about, Blackstone thought. He should have guessed, but coming from a country where people did not talk casually about assassinations, it was not entirely surprising that he hadn't.

He looked around. The place was certainly opulently furnished. There were porcelain vases, inlaid chests, tables and carved wooden chairs. Persian carpets had been laid on the floors, and in front of a bronze and crystal crucifix was a magnificent bearskin rug.

'This morning, the place was nothing but a gloomy basement – and look at it now,' Yusupov said, obviously proud of himself. 'I selected all this personally from our furniture store at the back of the palace.'

'And did you bring it here yourself?' Vladimir wondered.

Yusupov laughed. 'Of course not.'

'Then how did it get here?'

The question seemed to puzzle the prince.

'It was brought here by the servants,' he said – as if it was obvious that when *anything* was moved, it was moved by servants.

'And how many of them were involved in the operation?'

'I have absolutely no idea. My major-domo supervised the whole thing.' He looked around. 'I shouldn't imagine it was less than ten of them.'

'Ah yes,' Vladimir said softly, 'the fewer people who have suspicions there might be a conspiracy afoot, the better.'

'There will be four of us involved in this exercise in vermin control,' Yusupov continued, missing the point completely, 'though, of course, I will take the leading role.'

'Of course,' Vladimir agreed. 'Might I be so bold as to inquire who the other three will be?'

'Can I rely on your discretion?' Yusupov asked.

'Naturally.'

'In addition to Grand Duke Dimitri, there will be Purishkevich, who is a deputy in the Duma, and a Dr Lazovert. The plan is that when Rasputin arrives, I will bring him down here straight away. I will tell him that my wife is entertaining some other guests upstairs – there will be a gramophone at the head of the stairs, so it will certainly sound as if she is having a party – but that they will soon be leaving, and when they do, she will come and join us.'

'And have you remembered to supply some records for the gramophone?' Vladimir asked.

'Naturally!' Yusupov snorted. 'I am not an amateur, you know. But to continue: I will offer Rasputin some refreshment – wine and cakes – which Dr Lazovert will previously have poisoned. He will eat the cakes, and he will drink the wine, and then he will die. We will take his body and drop it into the Neva – we have already bought the chains to weigh it down – and the affair will be all over. Is that not a brilliant plan?'

'Breathtaking,' Vladimir said. 'With so much clever thinking behind it, I cannot see how it can possibly fail.'

Once they were back in the car, Vladimir said, 'There is a complication that has only just occurred to me – though I should have thought of it long ago.'

'And what complication might that be?'

'In all that has gone on, I had quite forgotten that you are still a policeman. And you *are* still a policeman, aren't you?'

'Not according to Scotland Yard,' Blackstone replied. 'According to them, I'm nothing but an escaped criminal.'

'Yet you are still a policeman in your head.'

'Yes, I think I'll always be a policeman in my head.'

'And as a policeman, when you hear that a crime is about to be committed, it is your instinct to try to prevent it.'

'Yes.'

'You cannot try to prevent this murder, Sam. I will not allow it. I will do whatever is necessary to stop you.'

'I'm sure you will,' Blackstone agreed.

And he found his thoughts returning to the first – and only – murder he had ever witnessed.

Blackstone is still a young man – he has been told that he is, in fact, the youngest sergeant in the British army. He has not been in India long, and on this particular day – the day of the murder – he is out on a routine patrol with a corporal, an Anglo-Indian who has seen twenty years' service on the North-West Frontier.

They sense the tension in the air the moment they enter the small village. It is a strange mixture of anger, fear and excitement, and they know that something significant is about to happen.

A large crowd has gathered at the centre of the village and formed itself into a circle around two men. The larger of the two has a sabre in his hand and is swaggering around the edge of the circle, cheered on by the other villagers. The other man – who is smaller and skinnier – is kneeling in the centre of the circle. He is sobbing, and every time one of the tribal elders offers him a weapon, he shakes his head.

'We have to put a stop to this,' Blackstone says.

'What makes you say that?' his corporal asks.

'The man kneeling down doesn't want to fight.'

'No, he doesn't, because he knows he wouldn't have a chance,' the corporal agrees. 'But whether he chooses to fight or not, he's already as good as dead.'

'And that's why we have to stop it,' Blackstone says.

'I'll give you three reasons why we shouldn't,' the corporal tells him. He starts to count them off on his fingers. 'The first is that even though this particular tribe considers itself a friend of the British, we probably wouldn't get out of here alive if we tried to stop it.'

'That's not a good enough reason at all,' says the idealistic young Blackstone hotly. 'Your first concern must always be to do the decent and proper thing, even if that puts your own personal safety at risk.'

'The second reason is that the man on his knees has raped and murdered three little girls,' the corporal says.

'How can you possibly know he did that?' Blackstone asks. 'We've only just ridden into this village.'

'And how can you know he didn't do it – or something equally terrible?' the corporal counters.

Blackstone finds he has no answer to that.

'What's your third reason?' he asks.

'You don't have the right to interfere,' the corporal says. 'Imagine you see a fox stalking a rabbit. You know the fox has to eat to live, so do you have the right to warn the rabbit?'

'I do if it's my rabbit,' Blackstone says.

'Exactly,' the corporal agrees. 'But the man on his knees over there isn't *your rabbit, is he?'*

'I shall want an assurance from you that you will not try to interfere, Sam,' Vladimir said, calling Blackstone's mind back from its time-journey to India.

'Your hand is in your pocket,' Blackstone said. 'Is it wrapped around your pistol, and is your finger even now on the trigger?'

'It might be,' Vladimir said.

'You can relax,' Blackstone told him. 'I won't interfere. Rasputin's not my rabbit.'

It was near to midnight when a large car, with Yusupov sitting in the back, left the palace and disappeared up the street.

'Felix has gone to fetch Rasputin from his apartment,' Vladimir said. 'If he and his little friends can refrain from making a complete pig's ear of things, the whole business should be over in an hour or so.'

'Something's been puzzling me,' Blackstone admitted.

'Indeed? And what might that be?'

'You asked Yusupov if he would tell you who the other conspirators were. You were very humble about it. But I could see, just from looking at you, that you already knew their names.'

'Of course I already knew their names, but by asking for them as a favour, I made him feel as if he was in charge, and someone as unstable as Yusupov needs constant reassurance of that. There's a danger that he'll fall to pieces before he has killed Rasputin, and so I'm doing everything I can to make sure that doesn't happen.'

'What about after he's killed Rasputin?'

Vladimir shrugged. 'After he's killed Rasputin, he can sit huddled in a corner and eat his own shit for all I'll care.'

'How many people *do* know about the plot?' Blackstone asked.

Vladimir shrugged again. 'It's impossible to say. I have taken the precaution of reading some of the letters Yusupov has written to his wife and parents, and while he does not actually say what he's about to do, they would have to be idiots not to read between the lines. And Purishkevich is even worse. He's openly boasted in the Duma press room that Rasputin will be killed in the palace and that Grand Duke Dimitri will be one of the assassins – none of which is at all surprising from a man who sometimes wears a red rose in his fly to show his contempt for the socialists.'

'And you don't think that the tsarina has heard any of the rumours?'

'The tsarina lives in a crystal bubble. She does not even know that the people beyond her palace walls are starving, so she obviously has no idea at all of just how much Rasputin is hated.'

'But when she learns of his death – as she must – she will want revenge,' Blackstone said.

'Most certainly,' Vladimir agreed, 'and there is at least one person who will be willing to exact that revenge for her.'

'General Kornilov,' Blackstone said, remembering Vladimir's story of the young military attaché who had prepared Princess Alexandra for her future life as the tsarina.

'General Kornilov,' Vladimir agreed.

The car returned at twelve fifteen, and now the conspirators had a new figure with them – a man in a fur coat and a beaver-skin hat.

Vladimir watched them walk across the courtyard and disappear down the steps to the basement.

'It will soon be over and done with,' he said.

But to Blackstone's mind, he did not sound entirely convinced.

TWENTY

I t was at around two o'clock in the morning that Yusupov paid another visit to the Renault parked next to the Moika Canal.

'Rasputin has eaten two cakes and drunk two glasses of wine laced with cyanide, and it all seems to have had no effect on him,' he told Vladimir, with a hint of hysteria in his voice. 'He asked me to sing him some songs. Do you hear me? *He asked me to sing him some songs!*'

'Calm down,' Vladimir said.

'The man can't be killed,' Yusupov replied, in what was almost a sob. 'He has supernatural powers.'

'He's a man just like any other,' Vladimir told him. 'If the cyanide did not kill him, it was because the cyanide was no good.'

'But Dr Lazovert assured me . . .'

'Do you remember the story of what happened to the circus elephant, somewhere in southern Russia?' Vladimir interrupted him.

'Yes.'

'Then there you have it. The elephant did not have supernatural powers, did it? It was simply that the poison had lost its potency. And that must be what has happened in this case, too.'

'But if I can't poison him, what *can* I do?' Yusupov whined. 'You must tell me what to do, Count.'

'It is not for a count to tell a prince how to act,' Vladimir replied. 'But,' he added, 'whatever you do, you cannot back down now – you have already gone too far for that.'

'Yes, I have, haven't I?' Yusupov agreed. And then he turned and walked back towards the palace.

'Tell me about the elephant,' Blackstone said to Vladimir.

'Yes, it is quite an amusing story – unless you happened to be the elephant in question,' Vladimir replied. 'This particular elephant was part of a circus, and his behaviour became so erratic that it was considered to be dangerous. It was decided to poison him, and since he was inordinately fond of cream cakes, a hundred of the cakes were purchased and laced with cyanide. The elephant ate them all – with obvious enjoyment – but it seemed to have no effect on him. So, in the end, they decided they would simply have to shoot him.' Vladimir paused for a second. 'And, given time, even someone as stupid as Prince Yusupov will realize that is what he must do with Rasputin.'

At just after three o'clock, Yusupov appeared again.

'Rasputin is dead!' he said excitedly. 'I shot him twice in the chest. The others wanted to help me, but I insisted on doing it alone. I am the hero who saved Russia, and my fame will live for ever.'

'You will certainly be remembered,' Vladimir replied ambiguously. 'The important thing now is to get rid of the body.'

'Oh, there will be plenty of time for that later,' Yusupov

said. 'First, Dimitri and Lazovert will drive to Rasputin's apartment – to give the impression that he had returned home – and then they will take his coat, hat and boots to the hospital train that Purishkevich runs, where Mrs Purishkevich will burn them.'

'Get rid of the body now,' Vladimir said firmly.

'You can't tell me what to do,' Yusupov said. 'You are a mere count, and I am a national hero.'

'He's a national idiot,' Vladimir said, as Yusupov returned to the palace. 'And refusing to move the corpse now had nothing to do with establishing alibis or burning clothes – he just wants more time to gloat over his trophy.'

'Isn't it about time we left?' asked Blackstone, who was heartily sick of the whole affair.

'No,' Vladimir replied. 'I want to stay and see just how many more mistakes they make.'

But even a man like Vladimir – who automatically always expected the worst – could not have anticipated just how badly things would go wrong after Grand Duke Dimitri had driven away again. Even Vladimir could never have guessed what was about to happen next.

A man, wearing a peasant blouse and baggy trousers, suddenly appeared in the palace courtyard at around four o'clock. He was staggering heavily and heading for the gate.

'That can't be . . .' Blackstone gasped.

'It's Rasputin,' Vladimir said grimly. 'It appears that when our new national hero, Prince Felix Yusupov, said he had killed the man, he was exaggerating somewhat.'

Another man appeared in the courtyard – a short fat man, with a pistol in his hand.

'Purishkevich,' Vladimir said.

The first two shots that Purishkevich fired appeared to miss Rasputin completely, but after the third the *starets* came to a halt, and with the fourth he fell to the ground.

Purishkevich rushed up to the fallen man and began kicking him in the head as hard as he could. Then Yusupov appeared, and together they dragged Rasputin back into the palace.

'You see,' Vladimir said to Blackstone, 'if we had left when you wanted to, we would have missed all the excitement.'

It was another ten minutes before a uniformed police officer walked up to the palace gate.

Vladimir seemed to have been expecting him.

'The officer will have been on duty on the other side of the canal,' he told Blackstone. 'In the middle of a still night like this one, he could not have failed to hear the shots.'

The officer's arrival had obviously been anticipated from inside the palace, too, and he was met at the gates by Yusupov and another man.

'Who's he?' Blackstone asked.

'Yusupov's major-domo,' Vladimir replied. 'Let us just hope it is he who is in charge now, and not our madcap prince.'

The prince, the major-domo and the policeman talked for a few minutes, and then the policeman left.

'Felix Yusupov couldn't organize an orgy in a brothel,' Vladimir said in disgust.

A few minutes later, the major-domo left the palace in the direction the policeman had gone, and when he returned, he had the policeman with him.

'Just how much worse can it get?' Vladimir asked, burying his head in his hands.

The policeman returned to his post for a second time, just before the car returned from its journey to Rasputin's apartment and the hospital train.

'Get rid of the body,' Vladimir said softly. 'For God's sake, get rid of the bloody body!'

The conspirators went back into the palace, and, at a quarter to six, emerged again, carrying a long object wrapped in canvas between them. They loaded their parcel into the car and drove away.

'*Now* we can go,' Vladimir said.

Vladimir was – understandably – very gloomy when they arrived back at his apartment. For five minutes, he listlessly played with his trains, and then he abandoned them in favour of the vodka bottle.

He drank as Blackstone had never seen him drink before, knocking back a quarter of the bottle in fifteen minutes, with no obvious sign of pleasure.

'I had nothing to do with Grigori Rasputin's assassination, did I, Sam?' he asked.

'Not directly,' Blackstone replied.

'Not *at all*,' Vladimir said emphatically, and now, with more of the vodka disappearing down his throat, he was starting to sound a little drunk. 'I had no part in the planning of it – it would have gone much more smoothly if I had – and no part in the execution of it. I was no more than a witness.'

Strictly speaking, that was true, Blackstone thought, but it rather overlooked the incident in which Vladimir had deliberately encouraged Rasputin to expose himself, as a way of strengthening Yusupov's resolve.

'If the tsar had instructed me – or anyone in my service – to protect Rasputin, then I would have been remiss in my duties tonight,' Vladimir continued, 'but, for all I know, the tsar may well have wished Rasputin dead, in which case it would have been going against his wishes to have intervened.' He took another slug of vodka. 'You think I am merely justifying myself, don't you, Sam?'

'And aren't you?' Blackstone asked.

'I suppose so – but I do know for a fact that the tsar was not as much under Rasputin's spell as the tsarina was, and that, two or three times, he became so angry with the *starets* that he actually sent him away. And who is to say he was not jealous of the amount of attention the tsarina was paying to a mere Siberian peasant?' He drank more vodka. 'Perhaps, after all, my master will not be entirely unhappy that the man is dead.'

'And will things in Russia get better now that Rasputin has gone?' Blackstone asked.

Vladimir shrugged. 'Who can say?'

'You can say – or, at least, you *think* you can,' Blackstone said. 'You have an opinion on anything and everything, and an absolute belief that that opinion is the right one.'

Vladimir nodded slowly. 'You're quite right, of course,' he said. 'I am so intelligent that sometimes it frightens even me.'

'So will things get better?' Blackstone persisted.

'No, things will not get better,' Vladimir said. 'The chances are that they will get much worse. When it was left up to Rasputin to decide what would be enacted and what wouldn't, at least a few of the decisions he allowed to get through made some kind of sense. But without his guidance, the tsarina will become more erratic than ever. And that, my dear Sam, is not the worse consequence of what has happened tonight – not by a mile.'

'Then what *is* the worst consequence?'

'Rasputin's death is the first rent in the cloak that has shrouded tsarism – and kept it safe – for centuries, and soon that rent will grow, and the cloak will be torn apart.'

'I'm not sure I know what you mean,' Blackstone admitted.

'Rasputin was known to be under the tsar's protection, and that should have been enough to ensure that no harm could ever come to him,' Vladimir explained. 'But now he is dead, and everyone can see that the tsar's protection is not as absolute as it was once thought to be. And if he could not keep Rasputin alive, are there not perhaps other things that he cannot do? The magic, you see, is starting to drain away.'

'Yes, I do see that,' Blackstone said.

'And if the *starets* can be killed, why can't a member of the aristocracy?' Vladimir asked. 'Why can't a member of the imperial family? Why can't the tsar himself? You must be careful when extracting a brick from the foundations, that it does not bring down the whole structure, and that was what Rasputin was – a brick in the foundations of tsarism.'

'If that's what you believe, then I'm surprised you allowed the assassination,' Blackstone said.

'We have already discussed that,' Vladimir said, a dangerous edge creeping into his voice. 'I did not *allow* it – I merely did nothing to prevent it. And if Yusupov had not killed Rasputin tonight, some other aristocrat – or some politician or some jealous husband – would have put a bullet in him before the month was out. He had many enemies.'

'You're splitting hairs,' Blackstone said.

'That is what Tanya said, the night she came here to show me the poster and demand that I do something about Rasputin,' Vladimir said. 'And do you remember what else she said, when I told her there was nothing I *could* do?'

Blackstone nodded. 'She said, "There are times when you make me so angry that I almost hate you."'

'I would gladly give my life for my tsar,' Vladimir said. 'If it would serve his interest to have me slowly tortured to death, then I would submit willingly. You believe that, don't you?'

'Yes,' Blackstone said, 'I do believe it.'

'I do not fear pain, and I do not fear extinction,' Vladimir continued, 'but I am terrified – to the very depths of my soul – by the thought of Tanya growing to hate me.'

TWENTY-ONE

17th December 1916 – Julian calendar; 30th December 1916 – Gregorian calendar

As they stood on the promenade at Brighton, looking out over a choppy sea, Patterson felt his own personal wave of depression roll over him.

'If we could find Max's lodgings in a big place like London, it should be easy enough to find Max himself in a piddling little place like this,' Ellie Carr said, with mock-cheerfulness.

But Brighton wasn't *such* a piddling little place, Patterson told himself – it was a town of over a hundred thousand people.

Besides, the clock was ticking. They didn't have six days to find Max – which was how long it had taken to find his lodgings in Collingwood Street. They didn't even have *one* day – because it was already ten fifteen, and at nine o'clock the next morning he would have to surrender himself at the police station.

'If we don't find him today, I'll keep on looking myself,' Ellie promised, reading his mind.

And what bloody use would that be? Patterson thought.

Ellie wasn't a trained police officer, and even if she did find Max, how was she ever going to get him to confess to anything?

A sudden feeling of shame and general unworthiness swept over him.

'I'll always be grateful for what you've done for me, Ellie,' he said, with a slight choke in his voice, 'and when I'm inside – with only four blank walls to stare at – I'll draw a great deal of strength from knowing there are still good people like you on the outside.'

'Oh, for Gawd's sake,' Ellie said, reverting to her cockney. 'You ain't quite dead yet, are you?'

Patterson smiled. 'No, I'm not quite dead yet,' he admitted.

'Then wait till they've screwed the lid down properly before you stop breathing,' Ellie told him. 'So where do we start?'

'Since we've got so little time left, it would be better if we split up,' Patterson told her. 'So you take the shops and all the pubs, and I'll check on the hotels.'

'Fair enough,' Ellie agreed.

She turned to look out at the grey sea and found herself wishing that – if only for a little while – the sun would come out.

From what they had learned of Max so far, he seemed like the kind of man who would indulge himself whenever possible, Patterson reasoned. And since twenty-four thousand pounds would buy him rather a lot of indulgence, it was likely that he had ignored the modest side-street boarding houses and checked into one of the swanky hotels on the promenade.

Working from this premise, he started his search in the Grand, which had been lavish with its use of Italian marble in its large foyer and was reputed to be the best hotel in Brighton.

The clerk behind the desk looked at him as if he was something the cat had dragged in.

'You're not a guest at this hotel, are you?' he asked with some disdain, before adding a reluctant, 'Sir?'

'Course I'm not,' Patterson agreed pleasantly. 'I'm an ordinary working man – just like yourself.'

The clerk did not welcome the comparison. 'Then if you're not a guest, I must request you to—'

'I'm here on a job,' Patterson interrupted him. 'I've come to pick up Mr Armitage and drive him to a very important meeting.'

'What name did you say?' the clerk asked.

'Mr Armitage,' Patterson repeated.

'There's no one of that name staying here,' the clerk said.

'Would you mind checking through the register, just to make sure?' Patterson asked.

The clerk gave the register the most cursory of glances. 'No, not here,' he said.

'Ah!' Patterson said.

'Ah what?' the clerk demanded.

'For business reasons, Mr Armitage sometimes travels incognito,' Patterson said. 'That means he doesn't use his own name.'

'I know what it means,' the clerk told him.

'And the problem is that he sometimes forgets to tell his staff what new name he's chosen.'

'A problem indeed – for you,' the clerk said unsympathetically.

'That's why I always carry a picture of him around with me,' Patterson explained, reaching into his pocket. 'Now if you'd care to look at it . . .'

'I have better things to do with my time than look at pictures,' the clerk said, turning away.

'But . . . but the last time a driver failed to pick him up from a hotel, he sacked the man,' Patterson said.

'I'm afraid that's no concern of mine,' the clerk said, starting to move towards the other end of the counter.

'And he got the manager of the hotel to sack the poor bloody clerk as well,' Patterson said.

The clerk stopped and turned around.

'I don't suppose that it would do any harm just to take a quick look at it,' he said.

But Mr Armitage was a stranger to the clerk at the Grand, just as Mr Bainbridge was not known in the Royal, and Mr Canterbury had never been seen in the Palace.

The air of optimism that Ellie Carr had displayed in the presence of Archie Patterson began to melt away almost as soon as she had left him, and after two hours of pounding the streets of Brighton – of seeing so many people shake their heads when she showed the photograph of Max – there was not even a trace of it left.

It was almost inevitable, she thought, as she approached yet another public house – this one called the Mariner's Return – that Archie Patterson – dear, lovable Archie – would end up going to jail for a long, long time. It was almost equally inevitable that Sam Blackstone would remain a fugitive, and she would never see him again.

A large part of her life – the only important part, aside from her work – was about to be wrenched from her, and knowing that Sam wasn't guilty (and Archie was only guilty of being a loyal friend) only made matters worse.

So although she would continue going through the motions – visiting every pub and shop in Brighton that it was humanly possible to visit, and showing the picture around – she knew, deep inside herself, that it was all pointless.

Vladimir had finally gone to bed at seven o'clock, looking so exhausted that Blackstone had been sure he'd sleep for hours, but he was up again at eight and had left the apartment by eight thirty.

When he returned, at lunch time, it was clear from the worried expression on his face that things had not been going well.

'You remember that the policeman made two visits to the palace last night, don't you?' he asked.

'Yes, I do,' Blackstone replied. 'It's not really something that I'm likely to forget.'

'Well, now I have learned why he came back that second time – and I'm sure that you'll find the explanation as incredible as I did.'

'I'm listening.'

'On his first visit, Yusupov told him that he and his friends had had a very drunken evening, and at the end of it they decided it might be fun to shoot one of the dogs. I should imagine the policeman was disgusted at the decadence of his so-called "betters" – I know I would have been in his place – but he accepted the explanation, because while it was undoubtedly an insane thing to do, he probably considers that most aristocrats *are* insane. At any rate, he went back to his post by the canal and would probably have thought no more about it if Purishkevich and Yusupov hadn't sent the major-domo after him.'

'Yes, why did they do that?'

'I assume because, at that time of the morning, there was no one else around who they could boast to.'

'They didn't tell him the truth, did they?' Blackstone gasped.

'They asked the policeman if he was a patriot who loved his tsar, and when he said yes – and what else could he say? – Purishkevich told him he should rejoice, because they had just killed Russia's greatest enemy.'

'And how did the constable react to that?'

'He didn't believe it. Who would? Nobody announces to a *policeman* that they've just committed a murder! So the constable – who I have talked to, and can assure you is not one of the world's great thinkers – asked himself why this important man would tell him such an obvious lie. And the answer he came up with was that it was a kind of loyalty test that was too complex for him to understand – and that what Purishkevich really wanted him to do was report the whole thing to his superintendent, which he did. The superintendent read the report and passed it straight up to head of the Okhrana, who read it himself and then immediately forwarded it to the Minister of the Interior.'

'Jesus!' Blackstone said.

'The police went to Rasputin's apartment to check on the family – and also to remove any compromising documents he might have left lying around. That alerted his daughter, Maria, to the fact that something was wrong, and she used one of her contacts in the palace to let the tsarina know.'

'So what will happen now?' Blackstone asked.

'I don't know,' Vladimir admitted. 'Rasputin's death was always bound to have consequences, but if it had been a smooth operation – a quick incision to remove a tumour from the body politic – I might have been able to control the damage. As it is, we are one step closer to disaster.'

It was only when Patterson asked about Mr Quinn in the Bellevue – by which time it was four o'clock in the afternoon – that the clerk, on being shown the photograph, said, 'Ah, you mean Mr Hansen.'

So he was using the same name as he had been using in London, Patterson thought. That was careless of him.

And it was strange that he should have chosen to stay in the Bellevue, rather than at any of sixteen previous hotels he'd checked on, which had all been much grander.

But those were minor considerations.

What really mattered was – after all their efforts – he had tracked the bastard down.

'Is Mr Hansen in his room now?' he asked.

The clerk glanced up at the key rack.

'Doesn't appear to be,' he said. 'Perhaps he's left a note saying where he can be found. A lot of our guests do that.'

He reached down and checked through the in-tray.

'Oh dear,' he said.

'No note?' Patterson suggested.

'Oh, there's a note, all right, but it's from my colleague on the night shift,' the other man said. 'It seems that before he went out for a walk last night, Mr Hansen ordered a room-service breakfast.'

'So what?'

'Well, we can assume that means he fully expected to be here this morning, doesn't it?'

'Yes.'

'But he never returned from his walk, and it's the night clerk's opinion – which I happen to agree with – that if he doesn't turn up by dinner time, we should inform the police.'

Shit! Patterson thought. *Shit, shit, shit, shit, shit!*

Ellie Carr stopped in front of the photographer's shop more to gather her strength than for any other reason, and if she looked at the display in the window, that was only because it was there to be looked at.

Part of the window was devoted to pictures taken in the studio.

There were family groups – the mother sitting on a chair with a saintly expression on her face, the father standing behind her, looking stern, and the kids on the floor, clearly uncomfortable in their best clothes and wishing they were somewhere else.

There were portraits of young women who saw themselves as romantic heroines and thought that being shot against a background of a painted forest could only add to their mystique.

And there were pictures of young men, posed in such a way as to emphasize their supposed athletic prowess.

The other half of the window was devoted to the second string in the photographer's business bow – his promenade photographs. There was none of the stiffness of studio poses about these photographs, because the subjects had not been posing at all. Instead, they had been captured in a moment of complete naturalness, and had only become aware of the photographer's existence when he handed them a ticket and told them they could collect their pictures the following day.

Ellie let her eyes glide over pictures of young men who were out for a stroll with their young ladies, and families exhibiting the true anarchy of family life.

And then she saw it!

And then she bloody saw it!

She opened the shop door. There was the sound of a bell tingling somewhere, and then a middle-aged, balding man in a mock-velvet jacket emerged from the back room.

'Can I help you?' he asked.

'I'd like to buy one of the photographs in your window,' Ellie said, fighting to keep the tremble out of her voice.

'I can't honestly say that I remember taking a picture of you,' the photographer told her.

'It's not a picture of me,' Ellie explained. 'It's a picture of my nephew.' She pointed to it. 'There he is – young Archibald.'

'Ah!' the photographer said cautiously.

'Is there a problem?' Ellie wondered.

'Well, yes,' the photographer admitted. 'I don't normally sell my promenade pictures to anybody but the subjects of them. Folk can be funny about other people having an image of them without their permission, you see. You might call that superstition, but that's just the way things are.'

'He *is* my nephew,' Ellie pointed out.

'So you say, but I've no proof of that, now have I?' the photographer countered.

'Would I give you a guinea for a picture of someone who *wasn't* my nephew?' Ellie asked.

The photographer licked his lips. 'A guinea, you say?'

'A guinea,' Ellie repeated.

'Well, I'm sure your nephew won't mind at all,' the photographer said. 'In fact, he should be quite flattered that his aunt is prepared to pay a guinea for his picture.'

'Yes,' Ellie agreed, 'he should.'

Vladimir and Blackstone stood on the Petrovsky Bridge, looking down at the water below. The river was partly frozen over, but in the sections that were ice-free, a number of divers were at work.

'The police received information that there was blood on the parapet, and when they came to investigate, they found an over-shoe on the ice, which Rasputin's servant identified as belonging to him,' Vladimir said. 'Was there ever a more incompetent bunch of conspirators?'

'It would be hard to imagine there could be,' Blackstone said.

'Now that they know where to look, it should not take them long to find the body, because it will be floating just under the ice.'

'Floating? I thought they were going to weigh him down with chains before they threw him in.'

'So they were – but in all the excitement, they forgot to.'

The divers had found nothing near the bridge and were moving further along the bank.

'Yusupov denies ever seeing Rasputin last night, but no one believes him,' Vladimir continued. 'The police visited the palace this afternoon. By then, the prince actually *had* shot one of his dogs – both to support the first story they told the policeman last night and so they might have some canine blood to cover the bloodstains left by Rasputin.' He paused. 'A man who will shoot his own dog,' he added, with a hint of anger in his voice, 'does not understand the meaning of loyalty and is capable of anything.'

The divers had selected a new spot in which to search, and two of them plunged into the river.

'The poor animal died in vain,' Vladimir said. 'The police found the traces of blood leading from the basement to the edge of the courtyard. It was obvious that *so much* blood could not have come from one dog.'

The two divers emerged from the water, shivering and shaking their heads. Two more plunged in to take their place.

'I hear that General Kornilov is angrier than anyone ever remembers seeing him before,' Vladimir said. 'He has been pacing up and down his office ever since he heard the news, and none of his staff dares go near him. It is not, of course, the death of Rasputin that has driven him into this rage – he doesn't give a fig about the *starets* – it is the effect that the death will have on the little princess who he has nurtured for so long.'

'He'll want to see someone punished for it,' Blackstone said.

'He will indeed,' Vladimir agreed.

The divers emerged from the river, and the moment they were on the bank again, they began waving their hands excitedly.

'They found the body,' Vladimir said fatalistically. 'I told you it wouldn't take them very long.'

'Will Kornilov want to punish Grand Duke Dimitri and Prince Yusupov?' Blackstone asked.

'Yes, he will – but he will not be allowed to,' Vladimir said. 'Dimitri is a member of the imperial family, and Felix – despite his inclinations in the other direction – is married to the tsar's niece.'

'Then who *will* he punish?'

'He will *attempt* to punish whoever it is that Yusupov – once he is backed into a corner – names as being the leading light of the conspiracy. And who do you think our Felix will choose to rat on?'

'It could be you,' Blackstone said.

'Yes, though I played no active part in the whole bloody mess, it could very well be me,' Vladimir agreed.

The pub next to the railway station was called – unimaginatively – the Railway Arms, and when Patterson entered the saloon bar at six o'clock, Ellie Carr was already sitting at one of the tables, waiting for him.

She looked cheerful enough, he thought as he crossed the bar – but then she hadn't heard his news yet.

He sat down opposite her.

'I found out where Max has been staying, but he'd already gone,' he said heavily. 'He left, unexpectedly, last night. He must have known we were on the way, but what I can't work out is who could have tipped him off.'

Ellie didn't look the least disappointed. In fact – to Patterson's astonishment – she was grinning.

'It doesn't matter,' she said.

'I should have given up then, but I didn't,' Patterson said. 'I thought, you see, that, in his panic, he might have taken refuge in one of the smaller boarding houses, so I checked them out as well. Nobody had seen him. He might be back in London, I suppose, or he might have finally fled the country, but whatever he's done, we'll never find him now.'

'It doesn't matter!' Ellie repeated.

'It *does* matter,' Patterson said, starting to get angry. 'Without Max, we have nothing.'

'Yes, we do,' Ellie told him. 'We have this!'

She laid the photograph she had bought for a guinea on the table.

'Another photograph,' Patterson said despondently.

'Look at it, Archie!' Ellie urged him. 'For Gawd's sake, look at it!'

With little show of enthusiasm, Patterson did as he'd been instructed.

Then a sudden change came over him. His eyes bulged, and his lip began to tremble. He picked up the photograph in shaking hands and held it up to the light. Then, not content with that, he twisted it around so he was viewing it from a different angle.

Finally, he laid it carefully back on the table.

'This changes everything, doesn't it?' he asked. 'It doesn't matter where Max has gone, because we don't need him any more.'

'Which is what I've been trying to tell you for the last five minutes,' Ellie pointed out.

Patterson picked up the picture again, as if to reassure himself that it was real.

'I never suspected . . . it never occurred to me . . .' he said.

'It never occurred to anybody,' Ellie told him. 'Why would it have?'

Patterson looked up at the bar clock. 'It's come too late for me to make any use of it,' he said. 'In fourteen hours' time, I'll be behind bars.'

'I know that,' Ellie agreed.

'And that means it will all be down to you.'

'So it would seem.'

'Do you think you can handle it?' Patterson asked worriedly.

'I'll do more than just handle it,' Ellie told him. 'I'll *enjoy* it.'

TWENTY-TWO

18th December 1916 – Julian calendar; 31st December 1916 – Gregorian calendar

It was mid-morning on New Year's Eve, and Sir Roderick Todd lay propped up – with a great many pillows – in his bed. He was now so ill that he rarely saw visitors, but he was not about to miss the opportunity to extract one last drop of sweet revenge from the Sam Blackstone saga, which was why he had agreed to meet the woman who was standing in front of him.

'You are, I believe, Inspector Blackstone's mistress, Dr Carr,' he said, in the thin, reedy voice that was all that was left to him now but which still managed to convey his disgust. 'That's right, isn't it?'

'No,' Ellie Carr replied.

'Are you saying that you do *not* visit his bed – that you do not sink into all kinds of debauchery together?' Todd asked incredulously.

'Oh, we do that all right,' Ellie agreed, 'though not quite often enough for my liking. It's the term "mistress" that I object to.'

'I beg your pardon?'

'And so you should. There's something rather unequal about the word "mistress", don't you think? Men talk about "my mistress" in much the same way as they might talk about "my dog" or "my horse". It's not like that with me and Sam. I'm his lover, and he's mine.'

'Are you really such a shameless woman?' Todd wondered.

'I try to be,' Ellie said. 'And now we've got your moral outrage out of the way, do you suppose we could get down to business?'

'Of course,' Todd agreed. 'You're here to beg for mercy for Sam Blackstone, aren't you? You want me to use my influence with the Yard – and with the courts – to get him a lighter sentence.'

'You couldn't be more wrong,' Ellie told him. 'I'm here because I have some information the police should know about, but, given the nature of that information, I'm not sure who I can trust in Scotland Yard.'

'Why should you trust me, when you say you can't trust a serving officer?' Todd wondered.

'There are a number of serving officers – and I've no idea who they are – who will either have something to lose by my evidence becoming public knowledge or something to gain by helping to suppress it. You, on the other hand, only stand to gain something if the evidence *is* investigated further.'

'You're not making any sense,' Todd said. 'What can I hope to gain? Can't you see I'm a sick man?'

'You're not sick – you're dying,' Ellie said.

Todd started coughing, and spatters of blood appeared on the bedspread and his nightshirt.

'You are a very callous woman,' he said, when he was finally able to speak again.

'I'm a doctor,' Ellie told him. 'I say what I see. And what would be the point of lying to you, when we both know that within a week – two weeks at the outside – you'll be gone.'

'My only wish is to live long enough to see Sam Blackstone gaoled.'

'Well, that isn't going to happen,' Ellie said indifferently. 'But I'll tell you what will happen. Any number of important people will turn up at your funeral and say what a fine policeman you were. They'll call you a relentless champion of justice and claim that you were determined never to rest until all the criminals in this fine country of ours are behind bars. They'll say it – but they'll know that it's all a load of old bollocks, even as the words are coming out of their mouths.'

'How dare you!' Todd gasped.

'You'll have spoken at such events yourself and used just the same platitudes,' Ellie said. 'And while you were delivering your speech, you'll have been thinking, "I remember the time when, to cover his boss's mistake, he buried a case," or, "He'd bend with the wind, that one, and when somebody in government asked him to back away, he'd do it without a second's hesitation." Tell me I'm wrong, Assistant Commissioner Todd.'

'We live in an imperfect world,' Todd said weakly. 'We all have to compromise now and again, or nothing would ever get done.'

'What I'm about to offer you is the chance to have somebody stand up at your funeral, say, "He did what was right – whatever the consequences," and really mean it. It's unlikely any of them *will* say that, of course. In fact, if you do what I want you to do, they'll probably hate you for it. But they'll know in their hearts that you *were* right – and that's as much of a legacy as any man can ever hope to leave behind him.'

'Go on,' Todd said.

'This is a picture of Max,' Ellie said, showing him the photograph they had found in the government warehouse.

'How do you know it's him?' Todd asked.

'I know it because Sergeant Patterson and I found the attaché case that was taken from Sam Blackstone at the docks, hidden in his lodgings.'

'You had no right to be there,' Todd said. 'You have no official standing at all.'

'The truth is the truth – whoever finds it,' Ellie said. 'And now we come to the part where I offer you the opportunity to do the decent thing. I want you to use your influence to gain access to a bank account.'

'Whose bank account?' Todd asked.

'His,' Ellie said, showing him the photograph she had bought from the seaside photographer for a guinea.

The train that pulled into Hamburg Central Station in the early afternoon was carrying mostly agricultural produce from the occupied Belgian territories, but one of the trucks – though not listed on the manifold as such – had been set aside for a variety of artistic objects which certain high-ranking German officers had decided would be much happier in Germany, in the homes of those same officers, than they could ever have been in Belgium.

The objects were all in packing cases, and the porters had been cautioned that this particular 'agricultural produce' was extremely delicate – and, indeed, might even shatter – so special care should be taken when unloading it.

It therefore came as something of a surprise to the two porters entrusted with the task to hear a furious banging noise coming from inside one of the longer, thinner cases.

'I didn't know cabbages could kick,' said one of the porters, a man not famed for his intellect.

The other porter grinned. 'That's not cabbages,' he said. 'It's onions. Belgian onions are well known for being fierce.'

'Are you sure?' the first porter asked.

The second porter sighed. 'It's not a vegetable at all,' he explained. 'It's either a man or an animal – and I'd put my money on a man.'

'Should we open it?' the first porter asked.

'It might be a good idea,' the second porter agreed.

It was a sturdy packing case, very well put-together, and it was two minutes before the porters had removed enough nails to be able to remove the lid.

'It *is* a man,' said the first porter, looking down into the case.

It was indeed, the second porter agreed, and a man who had
been bound and gagged with the same thoroughness that had gone
into the construction of his container.

The porters lifted the man out of the case, cut through his
bonds and removed his gag.

'Who are you?' the second porter asked.

'My name is Karl Hansen, and I am a Norwegian citizen,' the
man was just about able to croak.

Superintendent Brigham had never seen either of the two inspectors
before, and when they arrived at his office unannounced – and said
they wanted to question him – his instinctive reaction was outrage.

'I don't know what you think you're playing at, but I'll have
your jobs for this,' he said.

'There's no need for you to make this any harder than it has
to be, sir,' the taller of the two detectives said calmly. 'We have
been ordered to ask you some questions, and that is what we
intend to do.'

'On whose authority was that order issued?' Brigham demanded.

'Our superintendent—'

'Your superintendent! Good God, man, I'm a superintendent,
too. It says so on the door!'

'The order was given to us by our superintendent, but it came
down from the commissioner himself,' the shorter inspector
said.

It was a routine check, Brigham told himself – a random audit.
He was being questioned, but it could just as easily have been
any other superintendent in the Yard, and there was absolutely
nothing to be worried about.

'Very well,' he said, in a bored, long-suffering way. 'Let's just
get this over with.'

'Do you know this man, sir?' asked the taller inspector, placing
a photograph on his desk.

Oh my God, Brigham thought, looking down in horror at it.
Oh, sweet Jesus, no!

*How, in God's name, had they ever got their hands on a
photograph of Karl?*

'I've never seen him in my life,' he said shakily.

'His name is Max Schneider, and he is the man who escaped

with twenty-four thousand pounds of government money,' the inspector said.

'But he . . . he can't be Max,' Brigham gasped.

'Now isn't that interesting?' the inspector said. 'You claim to have no idea who he is – you've never seen him before in your life – and yet you're certain he can't be Max.'

'Have you checked your bank account recently, sir?' the shorter inspector asked.

'No, but I don't see—' Brigham said.

'We have,' the taller inspector interrupted.

'How dare you!'

'And we discovered that you're five thousand pounds richer than you were a month ago.'

'I . . . I've never put five thousand pounds – or anything close to it – into my account,' Brigham protested.

'We know *you* didn't put the money into your account,' the shorter inspector agreed. 'But somebody certainly did. And can you guess who that somebody might be?'

It couldn't have been Karl, Brigham thought. Karl had never so much as had a sniff of five thousand pounds in his entire life.

Unless . . . unless Karl really *was* Max.

He should confess now, while there was still a chance he would be believed, he told himself.

But he knew that he simply couldn't do it – knew that the shame of being thought a robber was nothing to the shame that would be heaped on him if he told the truth.

'We asked you if you had any idea where the money came from, sir,' the shorter inspector asked.

'No doubt you think it was this Max who paid the money into my account,' Brigham said, making one last desperate attempt to bluff his way out.

'We do,' the inspector confirmed.

'But why would this man – who I've never met – have given me five thousand pounds.'

'Perhaps we should show him the other photograph now,' the taller inspector suggested to the shorter one.

'Yes, that would be a good idea,' the shorter inspector confirmed.

The taller inspector placed the photograph on Brigham's desk.

The superintendent recognized the location – it was the promenade at Brighton.

There were two men in the photograph. They were walking side by side, and it was obvious that they were together. One of those men was Karl – and the other was himself.

White's had been founded by an Italian immigrant called Francesco Bianco in 1693. Its original purpose was to serve hot chocolate (then a great luxury), but it soon evolved into a gentlemen's club. The club offered men of quality two things they could not find elsewhere. The first was absolute escape from the company of women (wives and mistresses included). The second was the opportunity to squander their fortunes on the gaming tables.

The club moved from Chesterfield Street to much grander premises on St James's Street in 1778. But the spirit of the club was unchanged, and it was from his seat in the bow window of the new club that Lord Alvanley once bet a fellow member three thousand pounds that the raindrop he had selected would reach the bottom of the window pane before the other man's fancy.

The three men meeting in the club's dining room were all members, and they might even have described themselves as friends, but there was certainly no atmosphere of bonhomie that evening.

'Well, you certainly managed to get yourselves into a fine pickle,' said Courtney Hartington, who'd arranged the meeting.

The other two men – the Metropolitan Police Commissioner and the Permanent Secretary at the Home Office – exchanged nervous glances.

'I wouldn't have phrased it quite like that,' the Permanent Secretary said cautiously.

'Wouldn't you?' Hartington asked, with a note of surprise in his voice that fooled no one. 'The head of the Special Branch is caught red-handed – in collusion with a German spy – stealing money from His Majesty's Government, and you wouldn't call it a pickle?'

'It is certainly something of an embarrassment,' the Permanent Secretary admitted.

'I should think it will be more than an embarrassment when it comes to court,' Hartington said. 'It will be a full-blown scandal. The press will have a field day.'

'We . . . er . . . are not anticipating it ever coming to court,' the Permanent Secretary said. 'Max and his associates have escaped – and most of the money has disappeared with them. All we are left with is Superintendent Brigham, and there seems little point in putting him on trial.'

'You were happy enough to put my clients on trial,' Courtney Hartington pointed out.

'Your *clients*?' the Permanent Secretary repeated. 'Did I hear you say your *clients*?'

'Yes.'

'In the plural?'

'That is what an "s" added to the end of a noun is normally meant to indicate,' Hartington agreed.

'So who *are* your clients?'

'Didn't I say? They're Archie Patterson and Sam Blackstone.'

'But how can Blackstone be your client, when no one even knows where he is?' the Commissioner asked.

'I do know where he is – he's in Russia,' Hartington said. 'But to get back to the point, you *were* quite happy to put him on trial, weren't you?'

'We thought he was guilty,' the Commissioner said defensively.

'Whereas you *know* that Superintendent Brigham is guilty,' Hartington countered.

'It wouldn't have looked good for the Yard to have Blackstone standing in the dock,' the Commissioner said. 'It never looks good to have a bad apple on public display – but, when all is said and done, he is a mere detective inspector. If the head of Special Branch were standing in that same dock, it would do irreparable damage to our reputation.'

'So what will happen to Brigham?' Hartington asked. 'Will he retire due to ill health?'

'That is the plan – and we hope we can rely on you giving that plan your full support,' the Permanent Secretary said.

Hartington nodded gravely. 'Of course you can. I've had my bit of fun, teasing you over different treatment for different people – wicked of me, I know, though I just couldn't resist it – but I never really meant to oppose you in the matter. We are, after all, members of the same club – and I'm not just referring to this building.'

The Permanent Secretary nodded. 'As members of the establishment, it is our duty to stick together.'

'Just as a matter of interest, what will happen to Blackstone?'
Hartington asked.

'Since you seem to know how to contact him, you may tell
him that the charges have been dropped and he may return to
England,' the Permanent Secretary said.

'And Patterson?'

'Patterson is more of a problem. He is, after all, guilty as
charged, so he must stand trial.'

'Oh dear, that does make things rather difficult,' Hartington
said, shaking his head.

'In what way?'

'Well, imagine me questioning him in the witness box . . .'

'Surely, you'll be briefing a barrister to conduct the defence,
won't you?' the Permanent Secretary asked.

'Not in this particular case, no. I've promised Archie Patterson
that I'll conduct it myself,' Hartington lied. 'And I have a perfect
right to do so under English law, you know.'

'I'm sure you have,' the Permanent Secretary agreed. 'But
even so—'

'Now, where was I?' Hartington interrupted. He grabbed the
lapels of his jacket, as if he was already in court. 'I will ask my
client something like, "Why did you hold up the Black Maria
and free Sam Blackstone?" And he will say, "I did it because I
knew he was innocent." I will give a disapproving frown, as
though he's said something I've told him not to say under any
circumstances – that's an old barristers' trick, by the way, and
it always works on juries.'

'Now look here, Courtney—' the Permanent Secretary said.

'Then, with the frown still on my lips, I'll say, "You mean,
you *thought* he was innocent?" And what else can he reply but,
"No, at the time I only knew in my *heart* he was innocent, and
now I have the proof." "Proof?" I'll ask. "What proof?" "We
now know who the real guilty party is," Patterson will say. And
then he'll probably name him.'

'You don't have to adopt that line of questioning at all,' the
Permanent Secretary said.

'Of course I do,' Hartington said, sounding shocked. 'It's my
sworn duty to defend my client to the best of my ability.'

'The judge will know the right thing to do,' the Permanent

Secretary said firmly. 'He'll put a stop to that line of questioning before Patterson even gets close to naming Brigham.'

'I should hope he would,' Hartington replied. 'As you said earlier, we in the establishment must stick together, and I'll certainly be delighted if he prevents me from doing a duty that I will be finding personally distasteful.'

'Well, there you are, then.'

'But say that someone – one of my juniors, or one of the clerks – is outraged by what he sees as a distortion of British justice, and decides to leak Brigham's name to the gutter press. There are such people around, you know – people who, for some peculiar reason of their own, seem to regard the truth as paramount.'

'That sounded like a threat,' the Commissioner growled.

'It is certainly *threatening*,' Hartington agreed, 'but let me just say that if such information were released, it would have nothing to do with me, since, as I said earlier, I am completely on your side.'

'Is there any way out of this dilemma we seem to be facing?' asked the Permanent Secretary, who regarded Machiavelli as light bedtime reading.

'Yes,' Hartington replied, 'and it's really quite a simple one.'

'Then let's hear it,' the Permanent Secretary said, with a hint of resignation in his voice.

'We all know that the man who held up the Black Maria had the same build as Patterson, that he was wearing an overcoat identical to the one Patterson habitually wears, and that the sergeant is devoted to Blackstone and would do anything to save him,' Hartington said.

'Which would seem to make a cast-iron case against him,' the Commissioner pointed out.

'It would indeed, except that the man who held up the Black Maria had a pronounced limp, and Patterson doesn't,' Hartington said.

'There's nothing in the witness statements about him having a pronounced limp,' the Commissioner retorted.

'Not at the moment there isn't – but there could be,' Hartington said. 'And since, having ruled Patterson out, you're never likely to find the real culprit, those witness statements will never actually come under close scrutiny.'

'That's blackmail,' the commissioner said.

'I prefer to think of it as negotiation,' Hartington replied.

'If we drop all charges against Patterson, can we assume we'll hear no more of this?' the Permanent Secretary asked.

'I'd certainly be happy with that,' Hartington agreed. 'And I'm more than confident that I could sell the idea to my clients – Inspector Patterson and Superintendent Blackstone.'

'Sell it to *whom*?' the Commissioner exploded. 'If you think – for a minute – that I'll stand by while—'

'Shut up, Roger!' the Permanent Secretary hissed. He turned his attention to Hartington. 'I'm sure, Courtney, that Inspector Patterson and Superintendent Blackstone will be more than happy with the arrangement.'

Max could not complain about the treatment that was meted out to him by the porters in the hours following his rescue. They had given him food, and they had given him water. They had allowed him to wash and provided him with a set of overalls to replace the once-immaculate suit that he had managed to soil during the journey. Yet, for all their kindness, they still made it quite clear to him that he could not leave the station without permission – and that that permission could only be granted by the man in charge.

It was seven o'clock in the evening before Max was finally shown into the station master's office. The station master himself was a square-shouldered, balding man with a large moustache. A large portrait was hanging on the wall behind him, and but for the brass plaque that said it was of Otto von Bismarck, Max might have taken it for a picture of the station master himself.

'You did not have permission to arrive at my station in a packing case,' the station master said. 'Would you care to explain how it came about?'

Max laughed with what he hoped sounded like bitter irony.

'I wish I could,' he said. 'The last thing I remember before waking up in the packing case was eating a meal in one of Oslo's best restaurants.'

'One of Oslo's best restaurants,' the station master repeated. 'Yes, my men told me you claim to be a Norwegian.'

'I am a Norwegian. My name is Karl Hansen.'

'You speak very good German for an alien.'

'I've been taking lessons.'

'I have a problem,' the station master admitted. 'You say you are Karl Hansen, and I want to believe you. Unfortunately, the packing case in which you were discovered also contained a packet of documents which identify you as Max Schneider.'

Whoever had kidnapped him must have taken the documents from his room at the hotel, Max thought – and he cursed himself for not having burned the papers years earlier.

'Max is a friend of mine,' he said. 'I was looking after those documents for him.'

'It appears from the documents that this Max Schneider was born right here in Hamburg, twenty-six years ago,' the station master said. 'How old are you, Mr Hansen?'

'Twenty-eight,' Max said, though he hated to make himself older than he actually was.

The station master sighed. 'I can pick up the phone at this very moment and ring a dozen people who will be willing to come to the station to identify you. So wouldn't it be easier – for both of us – if you just told the truth?' he asked.

'Yes, I am Max Schneider,' Max admitted.

The station master nodded. 'Good. Now, according to some records I have just been studying, you went to England in 1909. Is that correct?'

'Yes.'

'A lot of other young men did the same. I applaud their spirit of adventure. So what else do we know? Ah yes, in August 1911, you received your call-up papers from the German high command. You were informed in those papers that you would be serving in the U-boat service. Is *that* correct?'

'Yes.'

'The submarine service is considered to be an elite branch of the navy, and there are many patriotic young Germans who would have given their right arms to serve in it, yet you, without making any effort, were one of those selected,' the official said. 'Do you know why that is?'

'No,' Max admitted.

'Would you like to know the reason?'

'Not particularly.'

'Well, I think I will tell you anyway. It is because your father has friends in high places and went to considerable trouble and expense to arrange that particular posting.'

The old bastard, Max thought – *the vicious, conniving, evil old bastard.*

'I spoke to your father less than an hour ago,' the station master continued. 'He said he'd wanted to give you the opportunity to serve your country with honour. He'd thought that in the U-boat service you might finally become the kind of son he could admire. And did you grab this golden opportunity with both hands?'

'I don't like enclosed spaces,' Max said.

'That is not the question I asked,' the station master said angrily. 'Did you – or did you not – grab this golden opportunity with both hands?'

'I did not.'

'So what did you do instead?'

'I changed my name and stayed in England.'

'And that is where you have been since 1911?'

'Yes.'

'You have never come back to Germany in all that time?'

'No.'

'So tell me, Herr Schneider, how did you manage to support yourself in a foreign country, where you could no longer even use your own name?'

Max sought for an acceptable way to describe how he had earned his living.

'I was an entertainer,' he said finally.

'Were you?' the station master asked. 'Well, let us both hope the appropriate authorities find you *entertaining.*'

PART THREE
Endgame

TWENTY-THREE

21st December 1916 – Julian calendar; 3rd January 1917 – Gregorian calendar

T he letter had been brought from England by Vladimir's own courier.
 It began:

> *Hello Sam*
> *I thought I'd just drop you a line to let you know how we've been getting on over here while you've been living the life of Riley in Russia.*

It ended:

> *So it's time to turn your back on the dancing girls and the champagne, come back to London and start being a right proper bastard, like all the other top brass.*
> *Yours sincerely,*
> *Inspector Archibald Patterson.*

Sandwiched between the whimsy of the greeting and the flippancy of the sign-off were ten pages of a tightly argued report in Patterson's careful, elementary school handwriting.

Blackstone read through the report once and then – aware that Vladimir, sitting behind his desk, was watching him closely – he read through it again.

There were a number of things he still found troubling about the report, and one of them was Brigham's role in the whole affair.

The superintendent had struck him as a bastard from the start – but not a *corrupt* bastard.

And Brigham had said he never wanted Blackstone to be the one to take the money to the docks.

'*Why me?*' Blackstone had asked. '*Couldn't your lads do it?*'

'*Yes,*' Brigham had replied, '*they most certainly could, and I would rather entrust it to one of them than to an inspector who has had what can be called – at best – a chequered career. But that option is not open to me. The man insists that you should be the go-between. He refuses to accept anyone else.*'

It would have taken a very good actor to carry that off – and Blackstone didn't think that Brigham *was* that good.

So the whole conversation only made sense as long as Brigham was actually what he appeared to be – a policeman who hoped to buy plans of submarine movements from a German agent and had been told by that German that Blackstone would be the only acceptable courier.

And that meant that it *was* Max – and Max alone – who had insisted that he act as the courier, that it had been Max – and Max alone – who had decided to frame him.

But why would Max Schneider – a man he'd never met – pick him out *specifically* to be set up?

It felt as if the truth had been held back by a huge dam. Now the dam had been cracked, and more questions came trickling through that crack, until they became a flood.

'You have gone very quiet, my friend,' Vladimir said.

'I was thinking,' Blackstone said.

'About what?'

'About how difficult it is, when you're continually being spun round on a whirligig, to see things as they really are. And I've been on a whirligig for some considerable time.'

'I'm not sure I know what you mean.'

'You're playing another of your games, aren't you?'

Vladimir smiled. 'Am I?'

'And this particular game is designed to find out just how smart I am,' Blackstone said.

'And just how smart are you?' Vladimir wondered.

'Is it at all likely that a minor official in the German navy would come across secret submarine plans?' Blackstone asked, postponing the question of his own intelligence until later.

'I should think it is highly likely,' Vladimir said. 'War sweeps away old-established procedures and demands new ones. And while these new procedures are being put in place, there will always be minor failings which the watchful can quickly exploit.'

'True,' Blackstone agreed. 'But how likely is it that this same minor official would be able to get several weeks' leave in the middle of the war?'

'That is less likely,' Vladimir conceded. 'But he could have just deserted, of course.'

'And if he did desert, what are the chances that this *minor* official – on the run from the German authorities – could get himself smuggled into England? And once he was in England, how would he go about recruiting at least two other men – and possibly more – to help him in his scheme?'

'When this Max of yours lived in England, he seemed to have more money than he could ever have earned legally, so perhaps he looked up some of his old criminal associates,' Vladimir suggested.

'How would you know what Max did in England before the war?' Blackstone asked.

Vladimir smiled. 'Ah, a mistake,' he said.

But it wasn't a mistake – it was all part of the game.

The soldiers were not the cannon fodder sent into battle unarmed to exhaust the enemy's supply of bullets, but crack troops who had seen heavy fighting on the Eastern Front and emerged from it bloody but unbowed. They had been spilt into teams, each one carefully briefed on its part in the death trap, and now that trap was about to be sprung.

They moved with speed, making little noise on the freshly fallen snow which had yet to become crisp.

The best marksmen – dressed in white camouflage uniforms – set up their rifles and tripods in the street and lay behind them on their stomachs, almost invisible in the snow.

Other teams entered the houses on the middle section of the prospekt through the back entrances and immediately began knocking on apartment doors.

'This apartment is being commandeered for a military operation,' they told those tenants whose lounges overlooked the prospekt. 'You are to go to one of the apartments at the rear, where you will be given shelter.'

'You will soon be receiving some unexpected guests,' they told the tenants at the back of the building. 'Once they have been admitted, you are to lower your blinds and lock your doors. You will not come out again until you are told to do so.'

They met with no resistance – no argument – because only a fool argues with heavily armed soldiers with bloodlust in their eyes.

'You hav' der money?' Blackstone asked Vladimir, in a fair imitation of the voice he had heard on the docks.

Vladimir's smile widened. 'I could easily have sent someone else, but – as you know – I have always had a flair for the melo-dramatic,' he said. 'When did you realize it was me?'

'About two minutes ago,' Blackstone admitted.

'And what tipped you off?'

'The fact that whoever it was waiting for me at the docks didn't have the two coppers who were on duty there killed. It would have been easier to kill them than to tie them up. It would have been safer to kill them. And Max – who we now know to be Vladimir – would have been hanged anyway if the police had got their hands on him, so he had nothing to lose by killing them.'

'So why didn't I kill them?' Vladimir asked.

'Because you knew that if I eventually found out, there would be no forgiveness, and I wouldn't rest until I'd avenged them by killing you.'

'Yes, you do seem to have an exaggerated sense of loyalty to your fellow officers,' Vladimir agreed.

'Do you want to tell me about the rest of it?' Blackstone suggested.

'Yes, why not?' Vladimir agreed. 'When the snippet of German submarine intelligence came into my hands, I saw immediately how I could make money out of it. And I needed the money. As the war progresses, my department is having to do more and more on less and less cash.'

'So you decided to steal it from us?'

'I decided to seek a subsidy from one of our allies without that ally actually realizing it was subsidizing me.'

'And so you became Max. And at what point did your devious

mind work out that this operation could achieve not just one objective but two?'

'Almost immediately.'

'So you set it all up to make it look as if I had been a part of the conspiracy to steal the money?'

'Yes.'

'And then, after allowing me to wander around London as a fugitive, stewing in my own juice, for a week . . .'

'You were quite safe. I had my men watching you all the time, and nothing would have been allowed to happen to you.'

'. . . after allowing me to wander around London as a fugitive, stewing in my own juice, for a week, you appeared and rescued me.'

'Correct.'

'The old gentleman I found collapsed in the alley was working for you, of course.'

'How can you be sure of that?'

'Because now I've got off the whirligig, I've started asking myself the questions that I should have asked at the time. And one of those questions was: if the old gentleman wanted some air because he was feeling faint, why didn't he take his coachman with him for support?'

'Quite right,' Vladimir agreed.

'Then the two thugs attacked me, and just before you slit the throat of the one straddling me, he screamed something like "Listen, this wasn't never part . . ." That wasn't a plea for mercy, Vladimir – it was a desperate complaint that things weren't going as they were supposed to.' Blackstone paused for a second. 'Was it really necessary to kill them both?'

'Strictly speaking, no,' Vladimir admitted. 'But it did add a certain extra verisimilitude to the scene. And you shouldn't mourn for them, Sam. They were quite willing to kill you. In fact, they were very disappointed when I told them that they couldn't.'

'It was just *too much* of a coincidence that you should appear on Battle Bridge Lane at just the right time,' Blackstone said.

'Yes, I always knew that was the weakest part of the whole plan,' Vladimir admitted, 'but fortunately you were too busy spinning on your whirligig to see the flaw.'

'What would you have done if Archie Patterson hadn't decided to rescue me from the Black Maria?' Blackstone asked.

Vladimir roared with laughter. 'You don't really think I'd have relied on fat Archie to spring you from the Black Maria, do you?'

'Wasn't it him?'

'Of course not! One of my operatives slipped Patterson a drug in the Goldsmiths' Arms, and while another of my men was freeing you, your fat sergeant was quite happily snoring away in a back alley.'

'Why was it necessary to implicate Archie by dressing your man in a coat just like his?' Blackstone asked, a hint of anger in his voice.

'Why should you be so concerned about that?' Vladimir wondered. 'It's true that Patterson went through two weeks of minor discomfort, but he did emerge at the end of it with a promotion.'

'I don't think his family will have considered it a minor *discomfort*,' Blackstone said stonily. 'Why *did* you implicate him?'

'For the same reason that I implicated you – but we'll come to that later,' Vladimir said airily. 'The important point is that once my excellent lawyer – Mr Hartington – had secured his release on bail, I set Patterson on the trail that would eventually – and inevitably – lead him to Brighton.'

'*You* set him on the trail?'

'Oh yes, I planted lots of clues. I even told Hartington to make sure he used the words "paper trail", which made Archie think – as I knew it would – of the government warehouse containing all those records.'

'You planted the attaché case and the railway ticket to Brighton in Max's lodgings.'

'Yes.'

'I know now why you insisted I should be the one to buy the case in the first place,' Blackstone said. 'You knew I'd mark it in some way, so it could be identified later. And it was very important that when Archie found the bag, he *could* positively identify it.'

'Just so,' Vladimir agreed.

'But why did you insist that I buy it from Harrods?'

'I knew that would worry you – and I wanted you worrying over the details that didn't matter, because that might stop you thinking about the details that did.'

'It was your men who placed the photograph of Max and Brigham in the photographer's window in Brighton, wasn't it?'

'How do you know that?'

'Because if the photographer had taken the picture himself, he would have given Brigham a ticket for it, and once Brigham was aware of the photograph's existence, he would have bought up all the copies of it.'

'You're quite right,' Vladimir agreed. 'One of my people took the photograph and then bribed the photographer to display it in his window. I had several ingenious schemes in play to make sure that Ellie Carr actually saw the photograph, but none of them proved necessary.'

'Why did you select Brigham to take the fall?'

'That had more to do with Max than with Brigham. In 1911, he was conscripted into the submarine service. He never did join it, of course, but you didn't know that, so he was the ideal person to hide behind.'

'So you knew Max before the war?'

'Yes.'

'*How* did you know him?'

'When he was lodging with Mrs Wilson, he held wild parties with the sole aim of making the other tenants leave, and when they did go, Max took over their rooms and moved his friends in.'

'I know about that from Patterson's notes.'

'And do Patterson's notes tell you *why* Mrs Wilson tolerated such behaviour?'

'She told him Max's friends were prepared to pay twice as much for the rooms.'

'And so they were. They could afford to, because what Mrs Wilson *didn't* tell Patterson was that she and Max were in part nership and were running a male brothel. And that brothel had some very interesting clients – military men and civil servants, for example.'

'So that's how you got to know Max – he was spying for you.'

'Yes, he did feed me a titbit of information now and again, though nothing of very great importance. Then he got his call-up papers from the German submarine service, and he went on the run. He still continued in his chosen profession – a man has to live – but now he was working independently. I kept tabs on him, because I knew that one day he might be useful to me again. And once I got the submarine plans, I knew exactly *how* I could use him, though, of course, he would know absolutely nothing about it.'

'Brigham was one of his clients,' Blackstone guessed.

'He was – and that made him perfect for what I had in mind. Even now, I'm willing to wager, he'd rather be thought of as a spy than as a pederast.'

'If the police had caught Max, the whole plot would have fallen apart,' Blackstone said.

'Yes, it would. And that is why I had him packaged up and sent home to dear old dad.'

As well as the camouflaged soldiers lying in the street, there were now men at the apartment windows and on the roofs. Twenty rifles were pointed at the window of the apartment on the first floor, another dozen at the front door of the building.

They were only waiting for the team with the battering ram to arrive, and then they were ready to go.

'I've been very patient, but now I'd like to know why you felt it was necessary to frame Archie Patterson?' Blackstone said.

'I did it because I knew that while you'd never come to Russia to save yourself, you might come to save Patterson.'

'You must have wanted me here very badly.'

'I did. I never really tried to hide that.'

'No, you didn't,' Blackstone agreed. 'I always knew you brought me here for a purpose, but I still don't know what the purpose was.'

Vladimir sighed. 'I will do all I can to prevent a revolution, but it will come anyway,' he said. 'At first, it will be a liberal kind of revolution, and the government will be made up of lawyers and journalists and other well-meaning – but ineffective – people. That will not last long. Within months, the Bolsheviks will have taken over, and then the situation will turn very nasty. They will hunt down anyone who has worked for the old regime, and they will eliminate them.'

'Then you'd better make sure you get out before that happens,' Blackstone said.

'I will stay,' Vladimir told him. 'I will die for my tsar, even though, by that time, there will probably be no tsar to die for. But Tanya must be saved.'

'And you think I can save her?'

'*I* will save her! Me!' Vladimir said fiercely. 'But you,' he continued, softening a little, 'will have the job of looking after her once she is safely in England.'

'You could have written to me and asked me to look after her. I would have agreed.'

'I know you would. You're a good man.'

'So if that was all you wanted from me, there was no need to bring me to Russia at all.'

'Ah, but there was,' Vladimir said. 'When I put the idea to her, she resisted – and she can be a very stubborn girl. So I brought you here so that she could get to know you – so that she could get to like you. And she does.'

'That's what all this was about?' Blackstone asked, astounded. 'You framed me, you framed Archie – and you killed the two thugs – just so that Tanya could get to like me?'

'She is very important to me.'

'I know she is. She's your daughter.'

Vladimir sighed again. 'I wish she was,' he said, 'but though I love her as much as any father can, she is not my child.' He pressed a button on his desk. 'We must wait a moment,' he told Blackstone.

The study door opened, and Tanya walked in – but this Tanya had her hair swept back, and this Tanya had no scar.

'The scar is a fake – a necessary disguise,' Vladimir explained, reading his amazement. 'Its sole purpose was to fool you.'

'Me? Why me?'

'Look at her, man!' Vladimir urged him.

Tanya was still standing hesitantly in the doorway.

Blackstone looked at her face and saw that it was almost achingly beautiful.

And then he recognized the source of that beauty.

The woman he'd seen on Nevsky Prospekt hadn't been Agnes at all. She moved too quickly – with too much of the grace of youth – to have been the middle-aged woman that Agnes would have become if she'd lived. It had been Tanya – eager for her first look at him.

And Vladimir was right about the scar – once he had seen it, it had banished from his mind the possibility of any suspicions being formed about who she really was.

'She's Agnes's daughter,' he said simply.

'You still don't understand, do you?' Vladimir asked. 'I lied about her age – I lie about many things. I told you she was older than she looks, but she isn't. She was born in 1900, which means that she is only sixteen.'

'She's just a kid,' Blackstone said.

'Just a kid,' Vladimir agreed. 'Tell me, Sam, when was the last time you were in Russia?'

'It was 1899,' Blackstone said.

'Call me Sam,' he'd told Tanya, when he'd visited her in her sick bed, and they'd seemed to be getting on so well with each other.

'No, I can't do that,' Tanya had replied, and there hadn't been any animosity or aggression behind it – it had just seemed like a simple statement of fact.

And yet she called Vladimir by his first name!

'Have you pieced it all together yet?' Vladimir asked.

'You're . . . you're not just Agnes's daughter,' Blackstone said to Tanya. 'You're mine, as well.'

'My mother didn't blame you for leaving her, but I did,' Tanya said. 'I hated you for it. But now I see that she was right, and I was wrong. We are in such a dirty business – and to be true to yourself, you had to keep yourself clean.'

'Would it . . . would it be all right if I held you?' Blackstone asked her.

'I would like that very much,' Tanya replied.

He raced over to her, flung his arms around her and felt a happiness he had never experienced before.

'Be careful, Sam, you're crushing the life out of her,' Vladimir said, with a mixture of amusement and envy.

Blackstone released his new-found daughter and turned to Vladimir.

'Thank you,' he said.

'There's nothing to thank me for,' Vladimir replied gruffly. 'If

I hadn't have thought you were up to the job, I would never have entrusted you with it.'

He opened the desk drawer again and produced a thick envelope.

'These are your travel documents,' he said. 'Tickets, false passports, money – everything you will need to get you safely to England.'

A small avalanche of snow suddenly fell past the window on its way to the street below.

'They're on the roof!' Vladimir said.

'Who are?'

'General Kornilov's men,' Vladimir said. 'I never thought he would go about it like this. It would have been so much easier – so much less dramatic – to try to kill me out in the open. But, of course, he *wants* drama – because he wants to impress the tsarina. He's as mad as she is.'

'Oh come on,' Blackstone said, 'even a mad general would never think of doing that.'

Vladimir stood up and walked around the desk, the travel documents in his hand.

'Take these,' he urged Blackstone. 'Take them now.'

The windows imploded, and the room was suddenly filled with an angry metal buzzing and the stink of cordite. Blackstone threw himself on Tanya at the first hint of the attack, but, even so, several bullets had already whizzed past them by the time they hit the floor.

The firing continued. The chandelier overhead swung to and fro as the bullets hit it, and then it crashed to the ground with a heavy thud, leaving the room lit only by the pale moonlight.

'Are you all right, Tanya?' Vladimir asked worriedly, as soon as there was a lull in the firing.

'Yes,' Tanya said.

'And you, Sam?'

'I'm fine,' Blackstone said, turning towards the dark shape that was slumped against the wall. 'How about you?'

'Unfortunately, I was not so lucky,' Vladimir said, and now Blackstone could hear the strain in his voice. 'I have been shot in the stomach, which, as we both know, will ultimately prove fatal.'

'Oh Vladimir!' Tanya sobbed.

'There is no time for pity – and no time for an agent as good as you are to give way to tears,' Vladimir interrupted her harshly.

'I'm sorry, Vladimir,' the girl said.

'There's no time for apologies, either,' Vladimir said. 'During the next round of covering fire, the general will try to get some of his men in through the front door, but he will soon regret it.'

The firing began again, round after round slamming into the back wall of the study, and now there was the noise of heavy feet rushing up the stairs.

Vladimir spoke, but his voice was so weak that Blackstone could not hear what he said.

The firing continued, and the hammering on the door shook the whole apartment.

They would be using a short battering ram, and whatever Vladimir believed, they would get inside eventually, Blackstone thought.

The explosions were so loud – so ear-shattering – that, for a moment, Blackstone believed they must come from right within the study. And then he realized that it was not the study but the corridor that had been blown up.

The firing stopped, as if the men outside were puzzled by the explosions and did not know what to do next.

Vladimir chuckled, and that chuckle soon became a painful gurgle.

'The walls and door are lined with steel,' he said, 'and the corridor, as you must have realized, was booby-trapped. I imagine it will have killed eight or ten of them. Now they will wait for reinforcements before they try anything else.'

But the reinforcements would come, Blackstone thought – and then it would all be over.

'Is there anything I can do to ease your pain, Vladimir?' he asked.

The Russian said nothing.

'Vladimir?' Blackstone repeated.

He was answered by silence.

'He's . . . he's dead,' Tanya gasped.

Well, at least it had been quick, Blackstone thought – at least he hadn't had to suffer for hours, as men with stomach wounds often do.

'Stay here,' he said. 'Don't move an inch.'

On hands and knees, he made his way slowly around the wall to what was left of the windows. When he had reached a point at which he could look out on to the street, he stopped.

After the recent fall of snow, the prospekt glistened in the moonlight like a tranquil and unwavering sea made up of a million tiny jewels.

There was no movement on the street, nor any in the houses opposite, but he knew that in both those places there were men with rifles watching the balcony and just waiting for him to make a move.

He wondered if he could trade his own life for Tanya's. But there would be no trading done that night. The general already had his life in his hands – and Tanya's, too – and was mad enough to want anything that had ever been associated with Vladimir wiped off the face of the earth.

So he would die, and the daughter he had only just discovered *was* his daughter – whom he already loved with an intensity that was almost frightening – would die as well. It seemed a cruel fate – but then fate could be cruel.

'Sam?' croaked a voice from the other end of the room.

So Vladimir was not yet dead, after all.

'I'm here,' he said.

'It's time for you and Tanya to make your escape,' Vladimir said.

The poor man was obviously delirious, Blackstone thought.

'We'd prefer to stay with you until the end,' he said.

'No,' Vladimir said. 'It can't be the end – not for Tanya. I . . . I need my control panel to my railway, Sam, and I cannot reach it. You . . . you must give it to me.'

There could be no harm in pandering to the wishes of a dying man, Blackstone thought, as he crawled back across the room and handed the control panel over to the Russian.

'At the back of each engine shed, there is a gate,' Vladimir said, 'and if the locomotives hit those gates with enough force, they will open them.'

'And then what will happen?' Blackstone asked.

'Then the engines will fly through the air and land in the street,' Vladimir said. 'But it is what happens *before* they land that is important.'

'I see,' Blackstone said.

'When I tell you to, you must both turn your backs on the prospekt and cover your eyes,' Vladimir said. 'You must count to three, and then you must jump over the balcony on to the street and make your escape.'

'We'll see how it goes,' Blackstone said.

Vladimir grabbed his arm. 'You must promise me,' he begged.

'Trust him, Father,' Tanya said. 'Trust Vladimir. He will get us out of here. I know he will.'

Trust him, Father!

They would not escape, Blackstone thought, but if Tanya died with the hope of escape still in her heart, then that was something at least.

'I promise,' he said.

Vladimir touched the control panel, and trains from all over the apartment began to speed towards the engine sheds against the outside wall. It was difficult to be sure in the faint light, but Blackstone thought there must have been at least a dozen trains on the move, and he marvelled at the way the dying man could still control them all.

Six trains were approaching the shed.

'Now!' Vladimir said urgently.

Feeling a fool, Blackstone turned away from the window and covered his eyes.

'One . . .' he counted silently.

He heard a slight click as the first engine hit its gate.

'. . . two . . .'

Even with his eyes covered, he was aware of the white light that seemed to fill the study.

'. . . three!'

'Now!' Vladimir urged. 'Go now!'

From the balcony, Blackstone could see soldiers with rifles walking around in a daze. The street was as bright as day, but that was nothing to what it must have been like when the phosphorous flares on the locomotives ignited.

He led Tanya across the room and lowered her off the balcony. Only when she had hit the soft snow below did he jump himself.

'Are you all right?' he asked.

'Yes.'

'Then let's get moving!'

They scrambled to their feet and began running down the street. Several times, they had to swerve around the blinded soldiers, but Blackstone could tell from the way they were moving that their vision was starting to return.

There was a side street thirty yards ahead of them, and if they could make it to that, they would be out of the soldiers' sights.

A bullet flew past them, and then another.

'Keep running, Daughter,' he said.

'I am, Father,' Tanya replied.

They had another ten yards to go before they would have some cover, Blackstone calculated – ten yards to go before they reached the gateway to a new life.